"Four stars! A lively piece of erotic fiction that explores how the wanton vagaries of fate turn a young girl's life around . . . bawdy and ribald." —*Romantic Times*

"This is a delightful contemporary take on the bawdy novels of past centuries, with a timeless heroine, subtle humor, and a wonderful cast of characters. There are plenty of erotic novels that are little more than a series of sex scenes strung together with a plot; *Madame Bliss* rises above that and is a very clever and well-told story with plenty of scenes that manage to be hot without seeming crass."

—Passion Postings

"An irresistible debut." —Fresh Fiction

Also by Charlotte Lovejoy

Madame Bliss

THE RAVISHING
of LADY MAY

AN EROTIC NOVEL IN THE COURT OF HENRY VIII

CHARLOTTE LOVEJOY

A SIGNET ECLIPSE BOOK

SIGNET ECLIPSE
Published by New American Library, a division of
Penguin Group (USA) Inc., 375 Hudson Street,
New York, New York 10014, USA
Penguin Group (Canada), 90 Eglinton Avenue East, Suite 700, Toronto,
Ontario M4P 2Y3, Canada (a division of Pearson Penguin Canada Inc.)
Penguin Books Ltd., 80 Strand, London WC2R 0RL, England
Penguin Ireland, 25 St. Stephen's Green, Dublin 2,
Ireland (a division of Penguin Books Ltd.)
Penguin Group (Australia), 250 Camberwell Road, Camberwell, Victoria 3124,
Australia (a division of Pearson Australia Group Pty. Ltd.)
Penguin Books India Pvt. Ltd., 11 Community Centre, Panchsheel Park,
New Delhi - 110 017, India
Penguin Group (NZ), 67 Apollo Drive, Rosedale, North Shore 0632,
New Zealand (a division of Pearson New Zealand Ltd.)
Penguin Books (South Africa) (Pty.) Ltd., 24 Sturdee Avenue,
Rosebank, Johannesburg 2196, South Africa

Penguin Books Ltd., Registered Offices:
80 Strand, London WC2R 0RL, England

First published by Signet Eclipse, an imprint of New American Library,
a division of Penguin Group (USA) Inc.

First Printing, May 2011
10 9 8 7 6 5 4 3 2 1

Library of Congress Cataloging-in-Publication Data:

Lovejoy, Charlotte.
   The ravishing of Lady May: an erotic novel in the court of Henry VIII/Charlotte Lovejoy.
     p. cm.
   ISBN 978-0-451-23314-1
   1. Courts and courtiers—Fiction.   2. Great Britain—History—Henry VIII, 1509–1547—
Fiction. I. Title.
   PS3612.O8347R38 2011
   813'.6—dc22   2010052289

Set in Berling
Designed by Alissa Amell

Printed in the United States of America

THE RAVISHING
of LADY MAY

CHAPTER ONE

"*I* will *not* squander my life here in this convent, Anne," whispered Margaret Roseberry to the girl who knelt beside her on the hard stone floor.

In their hands were stiff-bristled brushes for washing, the suds bubbling around the girls' red-knuckled hands as they scrubbed at the floor. For Margaret, this was yet one more punishment meted out to her by the abbess, this time for smiling from the window at the young carter who brought the firewood to the convent.

Not that punishment would change anything. Margaret had loved spying on him from high above, watching the way the muscles of his sun-browned arms had bulged beneath his shirt's sleeves as he'd tossed the thick-cut pieces of firewood from his wagon, and admiring how his shoulders had worked beneath the close-fitting leather jerkin he'd always worn. She'd been fascinated by his strength, imagining how those muscles would feel beneath her hands. She'd leaned forward over the stone sill, her heart racing both at the temptation he represented and from fear she'd be caught by one of the nuns.

Yet he'd been the one who'd caught her first. He'd stopped his work and turned his face upwards to look at her, holding one of the heavy pieces of wood in his arms, his thick fingers spread around the rough bark. She loved how the neck of his shirt was open, how the dark curls on his broad chest had shown against the linen. He'd tossed his dark hair back from his eyes and grinned suggestively at her, as if he could read her desire.

She'd smiled slowly and leaned farther over the sill, pressing her breasts against the warm stone as she offered them to his gaze. It had been easy enough to imagine those strong, muscled hands of his holding her breasts, squeezing them as the calluses of his palms rubbed over her nipples. He'd kiss her hard, his tongue deep in her mouth, and rub his rough, unshaven cheek against hers. Groaning with desire, he'd tear away her simple smock and hold her naked body against his.

She'd imagined herself sliding down lower to kneel before him, untying the laces on his hose so his cock would spring free, as hard and ready as the wood he carted. Then he'd lift her upwards and settle her on the edge of his cart, pulling her forward until he could slip that huge cock into her. With her thighs wrapped tightly around his waist, he'd plunge deep into her, opening her and filling her again and again until she fair screamed with pleasure, there before all the astonished onlookers around them in the abbey's sunny courtyard.

Her heart had raced as she'd imagined it all, and she'd leaned even farther from the sill towards him, so he must surely have seen her hard nipples pushing through the worn linen of her smock. What she might have done, what she'd longed to do, if only Sister Agnes had not discovered her then, pulling her roughly from the window and slapping her hard, as if that were all it would take to make Margaret forget the craving desire that tormented her.

Margaret hadn't cared. She'd do it again and much more besides, no matter how much it angered the abbess, for the carter was that handsome and she was that eager, and, ah, how much her body yearned for him!

"I am almost seventeen years, far too old to continue here as I am," she continued now to the girl scrubbing the floor beside her, frustration making Margaret shove the brush harder across the stones, "and I vow I will *not* see another birthday pass before I am free of this abbey and the sisters in it."

The other girl, Anne, glanced up at her uneasily, her plain face doleful beneath the equally plain linen coif that hid her hair. For her, the scrubbing was not a punishment but a chosen penance for the betterment of her immortal soul.

"You should not speak so, Margaret," Anne whispered. "You do not even know what you ask for! You should be grateful to be here in holy solitude, where you might lead a good and pure life rather than crave the wickedness and sin of the great world."

"What I crave is freedom, Anne," Margaret whispered fiercely. "You may wish to live here all your days, hidden away with only sour-faced holy women for companionship, but I want joy, and laughter, and amusement, and . . . and I wish for the admiration of men, too, Anne! If some pretty fellow were to enter that door, I vow I would go to him and kiss him sweetly for the pleasure of it!"

Anne gasped. "Have you ever done such a thing, Margaret? Have you ever let a . . . a man debase you like that?"

Margaret sighed in frustration. She hadn't, of course. How could she? But it wasn't as if she were ignorant of favors to be granted, or even boldly stolen. She'd long ago discovered a place in the chapel where, under the guise of being at her own reflections, she could hear the fine ladies visiting the abbey at their confessions. The first time Margaret had listened, she'd been shocked by what she'd heard, but the more she'd overheard, the more she'd longed to know.

These ladies spoke with astonishing freedom of how they'd sucked the cock of their children's tutor, or met with their lovers in hired rooms to fuck with the greatest abandon before looking glasses, or bid their footman to tease and lick their most private parts until they spent, and when they'd spoken too generally, the priest had urged them to describe their acts in more detail, so as to make a more complete confession. All this Margaret had overheard with breathless curiosity, their lewd confessions leaving her eager to experience such delights for herself in the world beyond the abbey's stone walls. The lustful acts they described to the priest had fired Margaret's imagination, and her blood with it.

"Nay, not as yet," she admitted. "But I would if such a man were to present himself for a kiss, and I'd do far more than that, too, if he were comely enough."

"Do not speak so, Margaret." Anne's pale cheeks colored with the shame that Margaret did not feel, and she made the sign of the cross. "May God preserve you and forgive you for such sinful desires."

But Margaret did not blush. "Where is the sin in joy?" she demanded. "Where is the sin in happiness? *That* was what I was made for, Anne, not to molder away behind iron gates and psalms, and if I could but—"

"Margaret." Sister Catherine's voice cracked as sharp as a whip, more than enough to make both girls scramble to their feet and curtsy over their scrubbing water. "Come. The abbess wishes for you."

The black skirts of her habit swinging heavily, Sister Catherine turned away without deigning to look back at Margaret. Margaret had time only to exchange a quick, resigned glance with Anne before she hurried after the nun, her bare feet leaving damp prints fading on the stone floor.

Uneasily Margaret wondered what she'd done now, for the only times she was called to the abbess's chamber were to be punished. She could only hope it would be over swiftly, willow switch stings to the back of her hand, rather than more floor scrubbing.

No wonder she sighed again. Oh, she knew she'd been cursed with rebellious, wanton blood that had no place in a Christian lady—the abbess had explained that to her many times—but she'd also seen how she'd been disciplined far more often than any other girl residing at the abbey.

That came from Margaret's other curse, of being an orphan without family or friends to defend her against the abbess's severity. No one ever arrived to visit her on Sunday afternoons, or sent a carriage to take her away for holidays. And though it was doubtless only one more part of her sinful nature, she longed to be loved, which in turn made her more rebellious still. Was it any wonder that the great, green world beyond the abbey's gray walls beckoned so sweetly, or that she dreamed of finding the happiness and joy that were so seldom in her life?

Sister Catherine knocked on the abbess's door, then pushed it open only enough for Margaret to slip through.

"May God have mercy on your sins, Margaret," Sister Catherine whispered sharply, and she gave the girl an extra little shove before she closed the door.

Margaret stumbled forward and fought to keep her feet, determined not to fall before the abbess, as doubtless Sister Catherine had intended. Somehow she managed her reverence, her head bent low, and in that position she waited, her gaze fixed on the stone floor.

"You may stand, Margaret," the abbess said with unexpected sweetness in her voice. "My lady, this is the girl you seek. Margaret, this is Lady Arabella Bruton, Countess of Wilyse."

Margaret stood as she'd been bid, her red-knuckled hands folded neatly at her waist. She had never so much as seen a countess, let alone been presented to one, and in her confusion she curtsied again.

Lady Wilyse sat in the abbess's own armchair, more imposing than any of the painted saints in the chapel. Even without the abbess's introduction, Margaret would have known that the lady in the chair was of high rank.

The countess was perhaps ten years older than Margaret herself, her dark-haired beauty enhanced by her noble bearing, and marked by eyes of so light a blue as to be almost silver. The countess's gown was a beautiful soft green embroidered in silver thread to match the unusual color of her eyes, and the ruffled linen at her wrists and throat was as fine as fairies' gossamer. Her peaked hood was likewise trimmed with silver thread and lined with crimson velvet, and long silver chains of enameled flowers set with pearls were draped around her neck. Her traveling cloak, also trimmed with the same pale fur, was tossed back carelessly over the chair, and her bright green kidskin gloves lay in her lap.

Margaret stared, marveling, trying to memorize every detail about the countess so she could savor it later. To be so grand as this, to sit while the abbess stood! What must it be like to wear such finery, to feel that soft fur against her skin and the weight of jeweled chains around her throat and the pale dust of powder on her cheeks?

"Good morrow, my lady," she murmured at last, unsure of what else to say. "You honor me."

"Silence, Margaret!" ordered the abbess. "You have no leave to speak."

"Fie, madam, but she does," the countess said with a languid air. "By the heavens, I vow you are the one who errs, not she. How dare you use her so? Not only do you dress her more meanly than a beggar, but you would dare address her by her Christian name only?"

"Forgive me, my lady, but it is our way with the girls here," the abbess said quickly. "We dress simply, and keep no worldly titles among ourselves as a way of remaining equal before God."

Lady Wilyse smiled, but with no humor. "To me, Mother Abbess, it would appear less humility than a way of claiming for your order what is not yours to take."

"My lady!" exclaimed the abbess, shocked. "I—we— would never willingly break God's own commandments!"

"Oh, nay, nay," said the countess. "But you *would* keep this young lady in complete ignorance of her lineage, so that if she chooses to join you as a novice, you might claim her as your own, and her fortune with it."

Margaret listened with astonishment. She'd never heard anyone dare speak in this manner to the abbess. And what was this of her own lineage? What secrets had the abbess kept from her?

"Forgive me, my lady," began the abbess, "but—"

"Silence, madam," Lady Wilyse said with a disdainful wave of her hand. "Do not weary me any further with your protests. I am aware of the laws of the church regarding maiden ladies in your care, and how quick those like you are to twist those laws for your own gain. To this lady's great good fortune, she is to be no longer in your care, but a ward of the Crown. His Majesty himself has entrusted me to collect her and bring her to him in London."

"You would take me away with you, my lady?" Margaret asked breathlessly, forgetting herself again before such a bewildering possibility. That she could be called a lady made no sense, for she knew she was an orphan whom no one wanted.

Yet Margaret was willing to believe whatever the countess said if it meant she would soon be free of the abbey. That she was to be collected—*collected!*—by order of His Majesty the King was beyond her hopes, her prayers, her most extravagant dreams, so far that she didn't dare trust it.

"You would not tease me, my lady?" she asked anxiously. "This is not another punishment for my sinful excesses?"

"A punishment? What could you know of sin in this barren place, my dear?" The countess smiled indulgently. "Faith, I'd give a crown that you're still a maid."

"Aye, my lady, I am." Margaret flushed. She'd kept her maidenhood, yes, but only from lack of opportunity, not from true virtue.

"Prettily said, and with rosy innocence, too," Lady Wilyse said. "The gentlemen at court will fight tooth and nail over you like a sweetmeat. Even His Majesty may be tempted."

"His Majesty, my lady?" Margaret asked. She had imagined the touch of a carter, not royalty. Yet they were both men, weren't they? If she could inspire love and desire in one, then why not the other? Her heart raced as she imagined what—and who—might lie before her. "His Majesty the King?"

"Oh, aye, none other than our mighty master Henry." The countess chuckled, narrowing her eyes a fraction as she studied Margaret. "Mistress Boleyn will not beguile him forever. Perhaps his eye will wander towards you. Ah, what pleasure it will be to oversee your education, and your success at court."

"I will strive to do my best to please you, my lady," Margaret declared fervently. "I vow I'll never disappoint you."

"Oh, child, do not make such a vow," the countess said mildly. "The first lesson of His Majesty's court is to please him above all others. The second would be to please, or rather *pleasure*, oneself."

"Consider the girl's immortal soul before you speak of these base, animal pleasures, my lady," the abbess sputtered indignantly. "How dare you steal her away for . . . for that?"

"You would rather I leave her in your clutches, Mother Abbess, to have every ounce of joy squeezed from her soul by your sanctimony?" The countess stood, drawing her cloak over one shoulder. "I should consider it my duty as a Christian to remove her from this place, even if it were not by His Majesty's order. You have read the royal warrant, and we are both bound to follow it. The girl will come with me. Come, Lady Margaret."

"Aye, my lady," Margaret said eagerly. "By your leave, I will fetch my clothes—"

"Nay." The countess looked her up and down, not bothering to hide her dismay. "I'll see to it that you are clothed as befits your station. Briskly, now, let us take our leave. I've had enough of mealy nuns and their false humility."

"I have as well, my lady," Margaret declared fervently. It wasn't a dream, but reality, and at last she felt safe enough in that reality to speak with boldness. "I will follow you wherever you will lead me."

"Do not heed this wicked temptation, Margaret," the abbess said, one final stern order. "Recall Eve in the Garden, and the dreadful price of earthly desire!"

Margaret tried to remember as she'd been bid, the last time she would do so. She tried, but all she could think of was the glorious future that the countess was offering her.

"Pray recall that your true home is here, Margaret," the abbess intoned, "and not among the wicked demons of the court."

Margaret looked at her evenly. "Pray pardon, Mother Abbess," she said, "but not one of the demons that I might find at court could rival those that I have found here for wickedness."

The abbess gasped, horrified, but Margaret didn't flinch, and the countess only laughed.

"Come with me, little one," she said, beckoning to Margaret to follow her. "I believe you will do better at court than any of us ever did think possible."

CHAPTER TWO

*L*ady Wilyse had taken an entire floor of an inn near the abbey for her use, not wishing to be bothered by other travelers. While she had been gathering Margaret, her servants had been busily arranging the rooms to suit her tastes and informing the innkeeper and his staff of her preferences and expectations. To Margaret's amazement, all these persons now hurried to present themselves to the countess, standing eager and ready to follow her further wishes, as soon as her carriage and outriders arrived in the courtyard.

But it was clear even to Margaret that no matter how her servants tried to oblige her, nothing would please Lady Wilyse, not in her present humor. Her conversation with the mother abbess seemed to have drained her completely, and even after she had slept in the carriage during the short drive from the abbey, she still appeared exhausted. With her eyes nearly closed and a scented, lace-edged handkerchief pressed to her forehead, she permitted two of the inn's young stablemen to assist her from the carriage, leaning heavily on their arms.

"Pray pardon, my lady, but what might I do to bring you ease?" Margaret asked earnestly as she slipped from the carriage behind the countess. She didn't care that she'd seemingly been forgotten. What concerned her most was the well-being of her newfound benefactress. Though Margaret had yearned desperately for freedom, that same freedom now yawned as vast and unknown as any distant ocean before her, and she feared what would become of her without the countess to guide her. "Is there anything I might fetch for you, my lady?"

"Oh, my dear, sweet Lady Margaret," the countess murmured weakly, her head tipped back against the broad shoulder of one of her stable-yard champions. Her gabled headdress had slipped askew, and a single glossy curl had come free of her coif, the dark lock making her throat look all the more ivory pale in contrast. "You are most kind, child. I will be well enough once I take to my bed. Now you . . . you are the one truly in need of aid. Poppy! Where is Poppy?"

"Here, my lady." A tall, round-faced girl near to Margaret's own age suddenly appeared to curtsy before the countess. Wisps of coppery curls peeked from beneath her cap, and freckles dusted across the bridge of her nose. Her apron marked her as a servant, but the rest of her dress was as cheerfully bright as her name, a scarlet gown with yellow sleeves, and a green scarf tied over her cap. "What is your wish, my lady?"

"This is the young lady I came to fetch from the abbey," the countess said, motioning towards Margaret. "You see her state. She has been kept worse than a common beggar. Take her to hand, Poppy. Wash her, polish her, dress her so I might see what manner of jewel I have uncovered for His Majesty."

"Aye, my lady," Poppy said, ducking in a quick curtsy to the countess, and another towards Margaret herself. "Good day, Lady Margaret. I am Poppy, and it is Lady Wilyse's desire that I am to belong to you, as your maidservant. This way, my lady, if it pleases you."

Unsure of what she should do, Margaret looked back towards the countess. "But perhaps I should remain with Lady Wilyse—"

"Lady Wilyse will be well tended by the others," Poppy said, and though her face was properly solemn, her eyes seemed to laugh as she watched the countess as much as carried away by the two young men. "For certain, she'll be recovered soon enough. This way to your room, my lady."

Gently, Poppy took Margaret's arm and led her inside and up the stairs to a large room at the end of the hall.

"This is your bedchamber, my lady," Poppy said, crossing the room to push the windows more widely open. "It's common enough, I know, but second only to the countess's, and the best to be had at this rough country place."

Margaret could only stare. How could she find fault

with any of this? The chamber was a corner room, with
large diamond-paned windows that overlooked the kitchen
garden. A honeysuckle vine curled along the windowsills,
filling the room with sweet fragrance from its creamy white
blossoms. The walls were freshly whitewashed, the better
to set off the dark, polished woodwork. A dining table sat
before one of the windows with a pewter bowl full of dewy
strawberries and a pitcher of wine with glasses besides. Two
armchairs sat nearby, invitingly set with fat red cushions.
On the floor a large trunk was opened to display an assort-
ment of ladies' clothes and other finery—clothes that, Margaret realized, were most likely intended for *her*.

But what she noticed first of all was the bed, larger than
any she'd ever seen, with thick carved posts and a head-
board and a footboard, heavy blue curtains and a matching
coverlet, and a feather bed plumped as high as a hummock
of new hay.

It wasn't just the size of the bed that captivated her, but
the sheer indolent luxury that it represented. At the abbey
she had slept on a hard, narrow cot in a long hall with a
score of other girls. They had never been permitted to lie
abed, and had always been roused before dawn for matins
in the chapel.

Yet this bed before her was clearly intended for more
than mere sleep, and meant, too, for more than one occu-
pant. With that bed looming before her, Margaret could
think only of the dire stories whispered among the other
girls, stories of honest countrywomen stolen away from

their homes and forced to serve wicked gentlemen in London brothels.

"That bed . . . It is so vast," she said uncertainly. "Am I to share it?"

Poppy laughed. "What, as if we were but poor low pilgrims at the most flea-ridden of inns, with a dozen of us tucked in together on our sides as tight as old pederasts?"

"I meant no such slander," Margaret said quickly, "nor did I intend to fault her ladyship's generosity. It was only that this bed did seem to me to be so vast for one person that I wondered if another would join me."

Again Poppy's laughter bubbled up. "Only if you wish it, my lady. That will be your choice, though—marry, you must be eager for a man if you long to quench your desires so soon after leaving the convent! Have you already spied one here at the inn to fancy? Should I make ready to open your door to him tonight?"

"Nay, there is no man," Margaret answered swiftly, blushing furiously at what the maidservant was suggesting. "How could there be when I've yet to be introduced to any man, gentle or no?"

"Oh, 'tis easy enough to lie with a man without any sort of introduction," Poppy said with breezy assurance. "Some women would say that it's much better not to know the name that belongs to the cock, my lady. They claim it sweetens the coupling by making it but a thing of the moment, without any empty promises or solemnity."

Margaret blushed even more deeply at such bold and

brazen talk—even if she herself had desired the handsome carter without ever learning his name. Still, her earlier fears rose again.

"Pray, Poppy, I must know," she asked, troubled. "Does Lady Wilyse mean me harm?"

Poppy's eyes widened. "Harm? Why ever would her ladyship wish you harm, when it is a rare honor for her to accompany you herself to London and His Majesty?"

"Then she . . . she has no plans to sell me to a brothel keeper in London?"

The maidservant laughed. "Pray forgive me, my lady, I should not show such mirth, but I cannot help it! True, there are many who would call King Henry's court a brothel, especially since Mistress Boleyn did come from France, but those mean-spirited folk speak only from spite or misguided prudery, not truth."

"Then His Majesty's court is not that way?"

"Nay, not at all," Poppy assured her. "Love and gallantry, pleasure and desire, all have their place at the palace, but only in the most agreeable fashion, as determined by His Majesty himself. And to fear that her ladyship would sell so fine a prize as you—a lady born!—to some common South-wark whoremaster with a stew. It would be the same as tossing a South Sea pearl away into the Thames!"

But Margaret's fears were not assuaged. "Why do you and Lady Wilyse insist that I am a lady when I know I am not? Why has she brought me here to this inn, to this room? I beg you tell me what plans she has for me."

Poppy stared at her with astonishment, her hands squared at her waist. "Her ladyship didn't tell you?"

Margaret shook her head. "She spoke to the mother abbess of how I'd been shamefully treated, and how I was to be taken to London and the king. But forgive me, it all did sound like the most fantastical story, with neither truth nor merit to it."

"Nay, there's no storytelling to it, my lady," Poppy said firmly. "It's true as the Testament. I've been with Lord and Lady Wilyse nigh all my life, and they're not the sort of grand folk to play jests. Even and all, her ladyship didn't come so far after you for a fancy, but because His Majesty bid her do it."

"But why should the king have any interest in me?"

"Because you're just as Lady Wilyse says," Poppy said. "You're Lady Margaret Roseberry, only daughter to the lamented Marquess of Hartwick and his lady, may they rest forever in God's immortal heaven."

"I am?" Overwhelmed, Margaret pressed her hands to her cheeks, and sank into one of the chairs. "But how can that be? If that were true, then why was I left at St. Beatrice's as a foundling? Why did no one want me?"

"There was only one that didn't want you, my lady," Poppy said with relish, "and that was your ward, and your master. Your father's brother—that who was your uncle— became the next Lord Hartwick. He'd no use for you, and would've rather you perished outright as a babe than to linger as a leech to his fortune. Mayhap that's why he gave you over to the good sisters, from being a burden."

"There was little that was good about them, Poppy," Margaret said bitterly. "Not in how they treated me."

"May God ever protect you from their like again," Poppy said piously. "Now none of that do matter, Lady Margaret, for your wicked uncle is dead, and all his fortune is yours. You cannot have the earldom, nay, from being a lady instead of a gentleman, but in time the king himself will find you a gentleman husband fit for your station, and see that you wed."

"So truly I am a lady?" Margaret asked, marveling at the wonders of Fate, and how in one afternoon she had risen from being an orphan of use to no one to a lady with a great fortune.

"You are, my lady," Poppy said, coming to stand behind Margaret's chair. "Or you shall be once I am done. If Lady Wilyse wishes to see you as a jewel, then I shall make of you the rarest and most precious of gems."

Briskly Poppy pulled the plain linen coif from Margaret's head, and with her fingers unraveled the tight braids that had always bound her hair. Next she drew a wide tortoise comb through her locks, over and over, freeing the curls that the braids had suppressed.

"There, now, hold steady," Poppy ordered, and shyly Margaret obeyed. Already her head felt somehow lighter, as if the convent braids had been one more restraint that had held her back. "Faith, my lady, but you've lovesome hair. How the gentlemen will sigh over it!"

"Only if they were to see it beneath my coif," Margaret

said. "If I'm a lady, I'll scarce walk about with my head
uncovered."

"It's because you're a lady that you'll have leave to do
exactly that," Poppy said, giving a final twist to one of the
curls. "At court the young ladies follow the style of Mistress
Boleyn, and wear only a coronet. Leastwise the ones with
hair so fine as yours."

She handed a small looking glass to Margaret so she
could see for herself.

"There, my lady," Poppy said proudly. "The sin came
from covering hair like that, not in showing it."

Margaret looked at her reflection and gasped. It was
not so much her hair alone that stunned her but her entire
self, now displayed to her. Looking glasses had been forbidden at the abbey as temptation to vanity, and while Margaret had glimpsed her face in the surface of water or in the
polished brasses of the chapel's candlesticks, she'd no real
notion of her appearance.

Yet in a day of shocking revelations, what she saw now
shocked her again. Her eyes were wide and blue, her mouth
red and full, her nose straight, and her cheeks marked with
the most charming of dimples. Her hair was the color of
burnished gold, tumbling in fat curls and waves over her
shoulders and down her back.

Now she understood why the carter and most every
other man who'd glimpsed her in the chapel or cloisters
had stared so at her, and why, too, the other girls had often

resented her. She was beautiful, and not even the mother abbess had been able to steal that from her.

"See, now, my lady? That's a face a man wishes to find on the pillow beside him," Poppy said with approval. "That's more than half the trick for succeeding at court, leastwise for ladies. You won't need to paint, either. You're fair and fresh without it."

Margaret blushed, and lowered the glass. "Lady Wilyse says I've much to learn. I told her I could read and write and speak French, but she only laughed, and said that wasn't the education she intended for me."

Poppy laughed. "Nay, my lady, I shouldn't think that it was! Her ladyship's a wise, worldly lady, and most popular with the gentlemen at the court, too. You should be honored to have her as your tutor."

Margaret twisted around in the chair to face Poppy. "Lord Wilyse must be most proud of having such an accomplished wife."

Poppy laughed again, even more heartily.

"Faith, he must be," she said. "His lordship serves the king as an ambassador to foreign courts and rules far from England, and is seldom on our shores. Her ladyship is his third wife, and much the younger. But he and Lady Wilyse have vowed not to pine for the other, and have granted the other the freedom to find amusement where they may, and not be lonely. But you shall soon see that all for yourself, aye? Now come, let us find you a suitable gown."

The maid bent beside the trunk, pulling out one gorgeous gown after another like silken clouds. "Not knowing what size lady you would prove to be, we were forced to bring many things in hopes we'd find one that would suit you. In time we'll have this stitched to fit you, as well as others new and made proper for you alone, of course. You'll need at least two score before you can appear at court. Ahh, this should do."

She shook out a pale pink silk gown trimmed with dark gray velvet ribbons and cuffs, and laid it across the bed with a fresh linen smock, stockings, and a boned linen corset. Eager to be rid of her old clothes, Margaret stood and began to unpin her gown.

"Nay, no need to take such care, my lady, not with that wretched shroud." Swiftly Poppy pulled the rough linen gown from Margaret's body, heedless of how the worn fabric ripped and tore. Margaret soon found herself without a scrap or stitch upon her body, and quickly she tried to reach for the new smock on the bed to cover her nakedness.

"Forgive me, my lady, but you are not ready for that yet," Poppy said, guiding her back to the center of the room. "First I must wash you properly, and grace you with a fragrance more befitting a lady than the base one you now possess."

Embarrassed to be so unclothed, Margaret flushed and covered her breasts with her hair and most of her private parts with her hands as Poppy brought a bowl and a pitcher of scented water.

"Fie, my lady, none of that false convent modesty," she said firmly as she dipped a washing cloth into the water. "That will be Lady Wilyse's first lesson to you. A lady should not be ashamed of her naked body, but should learn to glory in it, and take as much pleasure in it as any lover would do."

Margaret swallowed, and tried to make herself relax. The maidservant was right, of course. She'd no reason to be so shy before another woman, especially one as cheerful and well-meaning as Poppy. If modesty was another mark of her convent training, with no place at the royal court, then she must put it aside just as she had her old linen gown.

Besides, the room was warm, with the golden sun streaming in through the open windows to fall about her. She closed her eyes and breathed deeply, inhaling both the heady scent of the honeysuckle blossoms along with the sweet, spicy fragrance that perfumed the water in Poppy's basin. Yet when she felt the first touch of the warm, wet cloth on her bare shoulder, Margaret recoiled, unable to help herself.

"Be easy, my lady, be easy," Poppy said softly, as if Margaret were a child in her care. "There's no harm to my touch. Be easy, and quiet, and let me wash away your cares and worries."

The soft cloth swirled over Margaret's bare shoulder and along the dipping hollow of her collarbone, a kind of unexpected caress that was at once gentle, yet strangely warming as well. Carefully Poppy raised Margaret's arm and slid the

cloth along her side, over her ribs to follow first the narrowing curve of her waist and then the swell of her hip. She
stepped behind her, sliding the cloth down the long line of
her spine and over the full rounds of her bottom.

With her eyes still closed, it seemed to Margaret that
every other sense intensified as the cloth in Poppy's hand
laved across her flesh. She became aware of the sounds of
Poppy humming softly, and of the cloth dipping in and out
of the water, like a small lapping wave at her feet, and the
quickening of her breath as she parted her lips. The scent of
the perfumed water on her warm skin seemed to be intoxi-
cating, somehow magically blending with her own essence.

But she was most aware of how every tiny touch of the
wet cloth seemed to thrum across her skin like a caress,
every trickle of perfumed water becoming a teasing rivu-
let. She was far from chill now. Instead she felt as if she
were warmed from within, and unconsciously she began
to stretch and shift her body to meet Poppy's roving cloth,
anticipating where she'd next be touched. Yet when the
cloth discovered her breasts, she gasped at the sudden, sur-
prising pleasure.

"Aye, that amuses you, doesn't it?" Poppy said softly, her
lips close to Margaret's ear, again swirling her cloth around
the fullness of each breast. "Such pretty bubs you have, my
lady, each one the perfect size to fill a lover's hand."

As if to demonstrate, she reached around and cupped
her fingers lightly beneath Margaret's right breast, support-
ing the tender flesh. She rubbed the cloth over the nipple as

if to polish it, making it grow puckered and stiff. Margaret gasped again, restlessly thrusting her breast more deeply against the other woman's fingers.

"As red and plump as a small summer berry, my lady," Poppy said with admiration, chuckling at Margaret's guilelessness. "As ripe, too, I'd vow."

She circled her thumb to her forefinger and gently, gently tugged and twisted the nipple, turning it just enough to draw a small gasp of delight from Margaret.

"Ah, my lady, you did not know, did you?" she whispered slyly. "You believed these were meant for suckling babes and no more. You'd no knowledge of the pleasure they held, did you?"

She squeezed the rosy bud again, and Margaret shuddered. How could she have been so ignorant? Was this, too, commonplace at court, that maidservants would tease their mistresses so? Pleasure streaked from her breast through her body with a heat that stunned her, gathering low in her belly in a most curious way. She leaned back into the other woman's arms, both for support and to seek more of what she offered.

"You like that, my lady, aye," Poppy said, her voice a breathy whisper as she dropped the cloth to tend to both of Margaret's breasts. "Such an innocent! What of all those tales of the wanton lasses in convents, of how hot the sport becomes at night?"

"Not—not us," Margaret stammered, her thoughts too scattered to say more as Poppy tweaked and tormented her nipples. There had been nothing like this at St. Beatrice's, not even a hint of it. They'd been forced to sleep with their hands outside their coverlets, though until now Margaret hadn't realized the reason for it.

All that was changed now. If she'd known the pleasures her own body could hold, she would have willingly been punished even more. Now she covered Poppy's hands with her own, increasing both the pressure and the delight.

"The best part of innocence, my lady, comes with losing it," Poppy said, fair purring, as if she could read Margaret's very thoughts. "Lady Wilyse will see to that. Innocence traded for knowledge—knowledge that grows into pleasure. This is but the beginning, your first start."

"Aye, but—but the beginning," stammered Margaret, her thoughts confused as Poppy's ministrations to her nipples made her entire body betray her. She felt at once restless yet weak, eager yet uncertain, and already a slave to the sensations that Poppy seemed to coax from her with such ease, sensations that now seemed centered low in her belly.

Without thought Margaret pressed her thighs tightly together, as if that would somehow stop this new feeling, yet to her surprise it only made the heat within her smolder and glow, like a fire newly fanned.

She imagined the man holding her, eager to possess her in the same ways as the lovers of the ladies she'd overheard at their confessions. She pressed back against Poppy and groaned with frustration, desperate for something she could not yet describe.

"My poor lady, to suffer so," Poppy whispered, her breath warm against Margaret's ear. "The sweet ache has spread, hasn't it? Lower, aye?"

To demonstrate, the maidservant slid one hand from Margaret's breast along her ribs and lower still, over the dip of her navel to her belly. She spread her fingers, tangling through the golden curls clustered there.

"This is where the fever's hottest, isn't it, my lady?" She pressed her fingers lightly through the curls and between Margaret's thighs, then deeper still to dip into her maiden's passage. "Buried here within your lovely little nest?"

Margaret gasped at the startling intimacy of the touch, her eyes squeezed shut and her head thrown back against the maidservant's shoulder. Poppy's questing finger withdrew just enough to press between Margaret's nether lips and caress the little pip, slippery with desire, that was hidden within.

She was sure the carter would have touched her like this if they'd but had the chance. He would have stroked her with his thick fingers, and it would have felt even better than what Poppy was doing to her now.

Oh, she'd no words for what she was feeling; it was that indescribable. She felt her legs tremble beneath her, and her heart drummed so fast that she felt sure if it were not for the other woman's support, she would have sunk to the floor. She arched back against Poppy, shamelessly offering herself as her muscles stretched taut. Another stroke, another, another, and then her whole body seemed to fly apart as waves of the sweetest pleasure swept over her. She cried out softly, overwhelmed with the joy of it, and sagged, shuddering, into Poppy's arms. With her eyes shut tight, she didn't see the door to the bedchamber swing open, and she was still too lost in herself to hear it.

It took another shocked gasp beyond her own to rouse her, and an exclamation that ended in an oath to make her open her eyes.

And then, at last, she saw the astonished face of Lady Wilyse.

CHAPTER THREE

With a cry of surprise, Margaret tore free from Poppy and reached to where her discarded clothes lay. She grabbed her tattered smock, her thrashing arms tangling in the sleeves.

"Here, now, Lady Margaret, that's not needed," the countess said, laying a calming hand on Margaret's arm. "Be easy, I beg you. You've done nothing wrong."

"Oh, my lady, how can you say that?" cried Margaret. All she could think of was how she'd been a lady for less than half a day, and yet already she'd been caught behaving like the lowest of strumpets. She'd even been caught by the grand lady who'd rescued her, before whom she now stood shivering in her smock. Now she wouldn't be surprised if Lady Wilyse sent her back to the abbey at once, exactly as she deserved.

"Forgive me, my lady, forgive me," she cried, and buried her face in her hands, letting her unbound hair fall over her like a veil of shame. "I never meant to sin before you like this!"

"Nonsense, dear," Lady Wilyse scoffed. "What I saw—what I see—is no sin at all. If that is what you were taught, why, then such is the true sin."

"I only did with her as you bid me, my lady," Poppy said, as she curtsied. "I washed her, and dressed her hair, and tried to make her be at ease with her nakedness. I welcomed her among us just as you wished, my lady."

"Oh, aye, and showed her a bit of frolic, too." Lady Wilyse chuckled, so warm and forgiving a sound that Margaret dared to look up. The countess now showed none of her earlier weariness, but instead appeared refreshed and full of jollity, her handsome eyes bright and her cheeks glowing. She had changed from the elegant but weighty clothes that she'd worn to impress the mother abbess, and instead now had chosen a flowing loose kirtle of silver brocade over her smock.

"Did I spoil your diversion, Lady Margaret?" she continued lightly, almost teasing. "Perhaps it should be I who begs your forgiveness. Poppy has many accomplishments, and is most generous in sharing them to entertain others. She accompanied me to the French court, you see, where she learned many ways to beguile both gentlemen and ladies. Isn't that so, Poppy?"

"Aye, my lady." Poppy beamed at her mistress's praise, and came to stand behind Margaret. "I did try my best to please her ladyship."

"I am certain you did, Poppy." The countess laughed again, tipping her head back a bit to lightly run her fingertips along her throat. "But what do you have to say, my dear? Can you put aside your embarrassment long enough to admit that Poppy's . . . *ministrations* were not so disagreeable?"

Margaret shook her hair back from her face, determined to make sense of this new life of hers. If Poppy was not to be punished for what she'd been doing—nay, it seemed as if the countess had only praise for her actions—then surely she was safe from punishment as well.

"Aye, my lady," she said boldly, choosing her words with care. "I did find pleasure in it."

"She did indeed, my lady," Poppy said eagerly. "For all that she was among the nuns, I vow she'll prove as fine a pupil to your teachings as ever you've had. She is most wonderfully made for love, my lady."

"Is she?" the countess asked thoughtfully. "I'd hoped it would be so. Show yourself to me, my dear. I'd but a glimpse of you just now. That wretched smock hides you like a cloud before the sun. Pray do not be shy."

Margaret took a deep breath. If all the ladies of the royal court were like Lady Wilyse, then clearly the modesty she'd been taught would be of very little value. In truth she did have nothing to hide, and before she lost her courage, she swept away the old smock and stood naked before the countess.

Lady Wilyse's face lit with approval. "Ah, so you are as lovely as I guessed! A perfect Venus, aye? What the gentlemen will make of you!"

"She's worthy of a duke, for certain, my lady," Poppy said eagerly. "Have you seen such hair, my lady? Like spun gold, it is."

"A duke at least," the countess said, "and perhaps even higher."

She reached out to smooth Margaret's hair back over her shoulders, delicately uncovering her breasts. Despite her resolution not to be shy, Margaret blushed again. Whether from the warm breeze from the open window or Poppy's earlier attentions, Margaret's nipples remained taut and red, and the countess's interested scrutiny seemed only to make them tighter still.

"Beautiful," murmured the countess. She reached out and took one of Margaret's nipples between her thumb and forefinger and squeezed it lightly. At once the little nub grew more fiercely flamed, the russet skin around it puckering in happy sympathy.

So gentle a touch, not even a pinch. Once again Margaret felt the same delicious heat streak through her body as it had done before with Poppy.

But this time Margaret didn't gasp or draw away. This

time, she only smiled with a breath of a sigh, and relished the sensation that made her breast feel as if it were growing heavier, fuller, sweeter with joy.

She glanced past the countess and saw her naked self reflected in the diamond-patterned glass of the open window, her pale skin and golden hair shown over and over. She'd no notion of who this Venus might be, or whether their bodies did resemble each other's, as Poppy had claimed.

But she liked what she saw of herself now: a narrow waist, an amply rounded ass, and swelling hips to balance her full, high breasts. Having the two other women standing beside her as completely dressed as she was completely naked somehow made her feel more beautiful and more wanton, too.

The countess smiled knowingly. "Pretty creature," she said, "and not nearly as innocent as the abbess believes, are you?"

"Nay, my lady," Margaret whispered, not only because it seemed the answer that Lady Wilyse desired, but also because it was the truth. She was just beginning to realize it, and to revel in it, too. At heart she was truly no less wanton than those ladies making their confessions. She liked to show herself this way, and she liked being admired and praised. She had been graced with beauty, as rare a gift as any from heaven. Why shouldn't she be proud of that gift, and wish to share it with others?

Lady Wilyse chuckled. "Nay, indeed, you pretty creature.

You would tempt a priest to break his vows, if he should happen upon you like this, or—"

"Or me," said a deep male voice behind them. "Though having no vows of my own to break, I am as free to be tempted as she is to tempt me. Where did you find this delectable hussy, Arabella? Or do you mean her as a gift for me, a winsome toy that we might share between us?"

At once the countess turned about, shielding Margaret from the man, while Poppy with equal haste hurried to fetch a new linen smock from the open trunk to cover her. While it had been acceptable, even praiseworthy, to display one's naked self to other women, apparently it was not so before a gentleman, leastwise this particular gentleman.

It was a disappointing realization to Margaret; how much more exciting it would have been to stand unclad in the warm sunlight to be admired by a single gentleman than an entire flock of ladies!

But despite their efforts, the man had seen Margaret, and more—she had seen him. He had pushed open the door that the countess had left ajar and now stood just inside the chamber, his broad shoulders neatly framed by the heavy beam of the doorway. She guessed he was perhaps thirty years or near to it, with black cropped hair and a narrow black beard that made his jaw seem impossibly square. He'd a long, crooked nose that had been broken, and pale blue eyes that had, in the few seconds that he'd had to study her, seemed to take note of every inch of her unclothed body, and approved of it as well. He was elegantly though simply dressed as a gentleman, in tall boots with silver spurs and dark clothes marked with dust from the road. He'd already removed his gloves and hat, and a handful of dark curls clung damply to his temples. Although Margaret had no experience with gentlemen, she was instantly sure there was no other like him.

Not at court, not in London, not in England, not in all the world.

"Have you no decency, brother, to enter a lady's chamber without notice?" the countess demanded, clearly striving to distract the man. "What reason have you to be here at all? Why have you followed me to this place?"

"And what manner of greeting is that for your only true kin?" he asked, laughing. "Where is the kindness a brother should properly command?"

"You shall have it when you behave like a proper brother," the countess said curtly. "You still have not told me your reason for being here, Jasper."

Desperate to see more of him, Margaret fought through the clouds of linen as Poppy shoved the smock over her head and shoulders. So this gentleman was Lady Wilyse's brother. Now she could see a likeness in their coloring and height, if nowhere else. How could there be, when he was so thoroughly, so commandingly male?

"His Majesty told me of your errand," he said easily, "and I decided you might find it pleasing to have companionship on your journey. His Majesty agreed, and thus here I am."

He opened his hand gracefully, a gesture dismissive and yet also somehow beckoning to her, as if he wished her to be included in this conversation. He'd large hands with an undeniable strength to them, the kind of hands that could rein in a rearing horse with ease. It was likewise easy enough for Margaret to imagine those hands on her body, caressing her with the same freedom that Poppy had shown, filling his palms with her breasts and stroking his long fingers between her legs, in that spot that even now seemed to ache and glow for his touch.

But the countess had no such thoughts. "Fie on your company," she said, swatting away his open hand. "His Majesty sent you to spy on me, didn't he?"

"What reason would he?" he said. "I swear to you, Arabella, there was no such motive. I was weary of the court, and wished an excuse to leave it."

She regarded him suspiciously. "How curious that the court would of a sudden prove so tedious to you."

"Oh, aye, it was, it was," he assured her, "and what better way to relieve any tedium than to see what mischief you have found?"

He leaned to one side, openly trying to see past her to Margaret. His pale blue eyes, so much like his sister's, were regarding Margaret hungrily, like a lion or other bold beast might look at his prey, as if considering whether to devour her in a single bite, or two. Yet the more she looked at him in turn, the more she decided that being devoured by him could be the most desirable fate in the world.

"It's a sweet little mischief, too," he continued, his gaze not on his sister but on Margaret. "Come, now, Arabella, don't keep the wench to yourself. I've ways to amuse her that neither you nor Poppy can match."

"Not this time." Scowling, the countess turned and took Margaret by her arm. "Jasper, this is Lady Margaret Roseberry, daughter to the late Lord Hartwick. Lady Margaret, my brother, Lord Jasper Carleigh, Earl of Blackford."

"The heiress?" His dark brows rose with surprise. "The one buried away with the nuns? The one the king sent you to fetch for him?"

"The same," said the countess. "Who would have guessed she'd beauty to match her gold?"

But Margaret had had enough of being spoken over in this fashion. If she was in fact the daughter of a marquess, then shouldn't she have the right to speak for herself?

"I am the same that I was when I rose this day, my lady," she said firmly. "What you have told me regarding my rank and my fortune has not changed who I am, only how I am addressed."

"Now, that's the Roseberry blood in her speaking for herself, as sure as can be," the countess said with approval. "I knew as soon as that wretched mother abbess told me that not even beating could break the girl's spirit that it must be the true Lady Margaret."

"A beauty with gold and a wit to match," Lord Blackford said, his first surprise now marked with pleasure at her response. He took Margaret's hand and bowed low, the heavy gold ring he wore pressing against her palm. "It is my honor, Lady Margaret."

"And mine, my lord Blackford." His fingers were warm around her hand, exactly as she'd known they'd be, and she blushed, praying he'd no notion of where else she'd imagined his fingers to wander. Her wayward thoughts made her grow more flustered still by his touch.

Without any knowledge of how she was, as a lady, supposed to respond to the earl's attentions, she sank into a curtsy from habit. But because he still held her hand, her balance was unsure, and to her horror she began to topple to one side. At once he claimed her other hand as well to steady her, a small courtesy any gentleman might make.

Yet as inexperienced as Margaret might be, she sensed the difference between another gentleman's gallantry and how Lord Blackford now held her hands. He did not so much hold them as possess them. His fingers surrounded hers, then slowly slid lower until his thumb lay across the underside of her wrist. Gently he traced small circles over her pulse, the most subtle of caresses to warm her blood and make it quicken.

Still bent before him in her thwarted reverence, she looked up at him through the thicket of her lashes. He was smiling as he gazed down at her, and, further, into the gaping neckline of her smock to her breasts. It was enough to know that he'd looked at her, and as he rubbed his thumbs across her pulse, she could imagine him caressing her breasts as well.

Again she felt her nipples stiffen, pushing into the smock's fine white linen like the sheerest of veils. Even that felt too much, and without thinking, she let a small groan of frustration slip free of her parted lips. Startled by her own reaction, she swiftly lowered her gaze before he could read too much in her eyes.

Even then her gaze betrayed her. For though she might have hidden her wanton longing from him, she now stared directly at the front of his trunk hose. Directly before her was the unmistakable jut of his codpiece, black silk embroidered over with blacker ribbon, and she stared at it, fascinated.

She vowed she could almost see its shape, thick and strong as its owner, pushing against its silken boundary to find her. So close before her, the codpiece was like an intriguing, beautifully wrapped present that begged to be opened. She didn't know exactly what she'd find inside— she'd seen a male member only once, and that at a distance, when a worker at the abbey had not bothered with the privy, but untied his hose to piss against the garden wall— but she was certain that Lord Blackford's cock would be much more impressive.

Aye, all she'd have to do was tug at those beguiling little laces with the silver tips, untie the knot, and there he would be. She remembered the confessions she'd overheard, of how some ladies found pleasure in kissing and licking a man's cock, even taking his seed into their mouths. His *cock*: la, even the word excited her, and she swallowed hard.

Lord Blackford chuckled, and her guilty gaze flew up to meet his. Could he read her thoughts that easily? Or had her pulse grown so fast beneath his thumbs that he'd guessed?

Nay, this wasn't gallantry. This was seduction, and even an innocent like Margaret knew the difference. She also knew that she'd never wanted anything more than the man before her.

"That is enough, Jasper," Lady Wilyse said, her voice sharp with irritation. "Let the lady stand free."

"As you wish," he murmured, and slowly raised Margaret up to her feet. She wished he'd kept holding her hands. Already she missed his touch, and longed for more of it. As it was, she couldn't have looked away from those pale blue eyes even if she'd wished to.

"There was no need to set me free, my lord," she said, her words strangely husky. "I was well enough as I was."

Amused by her honesty, he smiled. "Did the prospect please you where you were, Lady Margaret?"

"It did, my lord," she said, thinking again of that tempting codpiece. "I found it a prospect with many possibilities to it."

That made him laugh, and the countess, too. "God's blood, hearken to such boldness in so young a lady! Surely that nunnery must have been more of a brothel, for her to speak so plain."

"Yet she vows she remains a maid," the countess insisted, "and I would that she remains so, Jasper, until I've brought her to London."

He shook his head in disbelief. "A maid? This lady?"

"I am, my lord," Margaret said firmly, though she flushed again, "and I will swear to it on the Scripture itself, if that will convince you."

"Nay, I've a better way to the truth," he said, and he turned towards the maidservant. "Poppy, you're as fair a judge as any in such matters. Have you tested her? Does she still have the maidenhead she claims?"

"Aye, my lord," Poppy said promptly. "Her passage is tight as a drum, my lord, with the sweetest parsley patch you'd ever fancy. But maid or not, she does possess an amorous nature, and takes to such play as quick as any stoat."

Margaret gasped with dismay, wishing Poppy had not spoken quite so freely of either her innocence or her eagerness.

Lord Blackford cocked a single brow. "'An amorous nature,' you say?" he repeated, his smile grown even more wolfish than before. "It's one surprise after another with you, Lady May."

"Margaret," Margaret said swiftly, not wishing him to confuse her with another lady. "My name is Margaret, not May."

"But 'May' can be used for 'Margaret,'" he said, "and it pleases me to call you so. 'Margaret' is a name for wizened saints and spinsters. You are more a 'May' to me."

Margaret smiled up at him, more pleased than he'd ever guess. No one had ever cared enough for her to give her a pet name like this. She liked it, too. If she was beginning a new life, then why not a fine new name to go with it?

"Truly, my lord?" she said breathlessly. She shrugged her shoulders, making her smock slide lower to reveal more of her breasts to him. "I am more a 'May' to you?"

"You are indeed." His gaze had followed her shifting smock and remained intent upon the rosy crests of her nipples, now barely covered by the fine linen. "As sweet and ripe as the first day of that merry month. My lady May."

He reached for her, and she swayed eagerly towards him. His arm was already half circling her waist when his sister stepped between them.

"Oh, aye, Jasper, I know you too well for this," the countess said, pulling her brother's arm away from the thoroughly disappointed Margaret. "You'll make the girl your lady May, only so you might raise your own rude Maypole for her to dance around."

"But I prefer it, too!" cried Margaret, already thinking of herself as May. "Cannot I decide how I wish to be called?"

The countess sighed with exasperation. "Call yourself whatever you please, so long as you keep yourself from my brother's path. Jasper, leave us at once."

He did not move. "But it's so late in the day, Arabella, and I've been long on the road. Surely we will sup together?"

"Nay, we shall not," the countess said firmly. "Lady Margaret and I are weary, and—"

"Lady May," insisted the newly renamed May, smiling as winningly as she could at Lord Blackford. "You must call me Lady May."

Lord Blackford laughed. "You see how it is, sister. Weary or not, Lady May wishes my company."

But Lady Wilyse would have none of it. To May's disappointment, the countess placed her hands firmly on her brother's chest and tried to shove him towards the door.

"Begone from here, Jasper," she ordered. "Begone!"

Much to May's delight, he remained, no matter how hard the countess shoved at him. "I will go only if you agree to let me ride with you tomorrow."

"I've a half dozen men-at-arms riding with me, Jasper," she said, "and my footmen are armed as well. What further could you add to that?"

"You can never have too many men riding with you, sister," he said. "You know as well as I that the roads are not safe for ladies, no matter how many attendants you have with you. I'd hate to learn that Lady May suffered at the hands of brigands."

The countess gave him an extra shove. "Oh, aye, no care for me!"

"Because you, dear sister, would like nothing better than to be bound and plundered by a pack of ravening highwaymen," he said mildly. "I know your tastes, Arabella, and your habits, too."

To May's astonishment, the countess didn't deny these sordid accusations, but only shrugged them away. "Speak as you please, Jasper, but I still intend to keep you as distant from this lady as I can."

"Pray let him accompany us tomorrow, my lady," May

pleaded. Though she wasn't sure what the word "brigand" might mean, she very much wanted Lord Blackford to be a member of their party.

More specifically, she very much wanted Lord Blackford.

"Please, my lady," she said. "I should feel far safer if we'd a capable gentleman such as Lord Blackford in our party."

The countess looked up to the heavens, or at least the ceiling. "Faith, child, you do not begin to know of my brother's capabilities! But no matter. Likely it is wise to have another sword with us on the road. Jasper, we leave at dawn. Make yourself ready then, or we leave you behind."

"You may depend on me to attend you, Arabella, though I know full well you'd wish I wouldn't." He turned towards May, with a graceful bow for so large a man. "Until tomorrow, Lady May. Sleep well this night, and dream only of me."

He touched his fingers to his lips, pressing lightly, and turned his open hand towards May, as if to make the kiss fly through the air to her. It was as pretty a piece of gallantry as May had ever seen—until Lord Blackford winked and slowly smiled to her, that same devouring smile that made her blood run hot with desire for him. He knew it, too, and as the door closed after him, she could hear him laughing to himself in the hallway outside.

"Now, that was trouble we did not need," the countess said crossly, taking the goblet of canary wine that Poppy had poured for her. "How vexing to have my brother appear like this!"

"I do not find it vexing at all, my lady," May said, still listening for the last fading notes of his laughter. He needn't have bid her to dream of him tonight, not when she was already certain she'd dream of no one else. "I am glad of it, and of him."

"Of course you are." Lady Wilyse didn't bother to hide her disgust as she sank into the nearest chair. "What female is there who does not brighten and cheer whenever my brother appears?"

"It's the black lion again, my lady," Poppy said darkly, "and another innocent dove ready to fall into his claws."

"Fie, Poppy, none of that 'black lion' nonsense," Lady Wilyse said with disgust. "My brother needs no further encouragement."

"Is that what he is called, my lady?" May asked. "I saw a lion carved deep on the gold ring that he wears. Is that the black lion?"

The countess sighed, and waved her hand dismissively. "There are black lions on our family's arms, marks of our fidelity to the king. That is the lion my brother wears on his finger, aye. But there are idle fools at court who choose to call my brother the black lion on account of his dark hair, and by how willingly maids will come to him to meet their own ruin. Lambs, they are called, and pray you are never among their flock."

May heard only the description, and not the warning that came with it. "His lordship *is* like a lion, my lady. A proud and virile lion, master of all and ready to prove it."

"If you believe that is so, then you are no better than the rest," the countess said with disgust. "Ah, if only you'd been plain or simpleminded, the way we all suspected, then none of this would be happening!"

"His lordship did not judge me plain, my lady," May said eagerly. "I could tell by how he looked at me. He liked my breasts in particular, and wished to touch them just as Poppy did."

As if to demonstrate, May cupped her hands beneath her breasts, raising them up like offered fruit. Her fingers grazed her nipples, and at once they again grew taut, poking lewdly through the linen.

The countess gave a little snort of disgust. "If I'd wanted more proof of your virginity, then that was it. Only blind ignorance of the act itself kept you from clawing away his clothes and clambering astride his cock here before me."

"And what if I wished to do so, my lady?" demanded May warmly, for warmth was in fact still coursing through her body. Having the countess describe so succinctly what she had longed to do to her brother only made that warmth glow.

"What if I wished to lie with him, here in this bed?" she continued. "Didn't you and Poppy both urge me to delight in the desires of my body? Didn't you tell me that modesty was false, that innocence was a burden?"

Lady Wilyse closed her eyes, as if the truth was too painful to bear. "I have said those things to you, aye, and I do not regret them. But not with my brother. Not with my brother."

"Pray, why not?" May demanded, tossing her hair back over her shoulders. "Has he some weakness, some secret deformity, that would make him a disagreeable partner? Or . . . or is he wed to another?"

"Wed?" asked the countess. "Nay, no longer. He was once, to a dutiful creature who bore him three sons in three years, and then dutifully died as well. Nay, there is no deformity to Jasper."

May dropped to her knees before Lady Wilyse. "Then why can I not wed him? You are taking me to court so the king might find me a husband. Why can't I marry Lord Blackford, and save His Majesty the trouble? Oh, pray agree to it, my lady. Pray agree!"

But the countess only scowled and shook her head. "Do not be a fool, my dear. You don't know what you ask."

"But I do, my lady," May insisted. Her head spun with the glorious possibility of being Lady Blackford, of having such a man all to herself for the rest of their lives. "I will never find another man who could suit me better."

"But he will always find another woman who will charm him after you, my dear." Lady Wilyse drank deeply of the wine, holding the goblet delicately between her fingers. "He has his sons. He has wealth, land, power. He has no reason to wed again, and never will. Not you, nor any other woman."

"Then I shall have him without marriage," May declared fiercely. "You say I have a fortune, too. What reason do I have to marry, either?"

"Because you are a woman, and a lady," Lady Wilyse said. "You could have all the gold in this world, yet you have no power until you have a husband. No woman does. In the end, even queens must marry to secure their futures."

May sat back on her heels on the floor to reconsider. "Very well, then, in time I will marry, when His Majesty says I must. But before then, I see no reason why I cannot have his lordship, too."

"You may take a score of lovers if it pleases you," the countess said firmly. "I care not if you do. But my brother must not be one of them."

"Pray why not?" May demanded, remembering again how much she wished to explore the mysteries of the earl's codpiece. "Or is there some reason you wish to guard his lordship from me?"

"You little fool!" The countess struck the now-empty goblet down on the table with ringing force. "It's not my brother I wish to guard but you. If you lie with him now, he will ruin you for every other man, and you will forever be discontented and unhappy. Now let that be an end to it."

But May knew it was only the beginning.

CHAPTER FOUR

*J*asper Carleigh, the fourth Earl of Blackford, had told his sister the truth when he'd said he followed her here to this inn because he'd been bored at court. He *had* been bored. The king had yet to return to London, instead dallying at Richmond longer than anyone had expected because Mistress Boleyn preferred it.

Jasper did not. Compared to London, Richmond was dull, with the same rounds of hunting and hawking and foolishness conducted around the same old faces. When he'd learned Arabella had contrived this ridiculous junket to rescue some long-lost lady buried away in a cloister, he'd been intrigued. His sister was by nature far too selfish and dedicated to her own amusements to run after an orphan unless there was some gain in it for her. He'd seen (and shared) enough of Arabella's diversions to decide that whatever she was doing would be more entertaining than watching the king snuffling like a spaniel in heat after Mistress Boleyn, and on a whim he'd requested permission to leave Hampton and join her.

But of all the possibilities he'd considered regarding his cheerfully debauched younger sister—were the nuns of this "abbey" she'd found this girl among really a retreat for devotees of Sappho, or perhaps even flagellation in the Italian manner?—he'd never imagined what he'd found. His sister and her maidservant, dallying with the rescued orphan, who had stood shamelessly naked before them. This orphan, too, turned out to be not the charmless waif he'd been picturing but the most delicious wanton he'd seen in years. She'd the face of an angel and a body made for deviltry, and for all her boldness, she was still a virgin, with a maidenhead ripe for his plucking.

Of course he'd have her. There was no mystery to it. Though he enjoyed the game of seduction as much as any man, he never doubted that he'd have any woman he set his mind—or his cock—to claim. Little Lady May was already so eager for it that he likely could have fucked her there before Arabella, if he'd wished to. The only question was why his sister was being so damned protective of the girl. They'd shared women in the past, hadn't they? Why should this one be any different?

No matter. Having to seduce her away from Arabella would only add spice to his conquest, and he smiled with

anticipation. Was there any finer way to pass the tedium of
the road than tutoring a young lass in swiving?

"The stable master's done as he should, my lord," said
Jasper's manservant Drumble, joining him in the box given
to Jasper's horse. "I found naught that was amiss."

Jasper nodded, pleased, for he was always watchful of
his mounts in public stables like this one. He valued his
horses too much to risk having a lazy stableboy short them
on their feed or water, and he'd come down here himself
after supper to make sure that his gelding was bedded properly for the night.

Drumble patted the large bay's neck.

"This day's journey was nothing to him, my lord," he said
proudly. A slight rascal of a man with sandy hair, Drumble
had been with Jasper since boyhood, and over time he'd
acquired the right to be as proud of his master's belongings
as he was of his master. "God's fish, he could travel twice
the distance we made today and scarce be winded! He'll be
fit for more tomorrow, my lord, that's for certain, even if
our pace will be slow following with the ladies."

"Aye, he won't be happy with that," Jasper agreed. "Having to walk beside my sister's coach won't please him at all."

"Nay, not at all," agreed Drumble, nodding sagely. "I
don't expect there's much to divert you in a place like this,
my lord, but the stableman told me that if you've an interest, they're putting a stallion to a mare this evening in the
field to the back. He said the stallion's a great strong brute,
the best stud in the county, and a sight worth the seeing."

Jasper nodded, and followed Drumble from the inn's yard. He kept a breeding stable of his own at Blackford Hall, and he was always interested in improving his lines. If this stallion proved his measure, then Jasper might buy him for his own stud. Besides, as Drumble himself had said, what else had he to occupy him in this dull village?

Not far from the inn was a small fenced pasture, with a few lanterns lit and hung from nearby trees against the coming dusk. Already a crowd of half-drunk men had gathered to watch, overseen by a blustering man in a red knit cap and leather jerkin, perched atop the fence. Clearly the man was the stallion's owner, from how he was boasting of his horse's merits and ability to sire foals.

Certainly the stallion looked able enough. Held by two sturdy grooms in the far corner of the pasture, the horse was exactly the great brute that Drumble had described, a large black with a white blaze. Though the mare was yet tucked safely in the inn's stable, the stallion must still have been able to scent her. He pawed the grass before him in eagerness, snorting and rolling his eyes and trying to pull his head free from the grooms.

Though none of the men recognized Jasper by sight, they knew at once from his dress and carriage that he was a nobleman. With many bows they quickly found him a choice place for viewing near the stallion's owner.

After the first few moments of awed silence at his presence, the men around him began talking again, too excited to keep still for long. It didn't matter what rank the men around him might be, thought Jasper with amusement. Lords and yeomen, even kings, all spoke the same coarse bawdry when it came to rutting.

"Porter's mare's a skittish one," said one man. "She'll lead that rogue a pretty dance at first, but he'll show her who's the master once he's fair mounted. There be no mercy in a stiff dick, eh?"

"Mare, bitch, or whore, 'tis all the same," said another. "Take them fast an' take them hard, an' hold steady until you spend in their cunts, an' not a care for how much they claim they don't like it, too. Their lot's to take our seed, and be grateful."

This brought a roar of laughter and approval. Jasper only smiled, and wondered idly how many of these men would dare speak such bluster before their wives. He'd often found that the men who crowed the loudest were the meekest of cocks.

Yet even so, Jasper found his own thoughts returning to Lady May. He wouldn't force her, of course—that wasn't his way—but he wished she were here with him now, to witness the stallion and the mare. Any coupling, whether between man and woman or lesser beasts, was bound to incite lust in the blood of even the shyest of maids, and Lady May was hardly shy.

At last another groom appeared, leading a neat chestnut mare into the pasture. She pranced sideways and coyly tossed her mane as the groom turned her to the fence with her haunches facing outwards.

At once the stallion came towards her, pulling his two grooms skidding across the grass to the delight of the onlookers. The mare raised her tail, beckoning him with her scent, and the stallion snorted and brought his nose to her hindquarters. Yet as soon as she must have felt his breath on her parts, she kicked backwards, teasing him.

But as the men had predicted, the stallion would have none of it. His cock had already dropped, as long as a man's forearm, and in one powerful lunge the stallion reared on his hind legs and over the mare. Pinned with his front legs over her shoulders, she must have realized her fate, for she spread her back legs to give him better access.

The stallion found his mark and drove into her in one stroke, his ballocks striking against her rump. The mare quivered from the impact, or perhaps from lust as well, and she widened her legs farther to brace herself for the fury of his attack.

Over and over the stallion thrust into the mare, his enormous cock glistening with their mingled juices. His black coat was sheened with sweat and his powerful muscles bunched and relaxed with every stroke.

There was no raillery now along the fence, no bawdy boasts or comments. Instead every man watched the rutting beasts in fascinated, almost reverential, silence. Jasper would have wagered a sizable sum that most were imagining themselves in the stallion's place. To be that thoroughly male, that potent, that dominating when it came to the carnal act of mating: what man would not consider it?

Jasper himself would freely admit that he found the

scene in the pasture arousing. While he preferred to win women by seduction, not force, the attraction of the stallion's mastery over the mare was undeniable. He was thankful that his codpiece shielded the insistent demands of his own cock, pressing hard for release.

From the horses before him it was an easy, swift leap to recall the Lady May standing naked in the sunlight, so much creamy pale skin tipped with the red of her nipples and gilded with the curls that fell over her shoulders and the tighter little fleece that guarded her quim. He hadn't been able to see her rump, not in the brief moment before Arabella had stepped between them, but he was sure it was as perfect as the rest of her had been, round and beckoning.

He could imagine her bent over a sturdy cushioned footstool, looking back coyly over her shoulder at him through that tangled golden hair as she presented herself to him much as the mare had to the stallion. With her bottom obligingly turned up for him, she'd part her legs to display her cunt, the rosy lips plump and wet with her desires and the dusky opening above.

She'd display herself for him much as the mare had for the stallion, fair begging him to use her, and he'd oblige just as the stallion had. He'd sink in deep in a single long stroke and bury himself in her cunt. She'd cry out with delight, that unmistakable, wordless sound that always inflamed him the more. He'd hold her by the hips to keep her steady, his fingers spread, and as his balls tightened, he'd drive into the full depth of her passage, again and again and—

"I vow I've never seen a stallion cover a mare better'n that, my lord," said Drumble with admiration beside him. "God's teeth, look at the head on that cock! As big as my fist, it is. No wonder there's so many foals come of it, eh?"

Jarred from his own thoughts, Jasper looked at the two horses. The stallion had spent, and the grooms had guided him off the mare. The black horse danced backwards, his enormous cock soft and dangling, with droplets of sperm catching the lantern's light as they scattered on the grass.

"Aye, there's much to admire," Jasper agreed. The stallion's performance seemed like an omen to him, an indication of the great pleasure he was sure to find with Lady May. "Go to the horse's owner, Drumble, and tell him I would know his price."

Drumble's eyes widened. "You would buy the stallion, my lord?"

"I would," Jasper said. "Pay him what he asks, and make arrangements to have the horse sent to Blackford Hall."

Jasper smiled and looked back to the black horse, still trotting proudly around the pasture with his tail streaming behind. They were two of a kind, he and this stallion.

As Lady May would soon be most pleased to learn for herself.

MAY HAD SUPPED with the countess in her room. After a lifetime of the abbey's austerity, the roasted meat and fowl, puddings, and other dishes that the inn's cook had sent up had seemed bewilderingly delicious and rich. But Lady Wilyse had deemed it coarse fare fit only for the country, and instead had devoted herself to the wine. She had made sure to keep May's glass filled as well, and when she announced it was time to retire for the night, May could scarce stumble back to her own room. She'd needed Poppy to help her undress, and as she sank into the novel luxury of the soft feather bed, she was sure she'd sleep forever.

But whether it was the unfamiliarity of the bed, the strange sounds of other travelers in the inn, the rare loneliness of sleeping by herself, or the rich food and wine, May woke deep in the night. No matter how she tried to compose herself, she could not fall back asleep, and at last she rose from the bed and went to the window.

The moon was still high in the dark sky, and she guessed it must be near to midnight, with many hours left before dawn. She could still hear men drinking in the taproom below, and the sounds of the cook barking orders to her staff as they cleaned the kitchen. Though it seemed late to May, it was clearly not so late to the rest of the world. At supper the countess had told her that if May had any need or concern, to come to her at once. Perhaps she, too, would be awake, and glad of company.

Cautiously she opened the door and made her way down the hall to Lady Wilyse's room. Candlelight shone beneath the door and she could hear voices within, likely the countess and one of her servants. May tapped lightly, but they did not hear her to answer. The door was unlatched, and May pushed it open a fraction, meaning to call to the countess.

But what she saw instead stole every word from her lips, and every thought from her mind.

The countess was on her hands and knees on the bed, completely naked save for her earrings and the long jeweled necklace that hung down over her breasts. Her hair was still elaborately dressed, too, the dark twisted braids pinned into place, which somehow made her undressed body appear even more decadently alluring by comparison.

With her, and equally naked, were the two young grooms who'd helped her from her carriage earlier. One knelt behind her on the bed, holding her tightly by the waist as he thrust his stiffened cock in and out of her. The second groom stood before her, his hands squeezing her breasts and tugging roughly at her plum-colored nipples as she sucked and licked his rampant cock with greedy abandon.

Though the countess's eyes were squeezed shut, it was clear even to May that she was thoroughly enjoying herself from the happy gurgles and moans she made each time the groom drove into her again. Her long jeweled necklace swung back and forth, glittering in the wavering light from the candlesticks around the bed. The two men also groaned and grunted, their heads thrown back in ecstasy, and their motions growing more urgent and violent by the moment.

May clapped her hand over her mouth to keep from

crying out herself. She knew she should retreat as quietly as she'd come and leave the three to their wicked play, but she could not make herself look away. It was one thing to have overheard whispered confessions of this kind of scene, but another entirely to witness one before her, and she stared both from shock and fascination.

So that was a cock in all its manly glory, red and thick and taut, and that was how a woman took one deep into her mouth, and that—that was fucking itself, a word she'd heard but never imagined like this. The countess arched her back and pushed her bottom back to meet the groom's powerful thrusts, and each time he withdrew, her fleshly nether lips clung to him, loath to part with him.

The longer May watched, the more she seemed to feel what the countess herself must be feeling. The feverish heat that Poppy's lascivious attentions had built in her belly earlier now returned to burn even more hotly, and her breath came short in her lungs.

She pressed her thighs together as if that might bring her relief, and when it only increased her restless excitement, she tugged up the hem of her smock and touched herself as Poppy had done. She had never done this before— such wanton, intimate acts had been strictly forbidden at the abbey, and deemed the most debasing of carnal sins— and from inexperience her touch lacked Poppy's practiced deftness.

With only instinct guiding her, she slipped her fingers between her legs. To her surprise she found that this part of her that was usually no more than a plump opening had swollen into full lips that were so sensitive that she sighed aloud.

Easing between, she discovered she was slippery and inviting, as if her maiden's nest longed to draw her finger within. More exciting still was the discovery of a tiny nubbin of flesh, sleek and round as a pearl, that was delicious to stroke and squeeze gently.

Over and over she played her fingers across this nubbin, unconsciously matching her rhythm to that of the footman driving his cock into the countess before her. It was almost as if she could feel that cock herself, buried deep within her. Her heart raced and her body trembled, and she panted in quick gasps that matched her finger's quickening game.

Her own touch, the lascivious scene before her, the desire that Poppy had already stirred within her, and the longing she felt for Lord Blackford all rushed together into a feverish blur. Her legs trembled beneath her and she was forced to lean against the door to support herself, yet still she could not look away.

Suddenly the groom who stood beside the bed jerked forward with a choked cry, pulling his cock away from the countess. A pearly essence sprayed from the tip, showering over the countess's shoulders and breasts as his hips continued to jerk wildly.

Yet instead of offending her ladyship, this offering of his spunk seemed to give her even more pleasure, and she suddenly threw her head back and cried out, pressing her ass more tightly against the groom who was working her from behind. In turn her response seemed to be enough to bring this man to his crisis, too, and with a bestial grunt he gave one final, forceful shove into her ladyship's cunt, so hard that she toppled forward onto the tangled sheets. He then collapsed upon her, the three of them now soaked with sweat and gasping for breath.

May's own release could not come quickly enough. With a helpless whimper, she fell back against the wall, her smock pulled high over her wide-spread legs as she struggled to find the pleasure that she was sure would be hers.

Yet even through the blinding haze of desire, she still somehow heard the footsteps on the staircase at the end of the hall. The countess had taken the entire floor for her party, and no other travelers would come this way. A servant, then, and with a little cry of frustration May dropped her smock and stumbled along the shadowy hallway towards the open door to her own bedchamber. The footsteps were heavy, a man in boots, and she hurried as fast as her unsteady legs would carry her, desperate not to be caught.

But the man was already at the top of the stairs, his broad form silhouetted by the lantern in the staircase. May looked, and gasped, and froze.

Lord Blackford.

Was his lordship sleeping in one of these chambers, too? Had his sister relented and let him share their lodgings?

Or had he perhaps come for her?

Though no manservant was accompanying the earl, he

appeared ready to retire for the night, his black doublet unlaced and hanging open over his white shirt and the sleeves unfastened and rolled over his bare forearms. In the half-light of the hall, he was in fact all black and white, from his dress to his dark hair, eyebrows, narrow beard, and the whiteness of his teeth as he smiled: a black lion exactly, thought May. He must have spent the evening among the men in the inn's taproom, for the odors of tobacco and ale clung to him, masculine odors that were enthralling to her for being so male and foreign.

"My lady May," he said easily, as if finding her here at this hour were entirely to be expected. "Good even to you."

To her shame, he claimed her right hand in greeting, the same hand she'd been using to pleasure herself. He raised it to kiss, and as he did, he must have breathed the unmistakable honeyed scent of her own cunny. She knew he did; he held her fingers there before his nose, inhaling deeply, as if her scent were the rarest perfume of the East.

He didn't remark it, nor comment as if in wonder. There wasn't any question. He knew where her fingers had been. His smile widened slowly, and with a small, confusing thrill of the danger he presented to her, she thought again of a great, ravening lion.

"Dear little May," he said, his rumbling deep voice low and full of confidence and amusement, too. "Pray what manner of mischief has my sister drawn you into this night?"

"No mischief, my lord," she said breathlessly. It was bad enough that her body still trembled from thwarted desire, but now it quaked from his nearness, too. "Not with her ladyship."

"Nay?" he asked, clearly not believing her. "Then why are you wandering about like a lost lamb?"

She could only answer the truth. "I awoke, my lord, and sought Lady Wilyse's company, as she had bid me to do if I were uneasy."

He glanced down the hall, then back to May. "Then why are you not with her still?"

May flushed. "Because . . . because there were others with her instead."

"Others? What manner of others, Lady May?"

She hesitated. Although she had been taught to trust the truth, and that no ill could ever come of so doing, the truth here might betray her benefactress's trust to her own brother. Yet the truth it must be; she knew no other way.

"Come," he coaxed, gently squeezing her fingers. "I doubt that anything you might tell me regarding Arabella will shock me. She is capable of every lewd folly and amusement, and I vow I've heard of them all, some from her own telling."

Now she, too, glanced towards Lady Wilyse's door, half expecting her to come sallying out to join them. As much as what she'd seen had seared itself to her memory, she still wasn't sure she could describe it, especially not to the man before her.

"Tell me, sweet." He raised her hand to his lips and kissed the back of it, a conscious intimacy that made her blush again. Whether she was being disloyal to the countess or not, she realized that she would tell him, and, more, that she wanted to tell him.

"Very well, my lord." She took a deep, shuddering breath. "Her ladyship is . . . is engaged with two of the servants of this house."

"Engaged where?" he asked. "Tell me. The three of them together?"

"Aye, my lord." The memory returned so vividly that the thrumming began again low in her belly, or maybe it was because she was describing what she'd seen to him. "The three of them were on her ladyship's bed. They— None of them were dressed, my lord."

He grunted, watching her so intently she could almost feel his gaze on her skin like a caress. "Not a scrap?"

"Nay, my lord, nothing." Without thought her fingers were working restlessly against his, threading in and out between them. "Except her ladyship wore her jewels, even— even as she did what she did."

"Tell me more, May. Tell me what was it she did."

"She—she was kneeling on the bed, my lord," she said, feeling feverish and daring. "One man stood beside the bed, and she was licking and kissing his—his staff."

"Was she?" he murmured, coming closer to her. "What of the other rogue?"

May leaned back against the wall, tipping her chin up towards him. "The other rogue was kneeling behind her, my lord, and he—he was pushing his staff in and out of her very fast."

"He was fucking her, then?" Idly, he reached out to run his finger along the gathered neckline of her smock, easing the linen lower over her breasts until only the very tips of her stiffened nipples were covered. "He was fucking her hard. Or is that word new to you, my innocent?"

She shook her head, feeling less innocent by the moment. She arched her back, lifting her breasts towards him, and as she did her nipples slipped free, framed by the ruffled linen. She made no move to cover them, nor did he, and she smiled up at him through her lashes.

"Nay, my lord," she whispered. "I have heard the word before. I would listen to women who came to the abbey to make their confessions, and they would use it."

"Then you should, too," he said, teasing her. "Say it, May. Speak it properly for me."

"They were *fucking*, my lord." To her own surprise, she chuckled, deep in her throat. What she was saying, what she was doing, standing here in her bare feet and smock— none of it seemed real to her, and yet she'd not wish it any different, not for all the world.

"The servant was fucking her ladyship," she continued. "And she liked fucking him, my lord. I could tell from how she moved with him. She liked it greatly."

"And you, May," he said. "Did you touch yourself while you watched them fucking?"

He raised her fingers again, but this time he slipped them into his open mouth. His tongue swiped around her fingertips, tasting her juices, his gaze locked with hers.

"As sweet as honey," he said. "As sweet as your cunny. Was it seeing them fuck that made your honey flow like this?"

She gasped, remembering, and pressed back against the wall to steady herself.

"Aye, my lord," she confessed. "Aye, I did. I could not help myself."

"Then do not try," he said, and at last he kissed her. He began lightly, his lips brushing over hers, but soon deepened the kiss, forcing her lips to part and sliding his tongue deep inside to touch her own. Startled, she tried to draw back, but he'd cupped the back of her head with his hand to hold her there, and after that first struggle she gave herself over to kissing him in return.

His beard grazed her lips and cheeks, and his chest was hard against her breasts. The more she kissed him, the more she liked it, and the more she realized how much being kissed by him—his tongue pressing and probing and stroking her with a ferocity that made her dizzy—was still only a teasing hint of what it would be like to have his cock inside of her, too.

His mouth left hers and she gasped, already missing him. He caught her breasts in his hands, lifting them free from the front of her smock so he could suckle them. He drew hard on one nipple, then flattened his tongue to swirl around the tip. He knew exactly how much to give her, the wet of his tongue and the pressure against the edge of his teeth, enough to make her whimper. If it were not for the wall behind her, she was sure she'd sink to the floor.

And if only he'd reach lower, and lift her smock. If only he'd touch her where she'd touched herself, kiss her there and push into her with his fingers, so much larger than her own, if only he'd fuck her, too, the way the groom had fucked her ladyship.

"Please," she gasped, shameless in her need. "Oh, please, my lord, pray fuck me now!"

He looked up at her with his pale eyes, letting her wet pink nipple slide over his lip and slip from his mouth. "You would ask that of me, Lady May?"

"I would, my lord!" she cried, frustrated and panting at the same time. "I would want that from you more than anything!"

He straightened, still caressing her breasts. "Would you, now?"

"Aye, my lord, I would," she said, desperation making her speak plain. Why wasn't he as feverish as she? "Am I . . . am I somehow lacking to you? Am I not worthy of your desire?"

"There's no doubt of that, little May," he said, smiling. "You'd bring a cockstand to a dead man."

He took her hand and pushed it down inside his trunk hose so she might feel his cock. She gasped: it felt enormous to her blind fingers, long and thick. The skin was velvet soft yet hot, and the blunt end of it was wet, weeping for her as her own cunny had done for him. Eagerly her fingers moved along his length to explore him, but with a grunt he pulled her hand free.

"That's enough, sweet," he said. "Enough for both of us, I would say."

"But why?" she cried. "If it is what we both desire, why will you not fuck me?"

"Hush now, hush," he said, quieting her by pressing his fingers across her mouth. "You are an innocent. You don't know what you ask."

"But I *do*, my lord, and I—"

"Nay, you do not," he said firmly, pulling her smock back over her breasts. "I do, and you do not. It will be my decision when I take you, not yours. You've many lessons to learn before you've earned that from me, sweet. And I say not this night, but another."

Mortified by his rejection, she shoved herself clear of him and ran to her room, slamming the door shut. She hoped he would follow, and with her heart racing, she stood on the other side of the door, listening for him to come. But to her sorrow, she heard his footsteps go the other direction, and finally down the stairs.

With a sob, she ran across the room and flung herself facedown on her empty bed. How could he refuse her like that? He'd wanted her. The proof had been clear enough, there in her own hands. He'd known, too, how much she'd wanted him. How could he have turned away?

With tears still streaming from her eyes, she rolled onto her back. She pulled up her smock to bear herself to the moonlight. She bent her knees and spread her thighs, and with one hand to rub across her nipples and the other brushing over her pearl and then dipping deep into her cunny, she soon roused herself to where she'd been before.

Her fingers moved swiftly, eased by her own wetness, and as the tension grew in her belly, she squeezed her eyes shut and thought of kissing Lord Blackford, how he'd pushed her back against the wall as he'd kissed her breasts to let her realize how much larger and stronger he was than she. She thought of his cock, how hot and demanding it had felt in her hand, and imagined how it would feel to have it there in her swollen passage instead of her fingers, stroking her and stretching her and fucking her hard like she'd witnessed earlier, only better because it would be *him*.

The tension broke suddenly, making her cry out with surprise and wonder. Her body buckled from the force of it, spasm after spasm that rocked through her entire body only to burst into a joyful, rushing relief that left her racked and spent. Afterwards she lay there, her legs still spread and her cunny and breasts still uncovered, as her heart slowed and her breathing calmed. This was what the mother abbess had warned her of, and what women and men both craved above everything else. She'd already understood that much.

But she also understood that it wasn't all, not by half, and for the rest she'd need Lord Blackford.

And by all that was holy, she would have him.

CHAPTER FIVE

*J*asper knew his sister well, and he knew she'd hoped to be able to leave the inn early, so early that he'd be left behind. On most days, this would have worked, for he was not by nature a gentleman who rose early, especially not without a better reason than to poke along in the dust of a lumbering lady-coach.

But today was different. He'd reason enough for rising well before dawn to be shaved and dressed, and being cheery about it as well. He was not about to give his sister the satisfaction of escaping without him, nor was he going to let her run away with a delectable prize like Lady May.

Ah, Lady May. There was part of him—the part of him that was his cock, mainly—that could not believe he'd walked away from her last night. He'd intended to go to

Arabella's rooms to speak with her, but instead he'd found Lady May, nigh drunk with lust in the hall.

A beautiful virgin, panting in rut and begging for him to fuck her! Not even he received gifts such as that, and after watching the stallion with his mare, he'd almost obliged her. But at the last, he'd realized the peril, and held back.

It wasn't that he'd any moral qualms about taking her maidenhead. He fully intended to claim both it and her. But to do so last night with her so willing would have been no sport at all. With so little challenge, he would have tired of her in a day or two, and that would have been that. All women were much the same to him after he'd had them, even the beauties like May. The pleasure came in the chase, not the weeping and clinging and maudlin protestations of devotion that came afterwards.

Besides, no good would have come in letting her believe he'd agreed to her demands like that. Faith, if he obliged every woman who begged for a taste of his cock, he'd never have a moment's peace.

Arabella was still having her hair dressed by candlelight when he came to her rooms. Poppy was furiously braiding one side of her hair with another maidservant on the other, and his sister complacently sipping a pint of ale to begin her day.

"Jasper," she said, grumpy, shifting only her eyes to see him without turning her head and disturbing the women arranging her hair. "Oh, pox on you. You're awake."

"Awake, and ready to escort you on your journey, my

lady sister," he said. "At least one of us will be sufficiently rested for the road."

"Aye, brother, I heard of your antics last even," she said, wincing as Poppy tugged and pinned her hair into place. "Buying that stallion for the sake of his performance with a mare! I vow the fellow who sold the horse to you must be laughing still for the price you paid."

"The horse is worth double what he asked," Jasper said. "It's a fortunate sale when both seller and buyer believes he's had the better of the other."

"But to buy beer for every man in the house afterwards!"

Jasper shrugged, dropping into the nearest chair. "The world can do with more goodwill and fellowship, and that was cheaply bought. We drank to the stallion and the many foals he shall sire for me. Though I have heard you tested the local stud last night yourself."

She looked at him sharply. "What do you say?"

"Only the truth," he said. "That you had two young squires attending your bed. Did they please you, Arabella?"

Irritably she waved away the two tiring women, who curtsied and left the room—though not, noted Jasper, before they'd exchanged glances that proved they were already quite aware of what had happened in their mistress's bed-chamber last night.

Jasper helped himself to a slice of the buttered bread on his sister's table. "It's no great secret, Arabella, nor do I care one way or another how you choose to arouse and amuse yourself. If your husband is unperturbed, then why should I not be?"

"Did one of those bastards tell you?" she fumed, striking her fist on the table. "God's blood, I paid them well enough to hold their tongues!"

Jasper smiled. "I'd vow they held a few other things about your person first. Was it their invention to tend to you from both ends, or did you need instruct them to your desires?"

She struck the table again. "I'll have their heads, the wretched little—"

"Hush, hush, Bella," Jasper said. "I heard it not from them. Likely they are too weary this morning to speak tattle of you to anyone else, anyway. It was your little virgin who told me."

His sister went very still. "Lady May? How would she know of it?"

"When she told me," Jasper said, "I feared you'd brought her to join in your antics as well."

He had, too. Wearing only her smock, May had come running down the hall towards him. Her hair was tangled and loose, her face so clearly flushed with arousal, her lips swollen and succulent, and when he'd taken her hand and smelled her cunny's scent upon it—ah, he'd been sure of it. What else was he to think, with so much proof?

But her stammering tale had told otherwise, and though she'd been spared being used by a pair of boorish servants for his sister's entertainment, she'd very nearly met the same fate at his hands instead. How close he'd come to pushing her back against the wall and lifting her pale legs around his waist and shoving his hard cock into her, even as she'd begged him for exactly that!

Not, of course, that he'd make such a confession to Arabella.

"How did she know?" Arabella demanded uneasily. "I made certain she drank so much when we supped that she should have slept the night away."

"She didn't," Jasper said. "She was awake, and saw you, and told it all to me. All."

"All?" Arabella smiled, turning sly. "Did she like what she saw?"

"It inflamed her, aye, if that is your meaning," he said. "But considering that she'd begun her day in a convent, your antics were much for her to see."

Arabella shrugged, and turned to her jewel box to choose for the day. "She will see far worse at court, and likely do far worse herself, so long as she keeps clear of you."

"Arabella." Jasper laid his hand on her arm. "I've never known you to act where there's no gain to you. What do you mean to do with this girl? What is your reason for claiming her?"

She looked sideways at him. "His Majesty asked this of me, and I am obeying."

"But why you, Arabella?" he asked. "Of all the ladies

of court, you are scarcely the one to be entrusted with the care and decorum of any maiden lady."

She drew her arm away from his hand.

"Perhaps because I am of a sufficient rank to make me fit for such an errand," she said. "Perhaps because the king cares less for how I amuse myself than my brother. Or perhaps because I was the one whose agents discovered the girl in obscurity, and suggested—gently, of course—to His Majesty that Lady May Roseberry might be an ideal new ornament to his court."

"An ornament!" He stared at her, aghast, understanding at once her real intention. "You mean to play the bawd by trotting this motherless lass beneath the king's nose?"

"A splendid ploy, aye?" she said proudly, returning to her jewels. "This girl is far more beautiful than either of the Boleyn bitches, and by the time we reach London, her innocence will have the enticing burnish of knowledge with it. Though her blood is impeccable, she has no family to meddle or expect reward. You'll see. She'll be exactly the sort of spice to make old Henry's prick rise one more time."

"The court is full of beauties, Arabella." Of course it was true that May was far more lovely than either Mary or Anne Boleyn, and true, too, that, virgin or not, there was an undeniable sensuality to May's beauty. He'd willingly attest to that, but then, he wasn't the king. "His Majesty is more than forty years old, and he has seen his share of young ladies paraded before him. What makes you believe this one will be different?"

Arabella smiled with triumph. "Because she will love him more desperately and more fervently than any other beauty in his experience. It will make him fall completely under her spell, Jasper. I am certain of it."

"You're mad, Arabella," he said with disgust. "I would never have guessed that you, of all women, would begin prattling over the power of love. Only poets and feeble women believe that. Men aren't ruled by their hearts, but by their cocks."

"And you are ever the cynic, Jasper," she said, unperturbed as she hooked gold drops set with garnets and pearls into her ears. "What you say is so with men your age and younger, when you are no better than that rutting stallion you bought last night. But when men age—even kings—they begin to fear their own mortality and impotence, and turn to love as the balm that will ease them in their dotage. Lady May Roseberry will offer that to His Majesty."

Jasper thought of the golden perfection of May, and then the grizzled, red-faced king who, it was whispered, was already too ridden with the French pox to ever get another child on any woman, young or old. By Jasper's reckoning, it would be a terrible waste of a perfectly good maidenhead. The lady deserved far better than the royal scepter.

"You are assuming that Lady May will do as you tell her," he said, "and pretend a great passion to the king. I would vow she'll consider him more like her grandsire than her lover, and show no more obedience to you than any other wench would, highborn or low."

"She will obey me," she said, "because I am her savior, and she will love the king because I tell her so."

She nodded as if to agree with herself, and closed the casket with her jewels. "You see how much favor the Howards and the Boleyns have garnered with the king because of those two wretched bitches of theirs. Why not our family as well?"

Jasper shook his head. "Because such a scheme could ruin our family as well as raise it," he said bluntly. "Our king is suspicious by nature, and sees plots everywhere at court. If he feels you are contriving to lead him to this girl, Arabella, then he will think nothing of sending you to the Tower for treason, or worse."

"His Majesty would never use a lady like me so," she said confidently. "You'll see. I shall do my best with the girl, and if the king takes notice of her, then we'll prosper. If she does not suit his tastes, then no matter. She'll wed someone, and soon vanish from court. But she will have amused me, and that will be enough."

Jasper laughed, and rose. "You sound like me, sister."

"Oh, aye, we are of a piece, aren't we?" She stood as well, and came to stand before Jasper. "But for now you must vow to keep away from the girl, brother. Leave her to me, and the king."

Jasper laughed, incredulous that she'd even ask this of him. "By my life, I'll never make any such vow to you!"

Arabella didn't laugh in return, but instead placed her hand flat on his chest in warning. "Leave her, Jasper."

"No promises, Bella, not in this," Jasper said, taking her hand from his chest to kiss her knuckles lightly. "For me it's always the challenge of the hunt rather than the quarry itself. Your warnings only make me want the girl more, not less."

She jerked her hand away from him. "A pox on you, Jasper," she said angrily. "You never will think of anyone but yourself."

"Nor do you, sister," he said mildly. "It's in the blood we share, you know. Now come. Enough of your schemes, and let us be on our way. The day, the king, and Lady May all await."

MAY STOOD IN the middle of her chamber, waiting for Lady Wilyse to call for her so they might begin their journey. Poppy had already dressed her as befitted her rediscovered station, and though May had never worn any clothes half so fine, she'd also never worn any that were so uncomfortable, and already she wondered how she would survive a long day of traveling in the countess's coach.

Over her smock May now wore layers of stiffened petticoats and a heavy gown with long, wide sleeves. For traveling her hair had been braided and pinned beneath a coif, and covered with a peaked headdress much like the one Lady Wilyse had worn yesterday. Also in readiness on the bed lay a long dark cloak and kidskin gloves embroidered with tiny curling flowers. She'd soft slippers on her feet and softer stockings on her legs, tied at her knees with bright silk garters.

And for the first time in her life, May had been laced into a corset, a stiff, unyielding undergarment of buckram, linen, and whalebone. The corset's straps dug into her shoulders, and the bones compressed her ribs and waist in a way that made breathing uneasy and bending impossible. That was much of its purpose, explained Poppy, for true ladies did not fling themselves about willy-nilly, but stood straight and unyielding.

But the most astonishing part of the corset in May's eyes was seeing—and feeling—what it did to her breasts, molding and thrusting them upwards in perilous, quivering display above the low, square neck of her gown. The sheer kerchief that Poppy pinned around her neck seemed to draw more attention to her breasts than to hide them, and the fashionable severe cut of her gown with its long, flat-fronted bodice only made them more noticeable still.

Every breath she took pressed her tightly bound nipples against the linen of her smock and the bones of the corset, just enough to make them ache for a more substantial caress. She felt enclosed, contained, held in by an unseen lover's arms. If yesterday her body had been awakened to pleasure, then today her very clothes seemed to be determined to make her continue the delicious torment and remind her of what she could not have.

But she'd other concerns about the journey today as well. Poppy had told her that Lady Wilyse was determined

to make good progress on their journey today, and that
May should expect to spend many hours, from before dawn
until after nightfall, in the coach. It would be just the two
ladies together in that coach, May and the countess, amusing each other for the entire long day.

Yet May was already miserably sure that when she finally
saw her ladyship that morning, her only thought would be
of how she'd seen the countess last, lustily engaged with
the two grooms. It was an impossible scene to forget. Even
now, as May struggled to forget what she'd witnessed, she
felt the first sympathetic flutters of desire in her belly, the
heaviness of longing that she now understood.

And how, too, would she feel when she met Lord Blackford again? She'd turned and tossed the whole night long as
she'd sighed over the memory of their kiss in the hallway,
how he'd stirred her and teased her only to abandon her
at the last, leaving her cruelly wanting more. She couldn't
decide which would be worse this morning: to have him
greet her warmly, but without any hope of further kind-
nesses from him, or to be ignored and feel the same rejection she'd experienced last night. Either way she'd have to
watch him from the carriage window, riding beside their
coach all the day long, and that, too, would be temptation
indeed.

Restlessly, May crossed the room to the window, determined to distract herself with the bustle in the yard below.
Though the countess had declared they would leave before
dawn, the first light was already up. Fragrant scents of

cooking rose from the kitchen as the cook prepared meals and provisions for journeys. Other travelers were preparing to leave, and grooms were hurrying to bring horses while servants carried trunks and other baggage.

Three men in livery were preparing to ride together, their horses standing ready. A third horse was being led out to them, a magnificent black stallion that snorted and pulled at the two grooms who were trying to control him. The stallion had only a halter, no saddle, though May doubted anyone would have been so foolish as to try to ride him.

Suddenly the stallion grew more agitated still, tossing his head and pulling hard against his leads as he tried to reach a saddled mare that stood waiting for her rider. To May's shock, the stallion's cock had grown dramatically, a long rod that dangled a good yard beneath his belly.

"Oh, now, that's a rare sight, my lady, isn't it?" Poppy said as she came to stand beside her. "It looks as if that great randy beast wants to show his worth, here before us all. No wonder his lordship paid so handsomely for him!"

"Lord Blackford owns that horse?"

"Aye, it was the talk of the inn last night," Poppy said. "That stallion's pride of this county, they say, and has stood stud to most every mare in it. His lordship saw him at it last night and, declaring him to be a prime beast, bought him outright for his own stables. Most likely he thought the stallion reminded him of himself."

"I thought his lordship was called the Black Lion," said May, "not the Black Stallion."

"Stallions, wolves, or roosters, it's all the same, isn't it?"
Poppy laughed, watching the horses, too. "I heard that brute
there was to be taken back to Blackford Hall this morn, but
it would seem the horse has another notion of how to begin
his day."

Fascinated, May could not look away from the stallion
as he pranced behind the mare. She clutched her hands
together, her palms damp. She could understand why Lord
Blackford would have bought him, for even she could see
how much alike they were, dark and dangerous and every
inch the rampant male.

Despite the best efforts of the grooms, none were able to
keep the stallion away from the mare, who in turn seemed
pleased enough by his attention. She'd already planted her
hind legs apart and raised her tail most obligingly, and in
the next instant the stallion was atop her, ignoring the saddle as he reared over her back.

Over and over the stallion thrust into the mare's quim,
his powerful hindquarters working hard to drive his enormous cock. May flushed, amazed and a bit ashamed at how
the sight of the two animals mating was enough to arouse
her as well. She found herself imagining herself to be the
mare and Lord Blackford the stallion, how she'd spread her
own legs so she might feel that powerful length plunging
into her.

"Marry, isn't that like every other male?" Poppy said,
laughing. "Begin the day with a cockstand, and only one way
to cure it with the nearest female." She glanced curiously

at May. "You've never seen a stallion at rut, my lady, have you? Nor any other beasts?"

"Nay, Poppy," May answered, her voice breathy with desire. "Not at the abbey. Such sights would not be proper for us to see."

The stallion had finished and dropped off the mare, his cock hanging limp and long, the head still swollen from his exertions. At once the grooms were able to pull him away, while the mare's owner rushed up to complain and shake his fist.

Now May spied Lord Blackford himself, coming to speak to the disgruntled owner. He was smiling broadly, and May guessed that he'd likely been laughing the same as Poppy. The man at once tugged off his hat and bowed, and after a few words from his lordship, he, too, was smiling.

"I tell you, my lady, they are all the same," Poppy said, chuckling still. "Look—there's Drumble with the final sweetening. Though that fellow should be pleased he's not been charged by his lordship for what that stallion just gave him, rather than expecting a reward for it."

Drumble must be Lord Blackford's servant, guessed May, as she watched the short, bustling man pass the mare's owner a few coins for his trouble. The now-docile stallion had been tied between the two other horses and was being quickly led away.

May leaned a little farther from the open window to watch Lord Blackford. Poppy was right. He did remind her of the stallion. He was dressed again all in black except for the white linen ruffles of his shirt at his throat and cuffs, with a black quilted doublet that showed off the breadth of his shoulders, black boots for riding, and black gloves on his hands. He moved with the same easy, virile confidence that the stallion likewise displayed. To be sure, his lordship did not snort nor paw at the ground, and his cock remained safely tucked in his hose behind his codpiece. But to see him there below her in the courtyard, his manly grace on display as he directed the grooms, she could think only of his strength and virility.

Had he watched the stallion cover the mare and thought of her, too? Had he imagined her turned away from him like the mare had, with his own cock plunging into the nest between her parted legs? He'd sworn that he would take her when he was ready, and in the manner that pleased him most.

Poppy had said that most men were like the stallion, and May remembered, too, how she'd seen the countess on her knees as the groom had fucked her from behind, much like the stallion.

Perhaps this was what Lord Blackford intended for her, and she felt her own cunny swell and tighten with secret anticipation.

Lady Wilyse's coach now drove slowly into the yard, with her own followers and attendants in her livery gathering with their own mounts.

Poppy sighed. "There we are, my lady. Lady Wilyse must

be ready at last. Once she's set, she'll not wait for anyone else. Join her now, if you please, and I'll fetch a servant to take your trunk."

She left the room, hurrying off on her errand. But May remained at the window, lingering just a little longer to watch Lord Blackford below. He was speaking to another man now, walking directly beneath her window as he continued his conversation, and she leaned over the sill to keep him in sight.

But of a sudden he stopped, and gazed up at her as directly as if she'd called and bid him to look her way. His pale eyes met hers, his gaze beneath his black brows every bit as piercing and direct as a hawk.

Then he smiled and his face softened, his expression proving his happiness both at being seen by her and at seeing her, too. He touched his fingers to his lips in the same salute he'd used to her the day before, and directed the kiss up to her at the window.

May blushed at being caught, and instead of making some graceful, winning acknowledgment of his attention, she scuttled backwards in confusion and away from the window with all the elegance of a sand-bound crab. Lord Blackford's bemused laughter followed her, rising up through the open window.

Mortified, May grabbed her cloak and gloves and left the chamber. If she was quick enough, she could reach the coach while his lordship was occupied, and thus be spared shaming herself further. But on the staircase one of the inn's young serving boys stopped her, tugging on the front of his knit cap in deference.

"If you please, my lady," he said. "Mistress Poppy said that she'd need of you regarding your trunk."

"My trunk?" repeated May uncertainly. She'd last seen her trunk still sitting on the floor of her chamber, not a minute before.

"Aye, my lady, aye, your trunk," the boy said firmly. "She bid me fetch you to her at once. This way, my lady, and I'll take you to her."

He waved vaguely in the direction of the yard, and with only a slight hesitation, May nodded and joined him, sweeping her heavy skirts to one side on the stairs. She'd have to trust Poppy in this as in everything else. Really, what other course did she have?

She followed the boy through the inn's center hall and into the yard. At least there was no sign of Lord Blackford, and she breathed a small sigh of relief at that.

"This way, my lady," the boy said, trotting ahead of her and into the stable. "This way."

She followed, blinking as her eyes grew accustomed to the murky shadows after the bright morning sunlight. The boy was far ahead of her, and with the unfamiliar weight of her skirts she was too slow to keep pace with him. She was so intent on trying to catch the boy that she didn't see the black-clad figure appear at her side until it was too late to dodge him, and too late as well to cry out before the man's gloved hand closed over her mouth.

Terrified, she kicked backwards, fighting to free herself, but the man was much larger and stronger, and he easily pulled her into a small room or closet used for tack, and shut the door, closing them together into the darkness of the windowless space.

"I'll uncover your mouth, my lady, but you must not scream," Lord Blackford said, for of course it was he who held her. His voice was low, a rough whisper meant for only her. "There are a score of men working in this stable, and if you draw them here, they will only see that you are with me, and tell the world of it."

He kept his hand over her mouth another moment, then slowly did as he'd promised. She gasped for air, more from fear than from suffocating. She could see nothing in the little room, and at once her other senses seemed to heighten.

She smelled the sweet hay that fed the horses, and the scent of the oiled leather harnesses and traces that she'd glimpsed hanging on pegs on the walls around her. She heard the voices of the grooms and stableboys talking and calling to one another just beyond the walls, exactly as Lord Blackford had told her, and the soft neighs and nickering of horses, too.

But what she felt most of all was how he was holding her, her back against his chest with his arm as tight as an iron band around her waist. Oh, she was truly like that helpless lamb now, caught in this lion's claws. She would never be able to break free of him, not when he held her like this, nor, if she was honest, was she even sure she'd wish to.

"What . . . what do you wish from me, my lord?" she demanded in a fierce whisper. "Do you wish to mock me further, or make more sport at my expense?"

"I'd never mock you, sweet," he said softly, his lips so close to her ear that she felt his warm breath against the sensitive little hollow beneath it. "I saw you at the window, and I wished to know if you saw what I did."

"I saw many things, my lord," she said defensively. "The inn's yard is a busy place."

"Aye, it is," he agreed. "But when I saw you at the window, you seemed most intrigued by the antics of my new stallion."

At once the stallion and the mare returned to her thoughts, exactly as he'd wanted it to.

"I do not fault you for it," he continued. "How could I, when I watched them, too? He's a black knave, that stallion. There are no niceties with him. When he sees a mare that pleases him, he takes her as his own, just as he did this morn."

"Is . . . is that what you wish to do with me, my lord?" In the dark space so redolent of horses and leather, she could not help but think of the stallion and mare. "To . . . to take me?"

"I speak of the horses, Lady May, not of us," he said.

"Did you take note of how willing the mare was to be served by so fine a stallion, how she turned to show him her rump to entice him to her?"

When May had first struggled against him, she'd bent over trying to break free, and she now remained awkwardly in that stance, leaning slightly over his arm with her bottom pressed against his loins and one of his legs between hers. Now he gently drew her backwards, making their bodies fit more tightly together. Even through the layers of clothing, she still felt the press of his well-filled codpiece pressing between the cheeks of her ass, just as the mare must have felt the stallion.

She gasped and shuddered at the realization, a palpable acknowledgment that he instantly seized.

"Aye, so you do know," he whispered, his voice rough in a way that thrilled May even more. He was moving against her in a definite rhythm now, making his actions match his words. "You remember that little mare, how she saw the stallion and knew what she wanted. It was plain as day. Her ears were back, her head was raised. How bravely she welcomed him, how she took him, how nothing would have parted her from having him!"

She was moving with him now, bending lower so to raise her bottom more fully against him. With his words to remind her of what she'd seen, both this morning and last night, she'd mindlessly spread her own legs apart. She was astride his thigh now, the hard muscles pressing through her linen petticoats and against her cunny, making the tender lips swell and grow more sensitive each time he pushed against her bottom.

She was panting, with an extra little catch in her breathing as he rubbed against her. Or maybe she was rubbing against him; she could not tell for certain. She was oddly disoriented in the dark, where every sensation was magnified. She felt as if she were melting within, the tension in her belly and quim as taut as they'd been last night when she'd brought herself to release, and through the haze of pleasure she realized she was close to that same joy again.

But would he take her now? Would he possess her like the stallion had the mare, and fuck her the way she so desperately wanted? As if reading her thoughts, he nipped lightly at the side of her neck, the same as the stallion had done to the mare.

"The mare knew what she wanted, May," he whispered roughly, "and nothing would stop her from having it. She wanted that stallion's cock, and she wanted his seed, and when at last she felt him come within her, she shook with the joy of it."

She whimpered and trembled, so much so that had he not held her against him, she felt sure she would have fallen forward to the floor. She scarce took notice when he held her forward to shove her skirts up and leave her bare and exposed, scarce noticed that he'd jerked open the front of his own hose.

But when he pulled her back close against him, she realized she was no longer riding his muscled thigh. Instead what she felt sliding back and forth between the wet, swollen lips of her quim was his cock, hard and hot and ready for her.

That thought, that touch, was enough to send her over the edge. With one last cry, she felt the tension burst in a rush of exquisite joy. She tumbled forward, and he caught her, holding her in the dark as she slowly came back into herself.

But it wasn't right. Innocent though she was, she knew that, and she knew the disappointment of it, too.

"You . . . you did not finish, my lord," she said, pushing away from him as she gulped for breath. "Not what you began. You didn't . . . you didn't . . ."

"I didn't fuck you." His voice was rigid with control. "Nay, it is not time."

"But why not, my lord?" In the dark she reached for him, finding his cock. It excited her to touch it, so thick around that she could barely circle it with her fingers. He was still hard, rampant and sticky with her spendings, but none of his own. Clearly he desired her. Why did he refuse to claim what she wished as well? "Now, my lord, pray now, if—"

"Nay." He turned away from her, and her disappointment grew as she heard him dressing himself. "Not now, sweet. Not yet."

"And I vow you are wrong, my lord," she said, frustration and disappointment adding an edge to her voice. "You are *wrong*."

She found the latch of the door and pulled it open,

slipping through it and into the stable. To her relief, none of the grooms were there to see her, and as briskly as she could, she began to hurry back to the yard where Lady Wilyse's coach would be waiting. She was still trembling from the violence of her release, and angry and confused by how he'd turned away from her again. Despite her agitation, she did her best to compose her face, determined to confess nothing to the countess.

She did not look back to see if Lord Blackford had followed her. She'd have to see him soon enough, and she'd decide then how best to address him.

"My lady!" Poppy ran to her in the yard and, after a quick curtsy, took her by the arm. "Where have you been, Lady May? I've been searching everywhere for you."

"Forgive me for troubling you," May said. "I was in the privy. I am unaccustomed to the wine and the spices of the food, and they . . . distressed me."

"Poor little dove," Poppy said, studying her face with concern. "Any fare would be too rich after the pious gruel those nuns eat. Your face is flushed."

"It is the heat of the morning, Poppy," May said wearily. "I will be well enough in time."

The countess was standing before the coach, curtly giving a final order to one of the men, a man that May recognized as one of the pair who'd shared her bed the night before. Both of them managed to keep their faces impassive, as if none of the shocking intimacies that she'd witnessed had ever taken place between them.

How curious, thought May, only to realize to her dismay that soon she'd be forced to do exactly the same when Lord Blackford appeared.

"I've found her, my lady," Poppy said, presenting May like a trophy. "She was in the privy, my lady. She's been unwell."

"Have you?" The countess's face softened with sympathy. "Are you feverish? You're flushed."

Wearily May shook her head, continuing the little lie as the best excuse. "I'll be well enough, my lady," she said. "The morning air will improve me, I am certain."

"Poor lamb." The countess patted her cheek. "And here I'd feared you'd been making merry with my wicked brother!"

"Nay, my lady," May said softly. "Nothing merry at all."

CHAPTER SIX

*J*asper rode beside his sister's coach ahead of the other riders, the pace so slow that he could have fallen dead asleep in the saddle and no one would have noticed. They had been traveling for hours now with only a short stop for dinner and to water the horses, and yet though the sun was already beginning to sink, they'd covered only a few miles. He rather wished he had fallen asleep, for mindless oblivion would have been infinitely preferable to the swirl of black thoughts that plagued him now.

He had never come so close to losing control with a woman as he had today with May Roseberry in the stable. He could not blame the girl. He was the one who was at fault, abandoning all his well-practiced control. It was one thing to paint seductive pictures in her ear to arouse her, but another entirely to begin to believe them himself. Another moment, and he would have been exactly the same as that rutting stallion, thrusting into her with no thought other than to get inside her and spend.

He was getting hard again just from the memory, and he swore under his breath. What was it about this girl that did this to him, reducing him to the most callow of mooncalves?

Nay, this was not how it was to be between them. He'd wanted to stir her a bit, as he'd done the night before, not have her shudder against him like that. Poppy had said she had a passionate nature, and faith, she was right. How the devil Lady May had lasted so long in a chaste nunnery was beyond reason. He could well imagine the mischief she must have caused for the abbess.

If in fact the king was to marry her off to some aged peer who'd already outlived several wives—the usual fate for young titled heiresses at court—then surely she would drive her poor bridegroom into his grave from exhaustion within a month. With a quim as hot as hers, there'd be naught left of the fellow but a scorched husk. It would be a waste, really, except that she'd soon become an eager, ardent widow, and doubly tempting.

As for Arabella's scheme to launch her into the king's own bed as a royal concubine, ah, he'd not see the future in that, either. He'd spent much time in Henry's company, and heard enough of his judgments of various women, from duchesses to serving wenches, to have an excellent notion of what pleased him and what didn't. The royal taste ran more towards the sly elegance of Anne Boleyn with her French airs.

Which was not to say that the king wouldn't desire Lady May; he wouldn't be male if he didn't. But Jasper was sure that Lady May, with virginal guilelessness, would not be to his carnal tastes, leastways not enough to unseat Mistress Boleyn. Though Mistress Boleyn, too, claimed she still had her maidenhead (which most of the court did doubt), she was also a bold and knowing lady from her time at the French court, and Jasper had heard that she spoke with great freedom of wanton acts to inflame the king further. Though May was learning fast under his sister's tutelage, she still lagged far behind Mistress Boleyn in that particular area.

Jasper had also observed that the king was a hunter, and like every other hunter, he'd not abandon his quarry until the capture, no matter how long the chase. Mistress Boleyn had been playing him with exceptional skill by denying him the final favor for a long time. Until she ultimately did, Jasper did not believe the king would seriously consider another woman.

As a hunter himself, this made great sense to Jasper. He recognized the impulse, and respected it.

But his sister, being a woman, failed to understand, just as she failed to see the spirit in Lady May. Arabella could talk all she wished about the girl obeying her orders.

Jasper's guess was that Lady May would never meekly follow the bidding of his sister or anyone else, and she'd certainly not love where she was ordered. She'd do whatever
she wished, and nothing less. Jasper had only to recall how
she'd left him so abruptly this very morning to see that.

He winced, remembering all too well. He'd intended to
bring her along gradually, the way that was best for seducing virgins, yet she was so damned eager that she'd fair
ordered him to take her maidenhead there in the stable,
and grown angry that he hadn't.

Ah, no matter now. He'd rein her in to his will soon
enough. Nothing good ever came of letting a restive filly
take her own lead. In the end, she'd follow his will like
every other woman, and the better for them both.

He glanced down into the coach. It was a great clumsy
thing, bright and gaudy with blue paint and red-spoked
wheels. Arabella believed in traveling in a style that drew
people running to gawk whenever they passed through a
village or town. Escorting the coach was a baggage wagon
with Poppy and her other personal servants as well as her
trunks, plus a half dozen liveried escorts who also served
as guards. The roads were safer under Henry than they'd
been in his father's time, but the risks remained, and Jasper
approved of his sister's caution—even if it was intended
more for show than safety.

But despite the coach's bright paint and cushioned seats,
it was still an uncomfortable way to travel, and not much

better than a common wagon. Passengers felt every rut and bump on the road, and breathed the dust that the lumbering wheels churned upwards. Because the day was warm, the leather curtains had been tied up, and Jasper could easily see the two women inside, like ornaments in a shopkeeper's window.

His sister was sprawled across one side, soundly asleep with her mouth hanging open. This was no surprise considering how busy she had been the night before, and how much wine she'd drunk when they'd stopped to dine earlier.

Opposite her sat Lady May, curled on the seat, her arms folded over her chest as she stared out at the passing landscape. She had shed her shoes and drawn her feet up on the seat, feet that in their white silk stockings seemed somehow charmingly vulnerable to him. Her cheeks were pink from the heat, and little wisps of her golden hair had escaped from her coif to curl beguilingly around her forehead and the nape of her neck.

She looked drowsy, too, her eyes heavy-lidded and languid, her lips parted, and her head tipped back against the cushions. In hopes of a breeze, she'd removed the sheer scarf from the front of her bodice, too, giving him a fine view of her high, round breasts, spilling out delectably from her tight lacing.

He had not spoken to her alone since she'd bolted from the stable this morning. Arabella had seen to that, guarding her little charge like a mother hen. Nay, more like a mother

goose, ready to hiss and clack and charge at him to bite if
he got too close. She'd had some tale of how the girl was
ill from what she'd eaten the night before. She certainly
hadn't been ill when he'd seen her, however, and he wondered if this was some quick invention of May's to explain
her time with him. If so, then he was duly impressed. To
have a passionate nature combined with the quick wit necessary for intrigue was a useful gift indeed.

He studied her, trying to guess her thoughts towards
him. She should be well content. She'd had pleasure enough.
And if he was any judge of women—which, in honesty if
not in modesty, he knew he was—then after that first taste,
she'd be eager for more of the next course.

He glanced again at his sleeping sister, now snoring, and
guided his horse more closely to the coach's window.

"My lady May," he called softly, though he guessed it
would take far more than that to rouse his sister. "How fare
you, sweet?"

Her drowsy eyes flew open. In an instant, she'd lunged
across the cushions to the window, grabbing the sill between
them.

"You, my lord!" she exclaimed in an indignant whisper.
"You would dare to ask after me, after this morning?"

"I would, my lady," he said, gallantly lifting his velvet
hat to her. "Especially after this morning."

" 'Especially'?" she repeated, her eyes round with outrage. *Especially*, my lord?"

He laughed. He could not help it; she was so delightfully upset over nothing.

"Hush!" she ordered. She leaned far enough from the window to cover his mouth and his laughter with her open palm. "Do you wish to wake Lady Wilyse with your foolery, my lord?"

Gently he drew her hand from his mouth, keeping possession of it. "After the prodigious amount of bad claret that my sister drank at that last inn, a pack of minstrels couldn't raise her."

She looked back towards the baggage wagon, traveling behind them. "You must not speak to me like this, my lord. Even if her ladyship doesn't take notice, then Poppy will, and tell her."

"Poppy will do no such thing," he said. "She's not a maidservant to tattle, and besides, she's too occupied with the driver to watch us."

He pointed back to the wagon, and she leaned farther from the window to see for herself. Poppy was in fact sitting as closely as possible to the wagon's driver with one arm tucked into his, and both of them laughing merrily together. The driver was a handsome rascal, and new to his sister's service and to Poppy, and Jasper was certain he'd soon discover the heady advantages to both.

"Here, now, take care, else you topple into the dust." He squeezed her hand, holding her fast.

"Would you care if I did, my lord?" she demanded, trying to pull her hand free.

"I would, very much," he said easily. Knowing he was dallying with Lady May while his sister was sleeping only a few feet away added an extra fillip of titillation that was all the more amusing.

She frowned and pouted, no determent at all.

"I assure you, my lady, I do care," he continued, smiling down at her. "It would be a great loss to me if you did."

He lifted her hand back to his lips. He kissed the back of it first, then turned it over and nipped at the soft pad of her palm. To his disappointment, her fingers smelled of the orange water that his sister carried with them for washing, a pleasing scent.

Yet it wasn't half so sweet as the honey of her own nest that had perfumed her hand last night—and his, too, this morning. Not that he truly expected her to pass the long journey by diddling herself under her skirts, but it was still amusing to imagine.

"You would *not* care, my lord," she said firmly, jerking her hand free. "If you did, you would not have treated me as you did."

He pretended surprise. "You did not find any pleasure, any joy, in what we did? Surely it did seem to me that you did."

"I did not say that, my lord," she said, flustered. "But while I had—had pleasure, you took none of your own."

Now his feigned surprise had turned genuine. Every other woman he'd known complained heartily of how men always satisfied themselves first and forgot to tend to them, and here was this lovely creature berating him for pleasing her instead of himself.

"As we rode this morn, her ladyship and Poppy both told me that the pleasure is much the greater when the man and the woman expire together," she continued, astonishing him further. "They say it is the height of selfishness for one to spend without the other, and . . . and I do not wish to seem selfish."

"You're not," he said quickly. "That is, in most examples it is the man who is the selfish one."

She narrowed her eyes at him. "That is what I thought, my lord," she said. "*You* are the selfish one, for refusing to take me properly and spending yourself, as I wished you to. You cheated yourself, and you cheated me, too, by only offering me half the pleasure and keeping your cock to yourself."

"Not for your first time, my lady," Jasper protested, his astonishment growing. So was his cock, too, as he remembered how close he'd come to fucking her outright in the stable, and how now, it seemed, that had been exactly what she'd expected him to do. She'd fallen forward at exactly the perfect angle for him, with her ass in the air. She would have been wet and easy from her own spendings, and with such a well-oiled passage, her pain would have been minimal. One good thrust, and her virginity would have been finished.

Oh, aye, he would have shown her pleasure then, and there'd be none of this whining from her now. This was what came of trying to seduce a wench with kindness. He shifted uncomfortably in the saddle, trying to arrange his hardening cock without her noticing.

"You don't know what you ask, Lady May," he said, striving to sound reasonable. "You could scarce wish me to have taken your maidenhead there in the stable."

"What I wish, my lord, is for you to leave me at once!" She turned from the window and flung herself across the seat, her skirts flying around her legs and stockinged feet as she buried her face in her hands.

It was not in Jasper's nature to beg, and he did not now.

"Very well," he said, gathering his mount's reins to turn away from the coach, "if that is what you wish, then I shall oblige. Good day, my lady."

"Nay!" As swiftly as May had hurled herself onto the seat, she now clambered back to the coach's window. "Nay, my lord, forgive me, that is not at all my wish!"

He wheeled his horse around and looked at her with his best gravity. She, however, was favoring him with her best, too, imploring him with her breasts heaving so mightily with her distress that they threatened to pop free.

"Pray, my lady, then tell it me," he asked as imperiously as he could. "What is this wish of yours?"

She ducked her head like a happy pup, and grinned guilelessly. "That I might see you naked, my lord, and view for myself that fine monstrous cock that I could but feel in the dark."

He laughed, more delighted than she'd ever guess. "That is all, my lady?"

"Aye, my lord, that is all." She glanced back over her shoulder to make sure that his sister slept still, then up in the direction of the coach's driver, as if remembering his presence for the first time. Doubtless he had overheard, but was too well trained to show that he had. Yet that was enough to make her laugh, too, a wondrous, bubbling laugh that seemed to capture the very sunlight in it.

"It only seems fair," she continued, "when you have already seen me as nature intended. You will oblige me, my lord?"

"As soon as it can be arranged, my lady," he said, laughing still as he drew his horse as close as he could to her window. "But first you must answer me a riddle. By my life, how did you ever sprout as you are from a convent?"

Her laugh dropped to a low chuckle as she pressed her teeth into the plump cushion of her lower lip.

"I sprouted, my lord," she said, "and I ripened, and then I dropped from that sanctified branch before I could cause the holy ladies more trouble, and how fortunate I was as a lowly windfall to be gathered up by her ladyship."

"More fortunate for me, I vow." He leaned towards her to kiss her, and she met him eagerly, the way she seemed determined to do everything with him. Between his horse and the coach, it was an awkward, bumping kiss, but not so clumsy that he could not slip his fingers deep into the cleft of her corseted breasts, then spread them to find the tight

little nub of her aroused nipple. Oh, aye, she was eager, and
so was he.

"As soon as you can arrange it, my lord," she whispered.
"As soon as ever you can."

DURING HER LIFE in the abbey, May had seen how the best
of intentions towards goodness most often faltered when
confronted by human frailty. But this was the first time
she'd experienced how very bad intentions could be foiled
as well, and also how much more disappointing it was.

Despite the promises that she and Jasper (for so she
had begun to think of Lord Blackford) had made to consider his nakedness together as soon as it could be arranged,
Lady Wilyse seemed equally determined to put every possible obstruction in their way.

For the next three days of their journey, her ladyship
never left them alone together, nor did she again conveniently fall asleep in the carriage. In fact she seldom left
May unattended at all, even ordering Poppy to sleep on a
pallet in her room with her, just to be sure May didn't leave
her bed at night to go a-wandering through the inn.

Now the long days of traveling in the lumbering coach
were filled with her ladyship's advice and education. When
the countess learned that May could read, she produced
books for her to pass the time, but books unlike any May
had ever seen. These books were filled with stories of fucking and little else, of men and women finding amusement

and satisfaction in every position and combination and manner that they could contrive.

As if the stories themselves were not astonishing enough, they were illustrated, too, in the greatest detail, showing those same men and women without a stitch of clothing or a coverlet to their beds. This permitted the artist to show every aspect of their couplings, of how exactly the man's cock would swell and thicken and stand with his arousal, and how the woman's cunt would so eagerly stretch to accommodate that cock.

May pored over the books, lingering especially on the pictures, which often made her so hot with her own sympathetic desires that she longed for a man to come do the same things to her here in her ladyship's carriage, and bring her relief.

It did not help to have Jasper so close, and yet so unattainable at the same time. A glimpse of his well-muscled, black-clad thighs, his tall boots and silver spurs, and the arrogant thrust of his sword in its scabbard against his leg as he rode by the coach—that was sadly the sum of what she saw of him, but more than enough to feed her feverish imagination.

Oh, Jasper would smile at her whenever he caught her eye, and make a pleasant observation about the weather or compliment her gallantly on what she wore, and even wink at her over his sister's back. But there were no heated kisses nor caresses exchanged, and certainly no repetition of what had transpired between them in the stable of the first inn.

Her ladyship told May that this separation from Jasper was for her own good, and for the sake of her future at court. She assured May that she would meet far more attractive gentlemen within the palace, men who were superior in rank, fortune, education, and comeliness, men who would wish to honor her with the sacrament of marriage, and give her the noble children and fine estates that were due to her by her birth and the fortune that had come with it.

Towards this end, each evening after supper she was trained by the countess, her lady's maid, and Poppy, all three determined to teach her the niceties of the court that she hadn't learned at the abbey. How to walk down a staircase without looking at her feet, how to smile without showing her teeth, how to dance with some manner of grace, even how to sit with her heavy, full skirts properly arranged—all of this and more May was made to learn during the warm spring evenings.

But while May listened in patient silence and did her best to follow the complicated lessons, inside she felt her old, familiar rebellious self rising up. Listening to Lady Wilyse describe the marriage that would be arranged for May made her almost wish she'd been left where she had been in the abbey, if the best she could expect from her life was to trade the prison of the cloisters for another ruled by a husband. And how could her ladyship lecture so often to her about the happiness of a wedded wife when she herself seemed content with a husband conveniently in a faraway

land, and a constant parade of young men to serve her in
his stead?

May did not want a husband, however nobly born or
wealthy, and especially not one who desired this false version of herself that smiled wanly and bowed her head with
meekness she did not feel. Nor did she want an estate to
manage, or children to rear. She was seventeen, and she did
not wish to see her life closed in and shuttered before she'd
had a chance to live it.

Besides, she knew what she did want. She wanted Jasper, and before they reached London and court, she would
find a way to have him.

But first, she would see him naked.

LADY WILYSE READ the letter that had been delivered to
her, then folded it once again, pressing the creases sharp
with her fingertips.

She smiled at May over the last dishes from their supper. They had eaten in her ladyship's rooms, as they always
did, for it was not proper for ladies to dine in the public
room of an inn. That was where Jasper took his meals, and
from the riotous laughter that rose up the stairs in the evening, those public rooms were a great deal more entertaining than supping alone with Lady Wilyse.

"This is very interesting news for us, May," her ladyship
said. "It would seem that on a whim His Majesty has post-
poned his plans to return to London, and prefers to keep

the court at Richmond, and his palace of Hampton Court. We will, of course, join him there."

"Not London, my lady?" May said, unable to contain her disappointment. London was said to be the greatest, most glorious city in Christendom, and she had been anticipating seeing it for herself.

"Not at present, nay," the countess said, waving for Poppy to refill her glass with more wine. "Mistress Boleyn prefers Hampton Court, and the king would do most anything to please her. But it's a pretty palace, newly built, with many diversions. Poppy, do you recall the maze?"

"Oh, aye, my lady," Poppy said, cradling the bottle of wine in her arms. "Who could not recall it? 'Tis a most cunning folly, Lady May, a puzzle-knot wrought of hornbeam hedges in the garden near the river, and contrived of a size for a man to lose himself within."

"More like a man and a woman, Poppy," the countess said, laughing at the memory. "They say the maze was made by order of Cardinal Thomas Wolsey when the palace belonged to him, to be used for holy reflections. But since the cardinal has fallen from favor and the king has claimed the palace for his own, the maze is used for more secular sport. Hornbeam, la! How many lusty horns have found employment in that garden?"

"Aye, Lady May, take care with that maze," Poppy warned, but in a teasing manner. "Don't venture within it in the company of a gentleman, unless you desire to lose yourself and your virtue with him."

May nodded, thinking at once of how she would be certain to explore this maze with Jasper as her guide. Doubtless he would know the answer to its riddle, just as doubtless he would know exactly which wrong turnings to take to make for the longest time for dalliance.

"There, now, my dear, you smile at the prospect," the countess said with approval. "I vow you'll find plenty to amuse you, and enough to forget London. Besides, Richmond will shorten our journey a bit. So long as the roads stay dry, we should arrive the day after tomorrow."

"Truly, my lady?" May's spirits rose with anticipation. Surely the court would be better than this journey, and with so many others about, she might also find more chance to escape the countess's watch and meet with Jasper.

"Truly," answered the countess, rising to leave the supper table. As she had done every night, she had changed from her heavy traveling clothes into more informal dress, even leaving off her stays so that her curvaceous body was clearly revealed beneath the lightweight linen as she crossed the room.

"Tonight we must have another lesson," she continued, "and a most important one. Poppy, the playthings. May, here, on the bed with me."

The countess sat on the edge of the bed and patted the coverlet next to her. May joined her, already intrigued. After the first day and night, there had been no more teasing play between them, only the tedious lessons on dance and manners, and there certainly had been no more amorous adventures with Jasper. She could only hope that tonight would be different.

And at once she saw that it would. Poppy handed the countess a long wooden box, beautifully inlaid with a representation of Adam and Eve in their unashamed and natural state in the Garden. With a sly smile, her ladyship raised the lid of the box slowly, building May's curiosity. Inside the box lay a half dozen neat bundles, each carefully wrapped with a length of brocade in a different jewel-colored silk.

"You know this night's lesson, Poppy," she said. "Which will be right for our Lady May? Which should I employ?"

"For the lesson, my lady, I would suggest the ruby," Poppy said, looking into the box over the countess's arm. "If it were for her amusement, then the sapphire."

Lady Wilyse glanced up with surprise. "Not yet, to be sure, not when we have guarded her so close!"

But Poppy only shrugged. "She's still a maid, aye, but she's learned to spend by her own hand well enough. I've heard her each night, wriggling and sighing with her own joy."

"Oh, my lady, forgive me," cried May, mortified. It was not that she was shamed by what she'd done, but that Poppy, whom she had supposed to be sleeping at the foot of her bed, had heard her. She'd been unable to help herself, nor had she wished to, really. It had been a poor second to Jasper himself, but after the whole day spent watching him astride his horse and growing more aroused at the sight by the moment, what choice did she have?

But the countess was unperturbed. "No matter, my dear, no matter," she said, running her fingers lightly over the silken bundles as she made her choice. "We have already discovered that you possess a passionate nature. Besides, if you know how to please yourself, then you will be better able to tell your lover what pleases you as well. So long as you keep your maidenhead intact, then I care not. I do think the ruby will do best for tonight's lesson."

She took up the bundle in the red brocade, and with great care unwrapped the silk until there in her hand lay the most extraordinary object that May had ever seen. Wrought from heavy red glass threaded through with specks of gold, the object was the perfect replica of a man's erect cock, ready to crow with its head uncovered.

"You are astonished, May," the countess said, coyly turning the glittering object in her hands. "Do you know what it is?"

"I know what it is intended to be, my lady," May said. "It is a representation of a man's member, cunningly wrought in glass, though marry, I cannot imagine the use of it."

The countess laughed.

"It is a representation, aye," she said, "and it is indeed most beautifully wrought. On one of my dear husband's many journeys to the distant state of Venice, a city remarkable both for its glassmaking and its debauchery, he observed similar objects as used by the courtesans of that place, and decided at once that I, too, would be amused by them."

She held the object to the candlelight, admiring it.

"They are called *deletti*," she said, "the Italian word for 'delight,' and truly few playthings are more delightful. My husband purchased this *deletto*, and its brothers, and brought them to me as a gift."

May pointed to the other bundles still in the box. "These . . . these are more of the same, my lady?"

"Oh, each *deletto* is different in his way," the countess said, "just as are gentlemen in their glory. My dear husband understands that just as even the most delectable of dishes will grow tiresome if consumed to the exclusion of all others, so it is with love."

May frowned. "Then you grant him permission to . . . to enjoy other ladies as well?"

"Of course," the countess said with surprise. "That is our understanding, and a fair and honest one it is, too. If I had not agreed, then he would not have visited the Venetian courtesans to have seen these among their belongings, nor would I have received my own gifts of these pretty baubles."

She leaned closer to May. "Now here, let us begin our lesson. When a gentleman is inflamed by love, his cock will grow stiff, and if the lady is fortunate, he will resemble this *deletto*, to show his interest in his lady."

"I know that, my lady," May said eagerly, thinking of Jasper, and, too, of what she had seen of her ladyship's own frolic with the servants. "When it is stiff, then he can thrust it into the lady's cunny, and push it in and out until they both feel the pleasure of it, and spend together."

"Such an apt pupil!" The countess smiled with approval. "But there are other ways to entertain a cock, May. There are times when the gentleman is weary, or would need a bit more encouragement from his lady to rise to the challenge of Venus. Then it is best for the lady to address him in the French manner."

"The French manner, my lady?" May repeated, doubtful. She had always been taught that in all things the English were superior to the French.

"Aye, the French," her ladyship replied. "You must recall that His Majesty is cousin to the French king, and that there is much shared between our two courts. Many English ladies and gentlemen attend the French king, and you will meet many French gentlemen and ladies at ours as well. And if they introduce us to such delightful practices, why should we not adopt them for our own? They say the two Boleyn sisters are particularly skilled in French pleasures. Here, now you must play the gentleman, and hold the *deletto* upright in your hands as if it were your cock."

May did so, laughing at the foolishness of it. La, to imagine having this great red thing rising from her loins instead of her neat little cunny!

The countess sank to her knees on the floor before her, and gently took the base of the *deletto* in her fingers. Slowly she dragged her tongue up and down its glittering length, striving to cover as much of its surface as possible.

"That is the first step, May," she explained, "and for many

gentlemen that is enough. To have you kneel before him, with your breasts convenient to his hands as you tongue his cock—what gentleman could not find that a lovely posture? But to continue: the most sensitive portion of the cock is here, on the underside. Tease it with your lips, just so, and mind you favor the head, too, and this small winking eye that is the font of his sperm. With practice, you might employ the merest edge of your teeth as well, but only with great care. No gentleman desires to be bitten."

May watched with interest, imagining herself licking Jasper's cock with such care. As beautiful as the glass *deletto* was, it could never possess the velvety firmness of the flesh-and-blood original.

"That is a fair beginning," explained the countess, drawing closer to May and the *deletto*. "But to bring the greatest pleasure to the gentleman, you must take as much of his cock into your mouth as you can, and suck it while again caressing it with your tongue whilst keeping your teeth clear. If done properly, this offers the most exquisite sensations to the gentleman, and some will even prefer it to our cunts."

She bent forward and took the *deletto* deep into her mouth, so deeply as to make its entire length disappear. Her red lips pressed close to the glass, a winsome sight, and then to May's amazement she sucked it with such fervor that she pulled the *deletto* from May's fingers, only to release it again as her lips slid up to the crest, only to plunge back down again.

The countess sat back on her heels. "I promise you it is not difficult, my dear, yet it is an accomplishment that will win you endless devotion from most any gentleman."

"Is the sensation enough to make a gentleman spend?" May asked.

"Aye, it is," the countess said, giving an extra fond stroke to the *deletto* as if indeed it were a genuine cock. "If you feel his ballocks tense and realize he is about to spout, then you can draw away at the last, and let him come outside your mouth. Some ladies choose to swallow his cream, and consider it Cupid's elixir. Come, now it is your turn."

Eagerly May took her place on her knees, with Lady Wilyse playing the gentleman. She followed every step as the countess had demonstrated, accustoming herself to having so large an object fill her mouth.

She closed her eyes and imagined the *deletto* as Jasper's cock. In the dark of the stable room, she'd held it for only a single tantalizing moment, which hadn't been nearly long enough. But it was sufficient to feed her imagination now, and the more she sucked on the *deletto*, teasing and stroking it with her tongue and lips, the more vividly she envisioned it as Jasper instead, and the more aroused, too, she became herself. The now-familiar ache grew low in her belly and in her breasts, her entire body longing for release, and surcease.

Without realizing it, she kept one hand around the base of the *deletto*, her wrist balanced on the countess's plump thigh, and with her other reached down to slip beneath her skirts to cover her own mound. Her nether lips were swollen with desire, and when she slipped a single finger between them, she shuddered as the pleasure vibrated through her body.

"Faith, she is the passionate jade!" exclaimed the countess. "I'd not have believed it if I'd not seen it myself."

At once May let the *deletto* slip from her lips, her breath coming in guilty, heaving gulps, but though she stilled her fingers on her quivering cunny, she was too close to spending to withdraw them entirely.

"Come, Poppy, we'll show her mercy," the countess continued. "Such an apt pupil! Pray hand me the sapphire. She has proven that she deserves it."

The countess gathered May in her arms and raised her onto the bed, pressing her gently down on the coverlet. She pulled May's hand from her quim, and May cried out— from the feel of her fingers dragged over her pearl, but also from disappointment.

"Nay, my lady, please," she gasped, striving to press her thighs together to find some sort of comfort. "Please!"

She thrashed her head to one side and saw Poppy coming towards her with another *deletto* of brilliant blue glass, much shorter in size, and with a flat, curving lip like a flower's petal to one side.

"There you are, little lass, there," Poppy said, fair cooing the words as she eased the sapphire *deletto* into May's passage. May cried out, bearing down against the delicious, shallow intrusion. Yet Poppy wasn't done with her. Gently with her thumb she pressed the petal against May's pearl, circling it lightly. At once May's back arched as her pleasure broke, waves of it rolling over her.

"Such passion, my lovely, such passion," whispered her ladyship, smiling as she bent over to stroke May's forehead to help calm her. "Who would not desire to possess you?"

But May . . . May cared for only one.

CHAPTER SEVEN

"So here we are, Bella," Jasper said as he walked across the inn's yard with his sister. He had been to the stable to see that his horses were properly cared for, as he always did, while he guessed his sister was perhaps inspecting the stable's grooms, as she always did as well. "One last inn, and one last night on this fool's errand. Is your little fledging swan ready to test her wings at court?"

"She had best be ready," Arabella said, brushing a spot of dust of the road from her skirts with her gloves. "Once we arrive at the palace tomorrow, I'll have no more time to spare for her education."

Jasper smiled. "What, are you weary of the girl already?"

"Not at all, brother, considering that I have kept her safe from you this far," she said, and smiled back at him with a triumph that he knew she'd no reason to feel. "I will not abandon her now. But with my guidance, I am confident that she will do well at court. If not with the king, then with some other grandee."

"Your *guidance*," he scoffed. "I can only imagine what rare advice you and Poppy have imparted on that innocent lady. Have you taught her anything of use? Who she must avoid at court, and who she must never ignore?"

"I've taught her how to smile and make her reverence and suck cock better than those Boleyn bitches," Arabella replied mildly. "That, and her beauty, are all any lady of her tender years needs to succeed."

He tried not to think overmuch about this new skill of Lady May's. There were precious few ladies at the English court who were willing to follow French customs like this, and to know that Lady May was already skilled at it was . . . inspiring.

Curiously he glanced about the yard. In this past week of travel, his sister had taken such care with Lady May that the girl had seldom been out of her sight.

"Where is the little pretty at present, Bella?" he asked as lightly as he could. "I wonder that you let her slip her leash at all."

"She hasn't," Arabella said. "I've only given her leash over to Poppy's care. She'll watch her every bit as closely as I do."

Or perhaps not, thought Jasper, a thought he wisely kept to himself. He had already made his plans for this evening, and Poppy was a sizable part of them. All this week he'd

observed how warm the friendship had become between
Poppy and the driver of the baggage wagon. He'd given the
fellow a few coins to help that friendship along, and in return
he'd made an assignation with Poppy for later this evening.
With his sister occupied with a groom or two, Jasper had
every right to believe that the lovely Lady May would be
quite alone, even lonely, and eager for his company.

Besides, it was the last night of their journey, and once
they reached Hampton Court, everything would be different. With her fortune and beauty to match, suitors would
be drawn to the girl like bees to honey. He wanted her, aye,
wanted her badly, but he wouldn't fight through a crowd
for any woman. It wasn't his manner. But if he could find
her alone tonight, then he could be sure she'd find a way
to come to him again in his own chambers at the palace.
Women were like that with him, especially delightful little
virgins.

"Why are you smiling, Jasper?" his sister demanded suspiciously. "I don't like to see you smile like that. It bodes ill,
and mischief, too."

He smiled still, and kissed her lightly on the forehead.

"No ill, I swear to you," he said. "As for mischief, look
to your own affairs, Bella, and worry not of mine."

"YOU ARE CERTAIN of this?" May asked the maidservant
clearing away the dishes from supper. "What Lord Blackford's man said?"

"Aye, my lady, I am," the woman said confidently, then gave a rolling laugh. "Drumble—that be his name—Drumble told me an' the cook's girl as he was passing us by. How his master the earl was of a mind to wash himself in the river, and how once he was determined, naught would stop him. Shameless, Drumble said his lordship was, then rolled his eyes to be most comical. Oh, my lady, how we did laugh and laugh!"

But May cared more for Jasper's shamelessness than his manservant's antics. "Did Drumble say where exactly in the river his master would be washing?"

The woman cocked her head towards the window. "I vow he'll most like go to the bend, my lady, where the water's deepest," she said. "It's not far beyond the kitchen gardens, down the path and beyond the fences and brambles. Beg pardon, my lady, but if you a-spy upon him, be warned that there might be others there besides. His lordship is a handsome-made gentleman, and if he'll be naked and shameless, why, where's the shame in the rest of us taking our peek?"

She laughed again, balancing the heavy tray against her quivering breasts. "Do that be all, my lady?"

"Aye, it is," May said, her thoughts racing ahead. Who would have guessed at her good fortune? To have both Lady Wilyse and Poppy away from guarding her at the same time as Jasper was said to be bathing in the river—la, was there ever such luck?

Of course she wasn't supposed to leave this chamber for any reason beyond a fire, but then she'd never limited herself to doing what she was supposed to. She'd vowed to see Jasper in his natural state, and here was her chance.

"That is, now that I have supped, I believe I shall retire for the night, to this very bed." May stretched her hands over her head and yawned extravagantly. "You see I am quite weary already."

"Very well, my lady," the woman said, though the bawdy grin on her face as she left the room showed she didn't believe May in the least. "But I wouldn't tarry if you've a mind to take the view of the river, seeing as Mr. Drumble was already on his way."

May only yawned again as the woman closed the door. She listened for the servant's footsteps to tread down the hall and the stairs behind, then raced to gather up her cloak. The evening was still warm from the sunny day, but she wanted the cloak more to hide herself than for warmth. Once she'd peeked from her chamber door to make sure no one else was in the hall, she hurried away, down the same way that the servant had come, through the back door of the inn, and into the kitchen garden. The inn was filled with travelers drinking and eating, the kitchen staff so busy that none noticed May as she slipped into the falling dusk.

Through the garden and beyond the fence and gooseberry shrubs: that was what the servingwoman had told her. Her heart racing with adventure and anticipation, May followed the narrow path down the hill.

She passed between a tall hedgerow and another, and before her were the gooseberries. She could see the river, too, with rushes along the banks and willows bowing low to trail their branches into the water. The moon was rising nearly as fast as the sun had fallen, and the evening sky was bright enough to illuminate all before her, almost as bright as day.

Almost as bright, aye, but infinitely different. The ordinary landscape seemed more magical by the rising moonlight, shimmering on the river's surface and turning every leaf and twig a silvery gray. The nightingales were just beginning to sing, too, their haunting calls adding to the scene's serenity, and May easily forgot the sounds of raised voices and crashing pottery and ironware from the kitchen behind her.

"Here, your lordship," called Drumble from the river's bank, not far from where May herself stood. "Here!"

At once May crouched down behind the bushes, where she'd be hidden by the shadows. She watched as Drumble rose from the grass, standing beside a dark bundle that she realized was Jasper's clothes and sword. It was only natural that the manservant would be here to guard his master's belongings. Not even Jasper would risk having his clothing stolen while he was in the water, and being forced to return to the inn dripping and naked.

Though that *was* worth imagining, and May smiled as she remembered how the maidservant, too, had been eager to ogle so handsome a man. What woman wouldn't?

Suddenly May heard a splashing before her, and Jasper's

head broke the surface of the water, dark and glistening. With both hands he wiped the water from his eyes and shook it from his hair like some large water spaniel. He spotted Drumble waiting on the bank and, with several long strokes, swam towards the shore. He reached the shallows, found his footing, and stood, rising clear from the water.

May gasped, overcome by the glorious sight of him before her. All those long hours in the coach when she'd been imagining what lay beneath his dark clothing were now rewarded. Shining wet in the moonlight, his body was long and lean and carved with muscles, without a bit of softness to mar the effect, his chest and shoulders broad and his belly taut and flat. She could see a swordsman's strength in his arms and the well-muscled thighs that came from being a masterful rider.

But what drew her gaze first was the sight of his cock and the balls below it, hanging quiescent before him. She had guessed at its size from her tantalizing touch in the dark stable, but clearly she'd guessed wrong. Even now, striding from the cool water, he was impressively long, and vastly more intriguing in flesh and blood than any glass *deletto* could be.

He was so beautiful there that she sighed aloud with unabashed pleasure—aloud, and more loudly than she realized. At once Drumble jumped to his feet, his dagger drawn to defend his master, and Jasper's gaze swung round to her hiding place behind the bushes.

Startled, she rose and drew back in confusion, determined to flee. But the edge of her cloak caught on a thorn in the bush before her, and as she tried to withdraw, it held fast, making her stumble. That was noise enough for Jasper to locate her, and in an instant he had reached the river's bank, grabbed his sword from its scabbard, and come charging towards her across the grass. Droplets of water flung from his naked body, and his gaze was so fierce that she cried out again as she struggled to free her cloak. He shoved aside the branches with the blade of his sword, and as she ducked back, he saw her at last.

"My lady May," he said, his face softening at once upon seeing her. "Marry, who would have guessed?"

"Good eve, my lord." Somehow May rose to her feet. She would not be intimidated, and though she trembled at the shock of having been discovered, she made her curtsy to him. "I . . . I trust you have enjoyed your exercise?"

"I'm enjoying this moment far more, my lady." He tipped back his head and laughed, drops of river water scattering over her.

Breathlessly Drumble reached them, and saw all. "Who is it, my lord, who—Ah, my lady!"

"It is indeed her ladyship, Drumble," Jasper said. "She would seem to have guessed my intentions to come call upon her, and joined me here instead."

"You would have come to me, my lord?" she asked, surprised.

"I would," he declared, "which is why I had come first

to the river, to cool and clean myself of the dirt of the road for you."

"For me, my lord?" She couldn't help but smile like a simpleton when he said such pretty things to her. "Did you then know her ladyship your sister had left me unattended?"

"And Poppy as well." He winked. "Perhaps I even gave them encouragement in that unattending."

He handed his sword to the servant. "Here, Drumble. I do not believe I'll need this to quell this particular intruder."

He had made no move at all to cover himself, standing boldly before her. Though she blushed furiously, May could not help but gaze at his cock, at last so close before her and bare to her scrutiny, and speak the first thought that came to her mind, however brazen.

"Perhaps I am safe from that sword, nay, my lord," she said, glancing up at him through her lashes. "But it appears you've brought another that might vanquish me if I do not take care to defend myself."

If he was surprised, he did not show it, but only smiled down at her with even more interest than before.

"Leave us, Drumble," he said without looking away from her. "I believe the lady would be more at her ease without you here."

Drumble shrugged and touched his forehead by way of respectful resignation, clearly well accustomed to such orders. He retreated back to the bank where Jasper's clothes still lay, to wait patiently and discreetly from sight.

His ready obedience made May giggle. "Do you do this often, my lord?" she asked. "Is it your habit to pursue ladies into the shrubbery whilst naked? Is this the form of hunting practiced at the royal court?"

"I should like to say that I often do," he said, setting his hands at his waist, "but in truth there are not many ladies who present themselves at the proper moment."

She glanced back over her shoulder towards the inn. They were hidden by the bushes from both the river and the inn above, as private a place as could be imagined. Which was likely just as well, considering how her situation would appear to anyone else, with her standing quite happily before a naked and dripping peer.

"But when we were last alone, my lord," she said, "I vowed to you that I soon would see you naked, and I have kept my word."

"You have at that," he said, grinning with pleasure at her boldness. "But tell me, pray. Now that you are here, do you like what you see? Am I all that you expected?"

"Oh, aye, my lord," she said breathlessly. "It is that, and far, far more."

As if in response to her praise, his cock began to swell and rise and lengthen as if it were a wild beast acting with a will of its own. She watched the change with fascination and delight, too, to know that she was the cause of such a delicious transformation.

His smile widened, and he leaned forward to take her face in his hands and kiss her. He took his time, his tongue dancing seductive circles around hers, yet also purposefully not drawing her close to him. She guessed this was another of his teasing games, his way of keeping her in his power through her innocence, and as much as it pleased her to be so carefully tutored by him like this, the slowness of his lessons frustrated her. She was ready for more, and faith, she was willing to show him.

She broke their kiss first, easing free of him. "We are almost equal, my lord," she whispered. "You have seen me as naked as Eve in the Garden, and now I have seen you, too, as naked as Adam."

"True enough, and equal, too," he said, holding his hands out at his sides. "Though I should scarce call this our earthly paradise."

"Nay, not as yet," she said. "Though surely I can make it so."

He tipped his head, intrigued. His hair was drying, springing into dark curls on his chest and around his now-rampant cock. "More equal, my lady, or more of a paradise?"

"Both, my lord," May said. "If you will but let me show you."

Not waiting for him to answer, she sank to her knees before him, her skirts fanning around her on the grass in the moonlight. His now-hard cock stood before her, the broad head uncapped and proud. For her, she thought, for *her*, and she smiled.

She rested her palms flat on the front of his thighs and leaned forward, taking only the tip of his cock between her lips. It was much different from the hard, chill glass that she'd practiced upon, hard and hot and yet almost like velvet to the touch of her tongue. He tasted still of the river, and yet salty, too, from the first drops of his seed that wept from the head's eye.

Fascinated by the difference, she let her tongue glide and play over the head and down the length, taking him deeper. She heard him groan, and beneath her palms she felt his thighs relax and tense as he pressed forward into her mouth. He tangled his fingers into her silken hair, holding her there. She smiled around his cock, and understood now that she was the one who had the power.

She opened her mouth more widely, as the countess had taught her to do, and she felt the sweet hardness of his cock slide deep against her throat. The *deletto* had not possessed ballocks, and now curiosity made her toy with them, gently fondling them in their sac. She felt him tense and swear softly with pleasure, and he pushed deeper into her throat.

In her lessons with Lady Wilyse and Poppy and with Jasper, too, she had been the one who'd received pleasure, the one made to feel the dizzying release that came with it. But this was the first time that she was the giver, and the one in control, and she was discovering that she relished this role, too.

Especially when it was Jasper, Lord Blackford, whose cock now filled her mouth and part of her throat.

It seemed so perfectly right, doing this for him, and the

intimacy and excitement of it had made her own cunny wet and full with her own building desires. She heard him groan, his fingers tightening in her hair and his cock tensing in her mouth.

"Free me, May," he ordered, his voice taut and rough. "Release me now."

She ignored him, holding him more closely with her hands and her mouth. Thanks to the countess's instruction, she knew what to expect, and she was eager to give him the same powerful release that he'd drawn from her in the darkened stable.

Yet she was still unprepared for the force of his spending, or the quantity of his hot seed as it suddenly filled her mouth. She pulled back with astonishment, swallowing as much as she could even as the drag of her retreating lips across his cock caused him to shudder and push harder against her. Though she tried to hold steady, he was too strong, and she fell backwards onto the grass, swallowing the last of his seed and gasping for air.

He threw himself on the ground beside her, gathering her into his arms.

"Why did you do that?" he demanded, his voice rough and his eyes full of fire. "I told you to release me. Didn't you know I'd spend?"

"I did, my lord," she said breathlessly, almost challenging him. "I did, and I wished it so. And faith, so did you."

He stared at her for a long moment. Then suddenly he grabbed her skirts and shoved them high, and with shocking speed he shifted lower, spreading her legs. She struggled with surprise and with excitement as well, but he held her fast, his fingers digging deep into the tender flesh of her thighs. She could not see his face behind the rumpled wall of her skirts, but not seeing only heightened the sensations more, and her eagerness with it.

He bent down and kissed the inside of her knee, his beard grazing across her skin. He kissed and nipped higher, pressing her legs farther apart, until he reached her cunny. She trembled with anticipation and curiosity, too, for though she guessed what he might do next, she wasn't entirely sure.

She gasped aloud as he kissed her mound, and gasped again with delicious shock when she realized he was licking the slit of her cunny with the flat of his tongue, over and over. She had already been excited from sucking him, but now she felt herself swelling further beneath his tongue, her arousal increasing so that she knew he must have tasted the honey that she felt slipping from her. With his fingers he gently parted her nether lips, dipping deeper into her as if he were devouring some delectable fruit.

Perhaps he was. His tongue sought and found her pearl, swirling and teasing so that every circling motion made her body tighten a little further. He eased a single thick finger into her, her passage so wet that though he stretched her, she felt only heat, only pleasure.

"Marry, but you are tight," he marveled. "Even after all that play with my sister and Poppy, you're still as narrow a virgin as any."

He slicked his tongue over her again, sending fresh riv-
ulets of pleasure streaking through her body. She stared
up at the moon, her fingers working mindlessly over the
soft, fragrant grass on which she lay. She loved this new
sensation of being entered, and having him stroke her from
within. Her hips rose from the grass, straining for more,
and she squeezed her eyes shut as her body arched and
begged for release.

With his finger sliding in and out of her, he pressed his
tongue wetly over her pearl, and her release broke. She cried
out, then cried out again as the spasms racked her body,
washing over her as surely as if it had been the river itself.

"Did I please you, May?"

As she gasped for air, her eyes flew open. The moon
overhead was gone, blotted out by Jasper's face. She smiled,
and reached her hands up to loop around his bare shoulders, his skin warm in the evening air.

"Are you pleased?" he asked again. "*Were* you pleased?"

"Faith, my lord, need you ask that of me?" she said
breathlessly, staring up at his pale eyes, the same color as
the moonlight itself. "All I would have now is for you to
make me entirely yours, and—"

"Nay." He pressed his fingers over her mouth to silence
her, reminding her of how she'd done the same to him
from the coach. The musky scent of her passion clung to
his hand, and when she pressed her lips to his finger, she
could taste herself, too. "Not here, not now, not like this."

"But I wish it," she said, reaching down to feel for his

cock. He was hard again, as she'd known he would be, and as ready for more as she was herself. She was lying here on her back with her petticoats rucked up and her legs spread, and he was beside her naked and with a cock so hard it must have pained him. What more was there for either of them to wish? "And you do as well, my lord. You cannot deny it."

"I cannot, sweet, and I do not." He kissed her hard, proving it. "But I would not take you here, behind a kitchen garden like some low serving girl. You are not that, May. You are not."

His face was so close to hers that she felt his breath on her cheek. A final few drops of river water fell from his hair onto her cheek.

"You are a rare creature, May," he whispered roughly, building heady images of desire for her, "and deserving of more. When I make you mine, I will take you in my own bed at the palace, where none will disturb us. I will kiss and savor every inch of your body, and I will bring your blood to such a fever of longing that you'll be nigh to perishing from it."

May closed her eyes, her heart racing anew as she let her mind envision what he was describing.

"Then, then, I will take you," he continued, "and destroy the last vestiges of your maidenhead. I'll bury my cock deep in your sweet nest, and I will fuck you—aye, I will *fuck* you—as no other man has ever fucked a woman, and fill you so that my seed will spill from you, and you will spend so hard that you will fair scream from the pleasure of it. *That* is what you deserve, sweet May, and that is what you shall have from me at Hampton Court."

He kissed her again, ravishing her with his mouth with the same ferocity that he was promising to do with his cock, and making her so breathless that it was as if she hadn't just spent.

"But why not both, my lord?" she begged. "Why not here, and there as well?"

"Because that is how I wish it," he said. "It is my will."

"It might be yours, my lord, but it is not mine!" she cried, her frustration spilling into anger. "That is not what I wish at all!"

She shoved him away and scrambled to her feet, and before he could stop her, she gathered her skirts and ran up the path and away from him. She didn't hear him behind her, but still she didn't dare slow her steps. Of course he'd have to stop to pull on at least his trunk hose and make himself decent before her followed her, though considering how he'd just rejected her, he might not bother to follow after her at all.

She swore to herself, using one of the new oaths she'd overheard from Poppy. She was so furious with him she could scarce contain it. How could he refuse her like that? How could he love her with his mouth as he had, then refuse her the rest? If he would not lie with her, then she would find some other man to oblige her.

She ran up through the kitchen garden the way she'd

come. But now the yard before the door was filled with men who'd spilled out from the inn's front room to enjoy the warm evening. They were lolling on benches they'd pulled outside and standing about with tankards and pipes, a noisy, rowdy crowd that May had no wish to pass through. Instead she kept to the shadows of the bushes, hiding her pale hair and face with the hood of her dark cloak, and hurried through the alley between the tavern and the stables to the stable yard beyond.

She could hear the nickering of the horses as they settled for the night, and the voices and laughter of the grooms with them. It would serve the great Lord Blackford right if she were to go to the stables and find some handsome, brawny stableboy, just as Lady Wilyse did. A stableboy wouldn't turn away from her, or be too proud to take what she offered. Tempted, she stood by the door, hugging her arms to her breasts beneath her cloak and wishing she could be as brazen in her needs as Lady Wilyse. Thoroughly miserable, her whole body ached with what she'd had, and what she hadn't, and against her will her thoughts went back to the day that Jasper had trapped her in a stable much like this one.

She groaned, and shook her head. Nay, as much as Jasper vexed her, no mere stableboy could compare to him. Best to return to her room before Poppy discovered her gone, and disconsolately she turned towards the door to the inn.

Suddenly three horsemen came thundering into the

inn's yard, accompanied by an entourage of servants and attendants and outriders with banners, all in handsome livery. May stopped to watch, as did everyone else, exactly as the gentlemen doubtless had intended. They *were* gentlemen, too, all three elegantly dressed and riding fine horses. Surely they must be bound to join the king at Hampton Court as well, or perhaps they had just left His Majesty.

The first man was clearly of the highest rank, his dress the most magnificent. He wore an elaborately worked chain of gold around his shoulders, and the scabbard of his sword was studded with jewels. The others deferred to him, content to let him lead, and from the number of attendants, May wondered if he was perhaps royalty himself.

Certainly he had the air of a prince. Though he was not tall, he held himself as if he were, and with an imperiousness that showed he expected to be obeyed. Dressed entirely in sapphire blue, a color that was bright even by the lantern's light, he had flaxen hair worn in the old-fashioned manner, cropped straight at his collar. His face was long and narrow, and with his beard trimmed to a point over his chin. There was something vulpine about him, too, a bit too much sharpness to his features: if Lord Blackford was considered a lion, thought May, then this lord would be a fox.

Servants rushed to attend the newcomer, and the innkeeper himself came bustling from the door, anxiously wiping his hands on his apron as he waited to greet the newcomer.

"Who is that gentleman?" May asked him as he stood beside her.

The innkeeper frowned, not wishing to be distracted, until he realized it was May who'd addressed him.

"Forgive me, my lady," he said, hurriedly bowing and touching his forehead in deference. "I did not see that it was you."

May pushed her hood back from her face, more interested in the blue-clad man than in whether she'd received the respect due her.

"Who is that, sirrah?" she repeated, her gaze drawn again to the gentleman. "The one who has just arrived?"

"Why, my lady, that is His Grace the Duke of Pomfrey," the innkeeper said. "I wonder that you do not know him yourself. He is cousin to His Majesty, my lady, and a wondrous grand lord in his own right."

"Is he indeed?" May said, marveling. To be sure, she'd been impressed by Lady Wilyse and Lord Blackford, but as highborn as they were, they'd never compete with a duke who was cousin to the king. For the last week, Lady Wilyse had spoken much of His Majesty, of his cleverness, his power, his strength, even his extravagant virility, that May had become very much in awe of anything to do with the king.

And now, here before her stood a duke with royal blood, the same blood as King Henry himself.

His Grace had dismounted from his horse, laughing

with the two other gentlemen with him. He was so grand
that, even now, he did not give orders to his servants himself, but simply stood in their midst and waited while
one took his horse and another brushed the dust from his
clothes, and yet another came trotting forward with a lantern to guide his way to the inn.

"He comes, my lady!" exclaimed the innkeeper, sinking
into so low a bow that May wondered that he kept his footing. "His Grace comes!"

Following his example, May, too, quickly curtsied low
and bowed her head, spreading her skirts as Lady Wilyse
had taught her. As she did, she realized she'd lost her cap
somewhere during the evening and that her head was
shamefully bare, and with a sudden jab of guilt she prayed
that no twigs or grass clung to her hair, or any other sign
remained of her activities with Jasper near the river. How
embarrassing that would be before a great lord like the
Duke of Pomfrey!

Without looking, she heard the men's footsteps ap-
proaching.

"Is His Grace's supper in readiness as ordered?" asked
one of the attendants.

"Aye, aye, everything is prepared, exactly as was ordered!"
exclaimed the innkeeper, so overwrought that his voice
shook. "Might I say how honored we are to be permitted to
attend to—"

"Who is this?" a man asked, and without raising her

head, May knew at once it must be the duke himself. "Her hair would bring joy to an alchemist's heart; it is that exact rare shade of pure gold. Your daughter, perhaps?"

"My—my daughter, Your Grace?" the innkeeper stammered in confusion. "I—I have no daughter, Your Grace, nor wife."

But May understood. It had been Fate that had made her lose her cap in the grass so that her bright hair might fall around her face, Fate that had sent her here to the front of the inn at this moment, Fate that had brought her here, to curtsy at the door. The duke meant her, and boldly she raised her head.

"If you intend me, Your Grace," she said, "then I am Lady May Roseberry, only daughter of the late Marquess of Hartwick, God bless my father's soul. I am honored, Your Grace."

She met his gaze, and smiled. He was younger than she'd realized at first, not so very much older than herself. He'd freckles, and his eyes were green with pale lashes and equally pale brows, which somehow made his face even more like a fox's. Those same eyes revealed far more than they should of his thoughts, or perhaps it was simply that because he was a duke, he'd no need to guard his thoughts the way that ordinary folk did.

Or, May thought with regret, the way that Jasper did.

No matter. In that instant, it was all she could do to watch the myriad of thoughts flickering through the duke's green eyes.

She saw that he was pleased with her beauty, and she could not help but blush from his approval.

She saw that he was surprised by her claim to noble blood, but pleased by it as well, as if he was relieved that she wasn't the innkeeper's daughter.

But what she saw most of all in his eyes was desire, a raw hunger so apparent that she almost stepped back before it.

Were her own thoughts and desires as easily read? Did he look at her and see that not a quarter hour before she'd been lying on her back beneath the moonlight, with her skirts tossed high and her thighs spread and a man's tongue burrowing deep into her cunny?

Her blush deepened. Could he tell that though she'd writhed from the pleasure of that licking, and spent hard, she'd still been left wanting for more?

Did he sense that beneath her gown and cloak, her nipples were hard as pebbles, pressed against the unyielding whalebone of her stays? Did he know that even as she'd curtsied so demurely to him, her pearl was so sensitive that she'd nearly whimpered from the motion? Could he guess that her cunny was still swollen and wet, and so eager for more that she'd actually considered finding a man from the stables to satisfy her?

Yet she did not look away from his gaze, instead letting him study her as long as he wished. And he did wish it. That was clear enough.

But was it equally apparent in May's face that she longed to be fucked, that her whole body ached for it, that the one thing she wished for most that night had been a man's cock, and that the one man she'd prayed would give it to her had refused?

But when His Grace the Duke of Pomfrey took her fingers in his gloved hand, she understood that he would not toy with her as Jasper had done, nor leave her unfulfilled. He would not care if she was a virgin. He *would* fuck her, and he would relish every stroke of it.

And from that moment, her life would never be the same.

CHAPTER EIGHT

For an evening that had started with such promise, Jasper could not begin to comprehend how far, and how fast, the night had sunk into a thorough disaster.

He was still tying the points of his doublet as he came up the alley between the stable and the inn. He'd never expected May to flee as she had, running away with all the haste of a rabbit before the hounds and leaving him to yank on his clothes as best he could before he could follow.

But then he didn't know what next to expect from her; she was that unpredictable. He'd never known a virgin like her. Here he'd reined in his own desires to let her grow accustomed to him, slowly seducing her with the greatest care imaginable. That was the way to win virgins, or it was with every other maid.

But May . . . May would have none of it. How she'd lasted so long in the nunnery was beyond him. First she'd crept down to the river to find him before he'd had the chance to come back to her. There'd been no demure shrieks of horror at his nakedness, or scurrying back to the inn. Nay, with her everything had been bold and eager, and before he'd realized it, his cock had been jerking away in her mouth.

Not that he hadn't enjoyed it. He enjoyed everything about her, and he could scarce wait to take her the way she kept begging him to do. But to quarrel with him and bolt away because all he'd done was lick her quim until she'd spent, and handsomely, too—merry, was there another maid like her?

He hoped he'd find her now before she locked herself away in her chamber for the night. A few more kisses and sweet words, a few wayward caresses, and he'd put things to rights between them. But one thing was certain: he wasn't going to wait any longer. Tenderness be damned. Once they reached the palace tomorrow, he'd take the first chance he found to bed her in his rooms, where there'd be no danger of their being disturbed. Otherwise she'd tumble into some other rogue's hands—and on his cock—and all the time and effort he'd put into seducing her would go for naught.

He raked his fingers through his hair, hoping he didn't look too disreputable, and turned the corner into the inn's yard.

And stopped short.

There before the doorway was the innkeeper and a score of others, gaping as if they were sitting in the pit at the playhouse. In a way, he supposed they were. Except that the players were Lady May Roseberry—*his* Lady May—and that damned rascal Pomfrey, gotten up like some bantam rooster in his usual infernal bright blue, and looking at her as if he meant to throw her against the wall and have her while everyone watched. Likely they would, too, and likely May would love every moment of it.

But God's blood, not if he could help it.

In a half dozen strides, Jasper was in the middle of the little group. He bowed curtly to Pomfrey, for by rights of rank he had no choice to do otherwise. But as far as Jasper was concerned, the civilities would end there.

"Blackford." Pomfrey smiled at him, keeping his lips together as he always did. "Good e'en to you."

"Good e'en to you, Your Grace." Jasper smiled, as much as baring his quite excellent teeth resembled smiling, and drew himself upright so he towered over the duke. He might be his inferior in rank, but in other matters he had the unquestionable advantage. Surely May could see that for herself, couldn't she? Or was she so dazzled by a dukedom that she failed to see the man who owned it? "You have made the Lady May's acquaintance, I see."

"Aye, the lady has done me the favor of presenting herself to me." The duke smiled at May, not at Jasper. "Quite boldly it was done, yet never have I been more pleased by a lady's impudence."

May tipped back her head and laughed, her lovely pale throat turned towards the duke, a pretty display of vulnerability. She'd learned that little trick fast enough, thought Jasper sourly; it had been much more pleasing when directed towards him.

"Lady May is much given to impudence, Your Grace," he said, determined to turn her interest back towards him, where by rights it belonged. "In the past week that I have journeyed in her company, I have seen many instances of it myself, and been charmed by them all."

May's eyes widened, and to Jasper's relief she turned away from the duke towards him instead, and to his even greater relief, she pulled her hand free of the duke's as well.

"Have you indeed been charmed by me, my lord?" May asked. "I would not have guessed it myself."

She gazed up at him with so little guile that Jasper immediately forgot his earlier irritation with her. No wonder Pomfrey was so interested: her face still had the delicious softness of a woman who'd recently spent, and all Jasper could think of now was getting her away from Pomfrey and the others so he might do it to her again.

"You should know my regards to you by now, my lady," he said, bowing slightly towards her. "Can you not trust the proof as it comes from my lips, my tongue, my very heart?"

She blushed furiously at that, leaving no doubt that she'd understood his meaning. Yet she did not look away, the way most ladies would, but met his gaze so evenly as to be a challenge.

"Indeed, my lord, you have given me that proof, and it has pleased me greatly," she said, "as I can but hope you were likewise pleased by my own fervency."

He'd not expected that, the little minx. "Surely you have my proof of that, too."

"I did, my lord," she said, and smiled slyly. "I demand only one final proof of it before I will be truly *satisfied* of your honorable devotion."

The duke frowned, and studied them closely. He was no fool, as Jasper knew well, and even a fool could likely read the real meaning behind this little exchange between Jasper and May.

"You appear well acquainted with this lady, Blackford," he said, his voice testy, though for May's sake his smile remained in place. He rested his hand on the pommel of his sword, an unmistakable warning that Jasper did not miss. "Is your friendship of long . . . standing?"

Jasper drew in his breath, but he, too, continued to smile. He dropped his hand to his own sword, only to recall to his chagrin that, in his haste to follow May, he'd left it behind in Drumble's care. By all that was holy! He doubted matters would actually progress to drawn swords—duke or not, Pomfrey would know better than to challenge him that way—but he hated to be forced to rely on words alone to defend May's honor.

"Nay, Your Grace," he said as evenly as he could. "I have known the lady but the few days of our journey. She is a perfect innocent, raised from the cradle by the blessed sisters of St. Beatrice, and only new released by them into the world."

"Into your care, Blackford?" the duke asked, raising his brows with skepticism. "What manner of cloister do these blessed sisters maintain? I wonder."

"A most ancient and venerable one, Your Grace," May said, speaking up for herself. "It was not a brothel, Your Grace, if that is what you suspected."

The duke gulped, and Jasper beamed at May. Who needed a sword when she could so ably defend herself?

"Pray forgive me, Lady May," the duke said, recovering as best he could. "I meant no slander towards the blessed sisters or yourself. I only wished to inquire as to why they would give one of their most precious charges into the keeping of Lord Blackford."

"But they didn't, Your Grace," said Arabella, sailing serenely into their midst. "Lady May was given into my safekeeping, and at the request of His Majesty I am accompanying her to his court. My brother did but fall in with us on our journey."

The duke smiled at Arabella, so warmly that Jasper wondered sourly if his sister had shared her favors with him as well. "Lady Wilyse, good e'en. It brings me joy to see you again."

"And I you, Your Grace." She curtsied belatedly, then stood to kiss each side of the duke's face in fond greeting after the French fashion. "You have met my dear Lady May, Your Grace?"

"I have had the honor, Lady Wilyse," he said, smiling once again at May. "A most precious jewel."

"More precious than the eye perceives, Your Grace," Arabella said. "She is an orphan, Your Grace, and now a ward of His Majesty, who will determine a husband for her in time."

"But not at once, my lady," May protested. "I do not wish to wed at once."

Arabella laughed indulgently, though with no real humor. "You will wed when and with whom the king decrees," she said, then turned towards the duke. "You see how she is, Your Grace. Very young, and in need of guidance. But I expect she will be much contested. Not only does she possess the beauty you see before you, but she also has a sizable fortune to match."

Arabella reached out to smooth May's hair, a simple gesture that could have been made from fondness; to Jasper, knowing his sister and her purpose, it had all the subtlety of a common procuress.

Nor did Jasper miss the new spark of interest in Pomfrey's eyes. Gold would do that to him. Although he was already rich as Croesus, he had a miserly soul, and was always wheedling for more lands and more gold. Of course his sister would know of the duke's infamous greediness, just as she'd know the duke had yet to find a lady who pleased him well enough to wed. If His Majesty failed to take interest in May, then there'd be little shame in claiming a duke who was the king's cousin for the girl instead.

Just not Pomfrey.

"It has been a long journey for us, Your Grace," Arabella said with a studied sigh of weariness. "You know how slowly we ladies must travel. God willing, we should make Hampton Court tomorrow."

Jasper couldn't keep back his snort of disgust. They could have reached the court days ago if his sister hadn't paused to savor every ginger-haired stableboy along the way, and she wouldn't be half so weary, either.

"Are you going to the court, too, Your Grace?" May asked eagerly.

The duke smiled at her warmly, too warmly, really. "I am bound there myself, Lady May. We stopped here to refresh ourselves and to sup, and to change horses, and then we intend to push forward to the palace this night."

"Ah, well," Jasper said quickly. "We shall be sure to see you there, Your Grace."

"Pray stay the night, Your Grace," Arabella said, resting her hand on the duke's blue sleeve. "Stay, and travel with us. The roads can be so treacherous for ladies, especially the closer we are to London. I should feel much more secure to add another sword arm to our little party."

The innkeeper smothered a gasp. To accommodate so large a party, and one with such high expectations, would sorely tax his resources.

"Please, pray do!" May exclaimed excitedly. "We would make a much grander show at the gate if we arrive as a single party."

The duke laughed. Jasper did not.

"Very well," the duke said. "I can never deny the wishes of ladies. We will stay the night, and ride with you tomorrow. And yes, Lady May, we will enter the castle with my pennants flying."

She grinned happily at the prospect, suddenly seeming achingly young to Jasper. She was seventeen, a woman grown. He'd discovered that himself. How constrained her life in the convent must have been, to be so delighted by bright scraps of cloth flapping in the wind!

The duke held up a single finger. "I will stay, aye, but on one condition. You must agree to dine with me, as my guests."

"We are most honored, Your Grace," Arabella declared. "Nothing would please us more."

But Jasper could think of a thousand things that would, and as he watched the duke offer his arm to May to lead her inside, he thought of a thousand more beyond that. Only one thing would please him now, and that was to claim May as his own.

IT WAS MUCH more interesting to sup with gentlemen than ladies, decided May, and far, far more entertaining than dining in the refectory at the nunnery, where they'd been forbidden to speak among themselves at all as they ate, let alone laugh and make bawdy jests and toasts as the gentlemen had done this night. There were four of them at table—Jasper, Lord Pomfrey, and his friends Sir Thomas and Lord Simon—and that was four more than she'd ever dined with at one time before.

Lady Wilyse had lectured her beforehand about how, being so young a lady, she should take care to say little in conversation, but instead to smile, and let the gentlemen guess at her thoughts. Lady Wilyse assured her that this was the expected manner for young, unwed ladies at the court, but May in turn had found it tedious to sit like a statue of stone and let the gentlemen strive to outdo one another in the compliments they heaped about her.

Though when she considered it, outdoing one another was truly what at least two gentlemen seemed determined to do. Both Jasper and the duke had sparred with each other the entire evening, and the more wine that had been drunk, the more obvious their antagonism became. May had fresh admiration for Lady Wilyse, who had somehow managed to ease the tension at the table again and again, and keep the two from blows.

Her ladyship had explained that, too, while Poppy had dressed May's hair: that the duke might prove a genuine suitor for May's hand, a most fortunate match if he could be brought around to it, yet one that Jasper would do his best to counter, not from any ill will towards May, but because he and the duke had never been friends.

Thus her ladyship had advised May to be at once charming to the duke, but not so much as to infuriate her brother. She was to be agreeable, but say nothing. Finally,

she was to behave as a lady should, even though May had
yet to determine exactly what that might be. How could
she make sense of being told one moment to be as dull and
solemn as a saint, and the next to practice sucking at the
spun-glass *deletto* in lieu of a flesh-and-blood cock? It was
enough to make her head spin far more than the wine that
she drank.

Yet as complicated and conflicting as all this advice
was to May, none of it was as difficult as minding her own
thoughts. She was thankful no one else at the table could
know them, else there would not have been any more talk
of her being a lady.

For each time she glanced across the table at Jasper, she
remembered what they had done on the river's bank behind
the kitchen garden. She saw him not as he sat here now, as
properly dressed as any courtier, but as a fearsomely male
creature rising from the river in the moonlight, his body
muscled and perfect and spangled with droplets of water.

And more: she remembered how she'd knelt before him,
the feel of his cock filling her mouth, how he'd groaned and
begged her to stop even as he'd tangled his fingers in her
hair to hold her close, the tantalizing little sac, cool to her
touch, that held his balls, the way he'd jerked and thrust
as he'd spent, and the salty taste of his seed on her tongue.

She stole another glance at him now, over the rim of
her wine goblet, to meet his gaze. She loved his pale eyes,
their seductive intensity. He'd looked at her that way this
evening when he'd kissed her, before he'd thrown back her

skirts and licked her cunny until she'd melted in blissful abandon.

The memory alone made her blush again, watching him as she remembered. He was watching her closely, too, not heeding the conversation between the others about whose horse was superior. His lips gleamed with the fat of the roasted fowl he was eating, yet it could have been her own juices that glistened there and in his beard. Suddenly he smiled, and from the wickedness of it she knew his thoughts were much the same as her own.

Swiftly she looked back down at her plate, fearing that someone else might notice the exchange between them. Lady Wilyse was speaking with much animation to the duke, telling some convoluted tale of two ladies at the court who'd fought each other over a talking bird who sang in French. The duke in turn was listening to this nonsense as if it were the most fascinating story he'd ever heard, and because he was enraptured, Sir Thomas and Lord Simon were as well.

None of them were paying any attention at all to May, and therefore none of them saw the little twitch she made in her chair, or the gulp that she couldn't quite suppress. Across from her Jasper was also listening to his sister, leaning back in his chair with his arms folded loosely over his chest. But beneath the table, May couldn't mistake the pressure of his foot against hers, rubbing gently and suggestively against hers.

She stared at him, wordlessly striving to gain his attention. Whether on purpose or not, he did not respond. May frowned, determined not to be ignored. Despite the pleasure Jasper had given her, she still hadn't entirely forgiven him for ending things as he had, and she wasn't prepared to let him forget it, either.

The table between them was narrow, the distance short. She slipped her foot from her shoe, and ran her toes lightly from his foot up the length of his shin to his knee.

Still Jasper did not look her way, but May was sure she saw the corner of his mouth twitch. Daring further, she slid her foot higher along the inside of his thigh, over his trunk hose. She watched his face closely for a response as she made small teasing circles with her toes along his thigh, inching ever higher.

Somehow he kept his expression even as if nothing were amiss, chuckling with the others at his sister's story. But when at last he shifted in his chair to move closer to May, she knew he wasn't nearly as unaffected as he was pretending.

She drew to the edge of her chair, reaching out as far as she dared without sliding off onto the floor beneath the table. Moving higher along the hard muscles of his thighs, her toes bumped into something harder still—that wretched shield of a codpiece—and she heaved a small sigh of impatience. Perhaps if she wriggled her toes the right way, she could find the space between the codpiece and the opening in his trunk hose, and find his cock, and—

"Lady May," the duke said, smiling, and every face at

the table turned expectantly towards her. "It is my custom to walk briefly out of doors before the final course of my supper. Pray would you and Lady Wilyse join me?"

"How delightful, Your Grace!" exclaimed her ladyship. "We shall be most honored to join you."

She pushed back her chair and stood, and at once the duke and the other two gentlemen did as well. Hastily May dropped her foot from Jasper's lap, and he stood as well. But no matter how she searched blindly about the floor, May could not find her shoe.

"Lady May," Lady Wilyse said, her voice carrying an unmistakable warning. "Come, my dear. We must not keep His Grace waiting."

"Forgive me, my lady," May said, pointedly not looking at Jasper from fear of laughing, "but I . . . I seem to have mislaid my shoe beneath the table."

Lady Wilyse's brows rose skeptically. "How could you have mislaid your shoe from your foot?"

"Such curious things do happen, Lady Wilyse," the duke said gallantly, and to May's mortification he himself bent beneath the table to retrieve her wayward shoe. Kneeling before her, he held it on his knee and beckoned for her foot.

"What a pretty show is this!" Lady Wilyse exclaimed. "Do not be shy, May, not when His Grace offers to assist you."

With no choice, May slowly raised her skirt a fraction and presented her stocking-clad foot. It wasn't that she was exactly shy. She knew she'd a neat little foot and ankle, made more pleasing still by bright green stockings. But she had chosen those stockings with Jasper in mind, not the duke, and it did not seem right to her to have His Grace now so openly admiring them and her leg inside them.

"There is no sin to maidenly reluctance, Lady Wilyse," the duke said, seizing May's ankle like a prize. "Indeed, it charms me."

His hands startled her with their strength, caressing her foot and toes with a freedom that only a man of his rank would dare. And yet to her consternation, she realized his touch did not displease her. Far from it: the more he stroked her foot, the more pleasurable it became, made all the more so by having him kneeling in subservience before her. It was only a few moments, but it was enough to make her breath quicken.

The duke noticed, too. How could he not? He was smiling his close-lipped smile, knowingly watching for her reaction much as she had earlier watched for Jasper's.

If they had been alone, she wondered, would he have pressed his suit, and let his hand roam higher? Would he have seen not only the color of her stockings but the color of her garters, and then the pearly pale flesh of her thighs?

Her wanton thoughts raced onwards, imagining him shoving aside the supper plates and lifting her back onto the table. With those same strong hands, he'd toss back her skirts and part her thighs, and then he'd enter her and fuck her with her legs around his waist, and—

"Pray do not forget the shoe, Your Grace," Lady Wilyse

said drily, not forgetting her own role as May's guardian. "She cannot go walking in the garden if she is unshod."

The duke did not reply, nor was he obliged to, being a duke. But he did finally slip May's shoe onto her foot and retie the ribbons himself, giving her foot a final, fond little pat when he was done.

"There," he said, rising and offering her his arm. "Now that you are shod, as Lady Wilyse desired, you can walk with me."

May took his arm, and he led her into the inn's garden—the same garden that she'd already visited that night. Following behind them at a respectful distance was Lady Wilyse, with Lord Simon and Sir Thomas on either side of her. May glanced back over her shoulder once, looking for Jasper, but he did not seem to have followed them, and she did not know whether to be disappointed that he hadn't, or relieved.

But the duke had a way of making her soon forget Jasper, and think only of him instead.

"I believe in being direct, my dear," he said, "and leave the sweet lies to the poets. I find you the most beautiful lady I have seen in years."

May smiled and blushed, for the idea of having gentlemen praise her like this was still a novelty. "Thank you, Your Grace. Though that does sound like poetry to me."

He laughed. "I vow it does, though I intended it as honest truth and no more. Mayhap this will sound less poetical:

I do not believe you are nearly as innocent as Lady Wilyse claims."

May stopped walking. "You are wrong, Your Grace," she protested. "I am a maid still."

He stopped, too, standing before her. His fair hair looked like gold in the moonlight, as bright as the rings on his hands and the large chain around his neck.

"You would swear to it that you are a virgin?" he asked, clearly not believing her.

"I am, Your Grace," she said fervently. "I have never known any man, or taken his member into my body, and I would swear it on the Holy Scripture itself, or by any saint you wish to name."

"Strong oaths for one who is convent-bred."

"Strong oaths because it is the truth, Your Grace," she said firmly. "No man can claim otherwise."

He took her arm, and once again began to walk with her. "Then you are a maid," he said. "We shall agree to that. But could you make the same vow regarding other freedoms you may have permitted?"

She frowned at him, unsure whether she could bluster her way clear again without lying.

"Then it is as I guessed," he said. "I saw it in your face today in the yard, and when I fastened your shoe, I could smell it in your scent. Only sex leaves a scent like that on a woman. You may contrive to make a fool of Lady Wilyse, but you will not do the same to me."

"I am sorry if I displease you, Your Grace." She didn't know whether to believe him. Could men truly tell such things of a woman? Shamefaced, she tried to pull her arm free of his hand to retreat. "Faith, if I am so distasteful to you, then I—"

"It's Blackford, isn't it?" he asked, holding her fast. "I saw how he did look at you, as weak-minded with lust as any mooncalf."

"I do not have to answer to you!" she exclaimed, then realized what she'd said. "That is, pray forgive me, Your Grace, but I need not answer such questions."

To her surprise, he laughed. "Nay, you do not. But that is why you beguile me, Lady May. You have none of the milky falsity of ladies who have been reared in the court. Mayhap in time you will acquire it, too, but now you are as God made you, and it pleases me. *You* please me."

He pulled her behind an outbuilding and from the sight of the others, and kissed her. He was only the second man that May had ever kissed, and from curiosity she could not help but compare him to Jasper. The duke kissed her with purpose, and with hunger, forcing her lips apart to thrust his tongue deep into her mouth. There was the same authority to it that he showed with everything else: a ducal kiss, she supposed.

Everything considered, she preferred how Jasper took his time, but she wasn't about to scorn the duke, not when she was still unhappy with Jasper. The duke tasted of the wine he'd drunk, and of urgency, too, an urgency that she soon found was as catching as a fever.

With a practiced expertise, he tipped her back into the crook of his arm, the heavy gold chain around his shoulder falling forward against her bare skin. Caught off-balance, she instinctively linked her hands around his shoulders to stop herself from falling. Clearly this was what he expected, because he made a smugly male grunt of contentment, and pressed his advantage by slipping his hand into the low, square neck of her close-fitting bodice to cup her breast.

"Ah, now, that's a plump little dove," he murmured with approval, and kissed her harder as he fondled her tender flesh. She felt her nipple tighten as he tugged and squeezed it, and she gasped into his mouth with surprise.

"That pleases you?" he asked, as if her pleasure were not evident enough. "You like that?"

"Aye—aye, Your Grace," she managed to stammer. She felt as if this eve she'd been aroused so frequently that it took next to nothing to do so again. Already she could feel the now-familiar gathering in her belly, the extravagant heat of it, and the sweet fullness growing in her cunny, and he'd done scarce more than kiss her and caress her breast. Caught as she was against his arm, she could not reach his codpiece to return his attentions, but she was tensing and relaxing her fingers into his shoulders much like a contented cat does, and she could tell from the grumbling sounds that he was making that he liked that, too. His mouth was grinding against hers, becoming more insistent, and she answered eagerly, tumbling into his sensual spell.

But then to her disappointment, he suddenly broke the kiss and set her back squarely on her feet. She felt as if she'd fallen from the stars to the ground, and none too gently, either. She opened her mouth, ready to inquire as to why he had stopped, when she saw he wasn't looking at her but over her head.

"Blackford," he said curtly. "Why are you here?"

Jasper bowed in perfect deference, but even as May put her bodice back to rights, she could see there was a hint of genial mockery to his smile.

"I was sent by my sister, Your Grace," he said. "The innkeeper has set the table with the next dish, as you requested, and she did not wish it to grow too chill for your tastes."

The duke simmered, his temper hot. "Tell your sister that I am not hungry, and that I care not for some country innkeeper's damnable dishes."

But Jasper's smile only widened. "Forgive me, Your Grace, but while you may not be hungry, I vow that Lady May looks to me to be nigh famished."

May pressed her lips together to keep from laughing. This was the greatest difference between Jasper and the duke: one could laugh and find humor in most anything, while the other was far too aware of his own place in the world to do so.

Even now an ominous vein throbbed in Lord Pomfrey's pale forehead, and his fists clenched tight at his sides.

"You need not feign ignorance, Blackford," he said. "I've already discerned that you have dallied with this lady yourself, so you needn't present yourself as her champion."

"Nay, Your Grace, I needn't," Jasper agreed. "Not with my sister keeping away any who might lay siege to the lady."

"Then for the lady's sake, I will carry her back to your sister. Come, Lady May." He grabbed her hand, and pulled her along after him. "But I shall not forget your interference, Blackford, nor your disregard for this lady's honor. I shall not forget."

The duke did not wait for Jasper's answer, but fair dragged May after him on the path back to the inn. Yet as May passed Jasper, he reached out and trailed his forefinger over the twin swells of her breasts, one after the other, then winked like the most sly of imaginable rogues.

May caught her breath at his audacity, but could not help but smile at him over her shoulder. Lord Pomfrey could vow up one side and down the other to defend her honor, but she would not forget what Lord Blackford had done, either.

And it was, she decided, a most pleasing memory to have.

CHAPTER NINE

*D*espite the excitement of the evening, May scarcely slept that night, and was the first of their party to be awake and ready to begin the final few miles of their journey. The day was warm and full of sunshine, and as May leaned from the window, even the very birds in the trees outside the inn seemed to share her joy. Why shouldn't they? For today was the day May would first pass through the gates of the palace to be presented to His Majesty the King of England, and she was certain in all her life she had never greeted a dawn with more excitement.

Because they were only a few miles from Hampton Court Palace, the rest of their party did not share May's haste, and were slow to leave their beds and rise. Much to her dismay, even Poppy was late with her breakfast.

"You're awake with the larks, Lady May," Poppy said, yawning broadly to prove that she wasn't, as she set the tray with May's breakfast on the table.

May bounded across the room to the table, plucking a bun from the plate. "That's because I wasn't awake all night heaving and sighing in the stable loft with John Carter."

Poppy started. "God's fish, my lady, who told you such a tale?"

"No one," May said, tearing the bun into tiny bites that she dropped one by one into her mouth. "But after I saw you nigh riding upon his lap on the wagon, cooing so sweetly, and then when you left me last night—"

"Aye, my lady, and did you mind that I did?" Poppy retorted. "I can tell a few tales of my own, about you and Lord Blackford *and* Lord Pomfrey, pitting them one against t'other with you as the prize. Her ladyship will not like that, nay, she will not."

"But she won't know unless you tell her, Poppy," May said blithely, "and you won't tell her so I won't tell her about you and John Carter."

"Aye, you're ready for court, my lady," Poppy said, half scolding, as she shook her head. "Secrets and more secrets, that's the way of court. Seat yourself, if you please, my lady, so I might dress your hair."

Obediently May perched on the bench and sat still, and Poppy began to comb out her hair.

"In truth I would not tell her ladyship your secret, Poppy," May said contritely. She'd spoken both in haste and in jest, and now thought better of her words. "I would never do that to you, not after the kindness you've shown to me."

"Oh, like as not she knows already, my lady," Poppy said with philosophical resignation. "Every servant and master has their share of secrets told and kept between them. Hah, what I could tell of her ladyship!"

May said nothing, remembering when she'd seen Lady Wilyse at sport on the first night. Less than a fortnight had passed since she'd left St. Beatrice's, yet already she, too, had her share of secrets.

"But little tales like those are not the ones that you'll find at Hampton Court Palace, my lady," Poppy said. "The ones there will be of much more importance, and consequence, too. A wrong word, a confidence misplaced, and there's the boat to Traitors' Gate and the Tower of London, and the headsman's block after that."

"But not for me, Poppy," protested May, startled and more than a little frightened. Until now all she had heard of the palace and the court was of its grandeur and its amusements. Lady Wilyse had never said a word of grim prisons like the Tower or, worse, of the executions and beheadings. "No one would see treason in so young a lady as I am."

"Nay, most likely not, my lady," Poppy agreed. "Not in you. But His Majesty does not like discord in his court, nor squabbles among his friends. He expects complete loyalty from those around him, my lady, and he tolerates nothing less. Those who cannot oblige him soon learn their folly, and to their sorrow, too."

"But I shall always be loyal to the king, and the queen as well," May said, troubled. "I would never be anything less."

"But you might cause such trouble, my lady," Poppy said, twisting and tucking May's hair into place. "Both Lord Blackford and Lord Pomfrey are among those closest to His Majesty, who honors them with his friendship and favors. There is no love lost between those two lords, nay, nor has there ever been, but before His Majesty they have been wise enough to disguise their dislike of each other. Now you have come between them, my lady, and we all did see it last night. But if you test and try them so far that His Majesty takes notice, who can say what ill may come of it?"

May twisted around to face her. "But I do not wish to harm either gentleman, Poppy. How could I?"

"Hush, hush, my lady, I did not say that you would," she said gently. "Play at love, my lady, and have your sport. You are young and beautiful, and pleasure is your due. But pray that you take care not to inflame those two gentlemen overmuch, or cause them to act so as to anger the king."

"Oh, I am so very ignorant of these matters, Poppy!" May said sadly. "How did you grow so wise?"

"For being a servant, my lady?"

"Nay, as a woman," May said. "How do I come to possess this knowledge of gentlemen?"

"It will come with time, my lady," Poppy assured her. "But pray take care to guard your heart while you do. The ways of the court move swiftly, and the gentlemen with it.

Soon enough you will learn which gentleman is no more than a bauble to you, and which will prove of lasting merit."

"I will, Poppy," May said solemnly. She had thought much of the tension between Lord Blackford and Lord Pomfrey last night. To be sure, it had been most flattering, to know they each desired her so much, but it had also been a bit bewildering, and far beyond her experience. "I will try my best, though I am not sure how to go about it."

"It's simple enough, my lady," Poppy said. "Never forget that your first loyalty is to His Majesty. Even the lowest boy who turns the spit in the palace kitchen knows that. His Majesty has promised to find you a husband. Trust him, my lady, as we all must do. If you but put His Majesty's wishes before any other, then surely you will prosper."

May nodded thoughtfully. When explained like that, her path did seem simple enough. It was also the same one that Lady Wilyse had advised, to please the king above all others. Good advice, and well worth her heeding, especially since this day she would ride into the palace courtyard in the company of both Lord Blackford and Lord Pomfrey.

Yet still she couldn't help herself from smiling. Why not, when this was sure to be the most glorious, most perfect day of her life?

"PRAY BRING YOUR head within the coach, May," Lady Wilyse ordered. "Recall that you are a lady, and deport yourself like one. It's not seemly for you to thrust yourself from the windows as if you were some sort of market-day puppet show."

With much reluctance, May drew her head back into the coach. It did not seem fair that she must be limited to what she could glimpse from the coach's windows, not when there was so much to be seen. They were close to Hampton Court now, and as the road turned before them, she'd seen the tops of the tallest towers and turrets of the palace over the treetops.

"Can you see the flags yet, Lady May?" Lord Pomfrey asked from his horse as he rode beside the coach. "They show that His Majesty is in residence at the palace."

"I can see nothing from where I must sit, Your Grace," said May crossly, glaring at Lady Wilyse. "I might as well be blindfolded, for all that I can know of flags and towers."

"I will be honored to teach you what you must know, Lady May," Jasper said, edging his horse in between Lord Pomfrey and the coach. "I'll take you to the highest tower at Hampton Court, so you might see the entire countryside spread before you like a coverlet of silken green, with the silver river across it."

"'A coverlet'?" Jostling closer, Lord Pomfrey made a barking laugh of contempt. "'A coverlet of silken green'? God's blood, Blackford, what manner of tripe is that? You, a poet?"

But Jasper did not turn to respond to his jeer, preferring to smile at May instead. "I've never been a poet, nay, Your Grace. But this lady's beauty so inspires me, I cannot help but speak poetically in her presence." He heaved an overwrought sigh to show his passion, but at the same time he winked at May, to show it was in jest, and she laughed.

"You may show me whatever you please, Lord Blackford," she replied with a teasing airiness that matched his declaration. "Propose the tower, and I shall happily oblige."

"The only one in the palace that you're meant to oblige will be His Majesty," Lady Wilyse said firmly. She leaned towards the window, brushing her hands through the air to dismiss her brother. "Away with you, Jasper. Don't put such idle notions into her head."

Lord Pomfrey chose to believe this did not mean him, urging his own horse closer, the curving plume on his hat ruffling in the breeze.

"The first towers with which you must concern yourself are those of the gatehouse, Lady May," he said, pointing ahead. "You can see them directly before us."

"Truly?" Forgetting Lady Wilyse's warnings, May eagerly thrust her head through the open window, her long hair trailing behind her.

She'd never seen any place as large or as beautiful as Hampton Court. Made of warm red brick, the palace rose before them, sprawling out on either side of a central gate with a magnificence that did not seem quite real. White stone tracery capped the bricklike lace, and dozens of crenellated towers and turrets thrust up into the sky. On some of these towers she could see the soldiers who guarded the palace, watching the road, their scarlet doublets bright spots of color in the sun. Most of the other towers, large and small, had ornate weather vanes or poles with flags that, as Lord Pomfrey had told her, proclaimed that the king and his court were there.

It was this thought that thrilled her most. In the palace before her would be not only His Majesty and his queen but the grandest nobles and other important folk of the entire country, and soon she, too, would be among them.

"Into the coach, Lady May, into the coach at once!" Lady Wilyse grasped her by the back of her gown and forcibly pulled her back to her seat. "Do you wish every guard and serving boy to ogle you? You are a lady, and you must behave as one!"

"It is as well, Lady May," Lord Pomfrey said. "I must take my place at the head of our complement. Adieu, my lady."

He touched his fingers to his hat before he left them, a small gesture that May knew was an honor from a gentleman of his rank.

"You are blessed to have captured His Grace's attention, my dear," the countess said with approval. "Heretofore he has not found any lady sufficient to his taste to take as his wife. In time you may prove to be the first, if it pleases His Majesty. That would be a mightily handsome arrow to have in your quiver, wouldn't it?"

"Such words, sister," Jasper said, once again replacing the duke beside the coach. "Here I did believe your avowed purpose was to keep any arrows, even ducal ones, from Lady May's quiver."

May laughed, delighted by the double meaning, but her ladyship only glared at her brother.

"Your place is at the front as well, Jasper," she said. "It's not seemly for you to be here, not as we enter the gate."

"I'll go," he said easily. "After one more word to Lady May. There is sure to be dancing in the great hall tonight, my lady. Will you honor me with your hand in the first dance?"

"The first by rights belongs to the king, Jasper," said Lady Wilyse. "You know that as well as I."

"I do, sister," he said. "But I likewise know that His Majesty does not dance as much at present as he once did, on account of the old jousting wound in his leg. Thus it is more likely than not that she will be languishing for a partner, and I would humbly present myself."

"Aye, my lord, I accept," May said quickly, before the countess could answer for her. "I will dance with you before all others, and I will visit the turrets, too, if you'll take me."

"You may rely upon it, my lady," he said, and if the duke had touched his cap to her, now Jasper touched his gloved fingers to his lips and tossed a kiss to her before he, too, went to the front of their little procession.

"I've warned you before against committing any folly with my brother, May," Lady Wilyse cautioned yet again. "Better to think of His Majesty, and your duty towards him."

But May still watched Jasper riding onwards as long as she could, his broad-shouldered figure so at ease upon his horse that he seemed more centaur than man.

She was weary of the countess's warnings, weary of being told whom she should love and whom she shouldn't. The awe that she'd first felt towards the countess had faded, or even tarnished, and while May still realized how much she owed Lady Wilyse for her present good fortune (which was, in short, everything), she also had begun to chafe under her near-constant advice. To be sure, the countess was not half as overbearing as the abbess had been, and far more generous. But May was ready to make her own choices, and risk her own mistakes, too.

And if that choice—or that mistake—included Jasper, then so be it.

The coach slowed to enter the gate, passing between a row of fancifully painted stone beasts—lions, unicorns, and bulls—so lifelike that May could only stare. In comparison the statues that had ornamented St. Beatrice's chapel had been clumsy, dull efforts, and once again she realized how much she had to learn and see of this new world of hers.

The armed guards bowed to the two lords in attendance as well as to Lady Wilyse as the coach entered the gatehouse arch. Slowly they circled in the enormous basecourt, the coach's ironbound wheels scraping over the cobblestones. Just as had happened at the inns where they had stopped, they were greeted with servants hurrying to the coach. But this was far different from any inn along the road. These servants all wore the king's scarlet livery, and moved with a brisk efficiency that May would soon learn was characteristic of the palace. His Majesty was not a patient man and expected his orders carried out swiftly, and to the lowest boy, everyone was in the habit of rushing to obey.

Lord Pomfrey was at once swept away with great ceremony, though he did pause to give May a cursory farewell, and a promise to see her when they gathered again later that evening.

Lord Blackford, however, whether from being of a lower rank or simply more attentive (as May preferred to believe), lingered beside May and his sister while his servants looked after his horse and belongings.

"We'll part here, Lady May," he said softly while the countess gave orders to Poppy. "Not by choice, but necessity. Sweet lady! I shall count the hours until I see you anon."

May had never heard so charming a speech, especially not delivered by a gentleman as handsome as Jasper while standing in the yard of a royal palace. She sighed with pure joy, and gazed longingly up into his pale eyes.

"Why must we part at all, my lord?" she asked. "Why will you not remain in our company?"

"Because we will lodge in different quarters of the palace," he said. "I have my own rooms, while you will be with my sister in hers."

"But I'd rather share with you!"

He chuckled. "How great a scandal that would make! You should be grateful you've a bed within the palace. It's no small honor, you know. There are plenty who come to court who are forced to lodge in other houses nearby, or even in the tents beyond the walls. To be granted permission to stay with my sister is a sign of the king's favor."

May sighed with disappointment. Clearly the easy familiarity that they'd enjoyed in the inns along their way was done.

"I do not care for the honor, my lord, nor the greatness of the scandal," she said wistfully. "I should still much rather share with you."

"As would I, sweet," he said. He'd drawn off his glove, and now brushed the backs of his fingers lightly across her cheek. She turned her face to meet his caress, relishing the scent of the leather that clung to his fingers, a scent she'd come to associate with him. It took so little now for her to become aroused, and she wanted him so badly that if he'd asked her to fuck him here, in the middle of the base-court, she would have agreed.

"How shall I find your room?" she asked, blushing at her own boldness in asking for what she so fervently desired. "You did vow to me that . . . that you would take me to your bed once we did reach the palace."

"Do you believe I've forgotten, my eager pet?" he said. "You will have no need to search for me, for I will take you there myself."

"When, my lord?" she asked breathlessly, searching his face. "Oh, my own dear lord, when?"

"Jasper, pray tend to your own affairs, and leave this lady alone," the countess said acidly, taking May by the arm. "Come, my dear, we must go to our lodgings."

She pulled May firmly after her, leaving May no choice but to follow. Longingly she looked back over her shoulder to Jasper, who raised his hand in farewell as he watched her leave, as still as a black-clad statue amid so much bustling activity.

"Marry, do not mourn so," the countess said with disgust as they climbed the stone steps to the nearest doorway. "It's not as if the rascal has perished. He's sure to be in the great hall tonight when you are presented, though if you'd even a grain of sense, you would avoid him as I have advised. Come now, don't dawdle, else I'll leave you behind."

May quickened her steps to keep pace with the countess, her skirts brushing over the wide-planked floors. She blinked, her eyes adjusting to the dim long hallways after the brightness of the afternoon sun. They passed down one long hallway, then up another flight of stone stairs, turned, and then turned again down yet another gallery. The halls were paneled in carved dark wood that gleamed from polishing, with whitewashed plaster above it and dark beams overhead. Many arched doors lined the halls, entrances to what May guessed must be lodging rooms for courtiers. The palace was so vast a place that she was sure she'd never find her way on her own, but become hopelessly lost.

The halls were crowded, too, not only with servants, but with many gentlemen of every age, all richly dressed and many with gold chains around their shoulders, as befitted their attendance at court. Attendants followed, and dogs, too, with handsome collars that reflected their masters' stations.

"Why are there so many gentlemen, my lady?" May asked Lady Wilyse. "I've not seen another lady yet, nor maidservant, either."

"It's the way of this court," the countess said. "There are next to no women waiting upon the king, as is proper. Why should His Majesty not have the best servants about him, which of course means men? As for the gentlemen you see about us now, why, quite simply more gentlemen will come to court than ladies. Gentlemen will tend to their business here and impress their loyalty upon His Majesty. They leave their wives at home to look after their estates, though; to be sure, most gentlemen are glad to be free whilst they are here."

"Do not the ladies have business here as well?"

"Perhaps." The countess smiled archly. "Some will serve the queen as members of her household. Some are here to find husbands or other betterment. And some are here for their own amusement, yes?"

May nodded, understanding, as she was meant to, that the countess herself belonged to the last group, and followed Lady Wilyse. She followed the countess, too, in keeping her eyes straight ahead and, beyond a polite nod of her head here and there, ignoring the comments of the gentlemen as they passed.

Some of these were mere greetings and pleasantries, but others were more blunt exclamations of appreciation for May's form or face, with a few low whistles besides. She liked to be admired—what woman didn't?—but not when she felt so overwhelmed. The crudity of their remarks shocked May, who'd expected better from wellborn gentlemen, but Lady Wilyse was unruffled.

"Your beauty attracts much attention, my dear," she said to May with approval as they made yet another turn. "Already gentlemen will be inquiring as to your name and fortune. By tomorrow, I vow you will have your first offer for your hand."

"But I do not wish to wed so soon, my lady," May protested. "I have told you that before. I have only left the abbey, and I've no wish to give over my freedom so soon to a husband."

"And I have told you, Lady May, that it will be His Majesty who decides who and when you shall wed, not you," the countess said, unperturbed. "Be easy, I beg you. Receiving an offer of marriage does not mean the king will accept it for you. True, His Majesty can act rashly, but I would venture he'll not do so in this matter. You are far too valuable a prize to be squandered, and he will consider well before he gives his consent. Ahh, here are my rooms at last. It would seem as if I have been away from court for a lifetime!"

Her return must have been expected, for the windows were open, and a large pitcher of fresh flowers, roses and pinks, sat on a table before the sill. The room was large and fine, with an elegant triple-arched window that opened onto the base-court, and tapestries hung on the walls. Little luxuries were scattered throughout the room: a coverlet of golden fur over the arm of a chair, a looking glass in a carved frame, a *prie-dieu* before a painted Madonna in a richly gilded triptych.

Lady Wilyse drew off her headdress as she crossed the room. Her servants appeared with her trunks and other belongings, and busily began unpacking the contents.

"The bedchamber is within, here," Lady Wilyse said, stretching her arms as she opened another door that had been left ajar. "Beyond that is the garderobe."

The word was new to May. "A garderobe, my lady?"

"A privy." Lady Wilyse smiled as she led May into the next room. "Each of the lodgings here has its own. His Majesty treats well those he likes and respects. My bed is large, as you can see. You will sleep beside me."

The bed was indeed large, filling most of the bedchamber, and could have slept four with ease. Like the rest of the lodging, the bed was handsomely appointed, with damask hangings and a coverlet to match, and plump, feather-stuffed pillows in fine linen pillow-biers. The countess was indeed being generous to offer to share such a bed with May. She'd no obligation to do so, and no one would have thought it amiss if she bid May to sleep on a pallet on the floor.

But this was Lady Wilyse, and May suspected that while she and the countess would sleep side by side together, there would also be other acts done together in that very large bed, acts that would please them both. She smiled, remembering those first evenings in the inns. It would not be the same as lying with Jasper, but then, she in turn could not offer the same delights to the countess that she had found with a pair of nameless stableboys.

Not the same, nay. But together they could still find a great deal of pleasure, both given and received. As if her imaginings were made real, Poppy began to unpack another of Lady Wilyse's trunks, pulling out gowns and smocks. As she turned to put these in the cupboard, May spied the silk-covered box that held the *deletti*, and her cheeks grew hot: not from shame, but from excitement.

The countess followed her glance, and smiled, too.

"Poppy," she said softly, not breaking her gaze from May's. "I find I am most exhausted from our journey, and in need of repose before tonight. Lady May, are you exhausted as well?"

"I am, my lady," May said quickly. "*Most* exhausted."

Lady Wilyse held out her hands to May. "Then come, my dear. There will be time enough this night for His Majesty and other men. For now, let there be only us."

Behind them, Poppy closed the door, and Lady Wilyse came to stand before her.

"Sweet May," she said softly. "What a lovely girl you are."

"Thank you, Lady—"

"Nay, don't, I beg you," the countess said. "Considering all that we have shared, it is past time that you began to call me by my Christian name whilst we are alone together.

Arabella, May. Pray call me Arabella, for what pleasure it will give me to hear my name on your lips!"

May smiled with happiness, and took the countess's hands in her own.

"Arabella," she said. "What a lovesome name it is! How you honor me, Arabella."

"It's lovesome because you speak it, May," she said, and as Arabella leaned forward to kiss her, May closed her eyes and parted her lips.

For all that May had tired of the countess's advice, she'd grown very fond of her as they'd traveled together. Now here amid the bustle and crowds of the palace, they were sure to spend less time together, and a well of affection rose up in May for Lady Wilyse.

Affection, and desire. As May returned Arabella's kiss, they each began to undress the other, soft hands easing and untying and unpinning and sliding away the layers of each other's clothes, leaving a tangle of silk and fine linen at their feet. Laughing happily, they pulled each other's hair free until May's golden curls tangled with Arabella's thick dark waves.

Together they fell onto the bed, and with the warm breezes of summer through the open window they caressed the other's skin, and their first foolery slipped away, to be replaced by a fiercer passion as their kisses became more heated.

Arabella had of course admired and explored May's body before, but May had never been able to do the same in return. Now, freely, she could. Just as she had relished her chance to suck Jasper's cock and learn his likes and dislikes, what had teased him and what had pleased him and what had brought him to fair explode so extravagantly in her mouth, she now would do for Arabella.

Lightly May ran her hand over Arabella's side as they lay together, following the narrowing curve of her waist to the swell of her hip. A woman's skin was different from a man's, as soft as silk velvet, and beneath her hand Arabella stretched like a large cat.

"Do you like that, Arabella?" May whispered, and chuckled, for the answer was abundantly clear. Arabella's nipples had already tightened into hard points, and as she rubbed her thighs languidly together, May smelled the sweet fragrance of her arousal. She reached forward to brush Arabella's dark hair back over her shoulder so she might take Arabella's breasts in her hands, so much larger than her own.

"Faith, how beautiful these are," May breathed, delighting in how the soft, weighty flesh overflowed her hand. Arabella's areolas were larger, too, and a delicious rosy violet color. Lightly May pulled and pinched her nipples until they lengthened beneath her touch, as thick around as May's little finger.

"Is it any wonder that men do gaze at you with such longing, Arabella?" she whispered, bending down to kiss her lightly as she continued to toy with her nipples. "Ah, what the gentlemen of this court would offer for a chance to be in my place with you now."

"But you see, my dear, that I'd not change places with any of them," she said, threading her fingers into May's hair to draw her face closer to her own. "Not at this moment, not if it meant being parted from you."

She rolled onto her back, taking May atop her, and behind the curtain of May's hair they began to kiss in feverish earnest, their tongues darting and dueling deep into each other's mouths. Arabella raised one leg, bending her knee to open her quim to press against May's thigh. May twisted to accommodate her, and realized that now her own cunny was opened wetly over Arabella's leg.

"Now, this is a rare convenience, is it not?" Arabella said, her voice low and throaty. "What need have we of gentlemen, my dear, when we've this clever posture to amuse us?"

She grasped May's ass, squeezing each cheek in her hands, and dragged May slowly along her thigh. May gasped, shocked by the pleasure of it: already plump with arousal, her pearl quivered beneath the pressure, weeping moistly against the other woman's skin. Unable to help herself, May began to rock back and forth on her own, the tension between her wide-stretched legs helping to build the sweetest torment.

She was gasping with each delicious stroke against her pearl, while below her Arabella, too, arched towards her own pleasure, the two of them so tightly twined that now

May could not have told whose cries belonged to whom, their juices blending together in sticky excess. Moving more quickly now, her head thrown back, May clung deliriously both to Arabella and to the very edge of control.

But as she hovered on the delicious precipice, Arabella suddenly slipped her hand beneath May and thrust her fingers deep within May's quim, pressing the pads of her fingertips hard against the sensitive, swollen walls of May's passage. With a shriek, May came and Arabella soon followed, the convulsions of their pleasure making May collapse onto the other woman in a tangle of arms and legs.

But while May lay gasping in satiated bliss, Arabella was not done. Swiftly she rolled May onto her back and clambered over her. Gently she spread May's thighs wide and, bending low, began to lick May's still-tender cunny with the wet flat of her tongue. May cried out with surprise, every nerve alive and the pleasure so perilously close to torment that it was almost beyond bearing.

Yet while Arabella held her fast, not letting her escape, May twisted around so she was beneath Arabella's own quim. The other woman's fleece was wet with her juice and ripe with her scent, and her full nether lips seemed to be begging for May's kiss.

Acting on instinct, May pulled Arabella's hips down towards her face and began to lick her with the same ferocity. Every movement that Arabella did, May repeated, until once again they both dissolved in paroxysms of delight.

Afterwards they lay together for a long while without

speaking, May with her head pillowed against Arabella's shoulder as Arabella drowsily traced tiny circles across May's belly.

"Ah, dear little May," Arabella whispered, kissing the top of her head. "There is so much passion in you, aye? So much passion!"

May only smiled, relaxed and content. It would not be the same when Jasper finally fucked her, not at all. But it had pleased her to lie with Arabella, and for now . . . for now that was enough.

CHAPTER TEN

"*B*lackford! Blackford, here!"

The king called to Jasper from the far end of the great hall, his voice booming as it always did over the evening's noise of laughter, chatter, and fiddles. He stood there, grinning expectantly, and beckoned, too, just to make sure Jasper had heard him.

At once Jasper made his way towards him, easing his way through the crowd that was gathered here almost every evening. The king liked the bustle and noise of crowds like this one around him, and he liked those crowds to be made of persons younger than himself. He was nearly forty now, not exactly fat, but fleshy, his face more florid than ruddy and his once-bright hair dulled with gray. Yet still he maintained he was as hearty and fit for life and ruling as he'd ever been, and who would dare speak otherwise?

"Your Majesty," Jasper murmured, bowing low before him. He'd already greeted the king once this evening, but such greetings could never be overdone, not with Henry. He sat in the tall-backed chair that served as his throne on these informal nights, the red cushion squeezing out beneath his sizable bulk.

Beside him the queen's chair was noticeably empty. Officially, she was said to be ill this evening, and had chosen to keep to her rooms among her ladies. But anyone with half a farthing's sense of this court knew the truth, and saw it, too, in the lithe person of Mistress Boleyn. Although she was ostensibly one of Her Majesty's attendants, she was here tonight as well, gliding among the other younger ladies and flashing her black eyes at the king.

Henry was watching her, too, his hunger for the girl so palpable that he scarce stopped short of licking his lips. Some said there was love, true love, between them as well, but Jasper doubted it. Kings did not bother with love; leastways this one didn't. His Majesty had been lusting after Mistress Boleyn for what seemed like years now, and if the tales were to be believed, she'd still not granted him any serious favors with her person.

Jasper smiled, imagining how the king would respond and act when she finally permitted him in her bed. Passion that long denied could be violent indeed, and without much effort his thoughts turned to his own Lady May Roseberry. Ahh, when he at last got between her thighs and into her nest and—

"Come beside me, you grinning jackal," the king said, striking the arm of his chair to show where he wished Jasper to stand. "You must tell me all, Blackford, every morsel. Omit nothing!"

"Of what, Your Majesty?" Jasper asked mildly, though he knew the king well enough to be able to guess.

"Of what? God's blood, man!" He struck his fist again on the arm of the chair. "The lady, Blackford, the lady! Lady Margaret Roseberry. My newest ward. The one your sister has brought to court this very day. What of her, eh? What can you tell me?"

Jasper made a small bow. "I can tell you that the Lady May's beauty is even greater and more surpassing than her wealth, Your Majesty."

"'Lady May'? 'Lady May,' not 'Margaret'?" The king regarded him slyly. "You have become that familiar with the lady on your journey?"

"Nay, Your Majesty," Jasper said, cursing himself for that small unthinking betrayal. "It was the lady's choice whilst we traveled that she be called May rather than Margaret. I misspoke to call her that."

"She can remain Lady May for all I care," the king said. "But pray tell me more of her beauty. Pomfrey here tried, and might as well have been describing a stone in the wilderness; the fellow has so little poetry to his soul. Isn't that true, Pomfrey?"

Standing on the other side of the king, the duke bowed in rueful acknowledgment.

"It is true, Your Majesty," he admitted smoothly, "though only because the lady is so beautiful that she defies any man to describe her."

"No woman is beyond description," the king said bluntly. "You try, Blackford. Tell me of the lady. Is she short or tall in stature? Is she fair? Is she plump?"

"She is very fair, Your Majesty," Jasper said, trying not to think of Pomfrey in any connection to May. But in this the king was right. The duke had no poetry to his soul, which was certainly reason enough that he did not deserve May.

"She is of a middling height," he continued, "and she has hair as bright and golden as a new-minted coin, and eyes as blue as the sky, and skin with the velvet blush of a damask rose. As to whether she is plump—she is plump where she needs be, Your Majesty, ripe and fulsome to fill a man's hands."

The king roared with delight at that, as Jasper had known he would. His Majesty was in many ways an easy master to please. Yet as cynical as Jasper might claim to be, he realized, too, that he'd not spoken entirely from calculation. May was exactly as he'd described. He hadn't exaggerated to entertain the king. She truly was that beautiful—more so, really, for how can words describe something as intangible as a woman made for desire?

But as he spoke, he'd realized something else as well. While he'd always considered himself a true courtier, willing to say and do whatever was necessary for his king, with May it was different. He didn't want the king to be enchanted by her, and unlike his sister, he didn't want to see her in the royal bed. The thought of the king's thick-fingered hands pawing her pearly flesh sickened him.

Jasper had never felt this way about a woman. It perplexed him, and worried him, too. Women were women: there was always another one waiting. There shouldn't be anything so vastly different about May Roseberry that he should consider keeping her from his king, if his king so desired her. To do otherwise would be disloyal, even traitorous, and Jasper certainly had no wish to have his short, very sweet life ended abruptly in the Tower for the sake of a woman.

"So have you had her, Blackford?" His Majesty demanded, his small eyes gleaming with salacious delight. "Confess it, man. I know your sister would have tried her best to keep the lass from you, but I know you, too. Did you pluck this sweet damask rose that comes so fresh from the convent? This Rose-berry?"

The other gentlemen in hearing all roared their approval to flatter the king's wit.

But Jasper only sighed mournfully, and shook his head. "She is a lady, Your Majesty, soon to be of your court, whilst I am a gentleman of honor. I'd not tell her secrets before she's even come among us. That would not be fair, would it?"

That, too, made the king roar with delight. "Then you *have* had her!"

Jasper only smiled and bowed, knowing that would be enough.

"Look, Your Majesty!" one of the other gentlemen suddenly exclaimed, pointing to the far end of the hall. "The lady herself, in the company of Lady Wilyse."

Every man looked to where he pointed, including the king and Jasper himself.

His sister was slowly making her way through the throng, nodding and smiling and greeting those she knew. May was with her, radiant in a gown of palest yellow that made her seem to glow like a rare flower among the darker dress of the gentlemen. She wore a curving French coif that framed her face, and when she turned, her hair fell below the black veil like a curtain of gold.

Arabella took her time, knowing how to build the king's anticipation and his desire with it. Jasper would grant her that. There were few things about inflaming men that his sister did not know. In some ways it was a shame that she'd been born so high, for she would have made an excellent bawd.

At last the two women came before the king, the crowds parting like the sea to let them present themselves. They curtsied deeply, heads bowed, and breasts presented, too. Jasper had always liked that particular feature of curtsies, how the posture of a proper reverence combined with a low-cut gown for court displayed a lady's breasts as freely as if they were offered on a platter for his consideration. At least that was how May's breasts looked to him now, round and sweet and high, and ripe for his touch, his lips.

"Your Majesty," his sister said, rising as soon as the king bid her leave to do so, while May remained low, with her head bowed over the floor. "May I present your ward, the Lady Margaret Roseberry?"

The king nodded, eagerly leaning forward on his throne for his first true look at the lady's face. Arabella whispered something, and May rose slowly, lifting her face towards the king like a flower towards the sun.

Jasper saw it at once. The rosiness of May's cheeks, the swollen pout of her full lips, the humid languor of her lovely eyes: he'd seen her like this before, and he knew how she'd come to be so, because twice before he'd brought her to a similar state himself.

She'd just spent, the wicked little creature, and spent well. Pleasure was still spangled across her face, as much as trumpeting her passion and her willingness to the world. No male with half a breath or a cockstand would mistake that look for anything other than what it was. However Arabella had managed it—and Jasper wasn't sure he wished to know—she could not have made May look more delectable.

Jasper himself was hard for May already, and his head was filled with only the thought of whisking her away from this place and taking her properly, the way she wanted and deserved. He didn't doubt that it was likely the same for every other man in the room who'd glimpsed her.

Including His Majesty the King.

God help him, how was he going to survive this eve?

LADY WILYSE HAD taught May exactly how she must make her reverence to the king. It could not be the groveling subservience that she'd been taught at the abbey, where all that had mattered was how far she could debase herself on the stone floor before the mother abbess.

Nay, this must be something else entirely. It was true that the king wished to see her demonstrate her loyalty to the Crown as his devoted subject. But, as the countess had carefully explained, His Majesty would also expect her to appeal to him more simply, as any ordinary woman might to an ordinary man.

May needed to curtsy with grace and elegance, and more than a little seduction, too. She was to sink low and spread her skirts in the same motion, as if beginning a dance.

She must bow her head to show her meekness, but keep her chest raised, so that His Majesty might survey the beguiling sight of her breasts as they threatened to spill forward from the neck of her gown. Her ladyship had taken much care with that as they'd dressed her, easing May's breasts higher herself while Poppy had pulled the lacings in her stays more and more tightly until she could scarce breathe.

But then that, too, had been part of Lady Wilyse's

preparations that afternoon once they'd finally left the countess's bed. Everything had a reason.

The shallow breathing caused by the tight stays would keep May's lips parted, as if waiting for a man to kiss her. The color yellow of the silk gown she'd been dressed in had been chosen to make her stand out among the more somber colors of the other courtiers. There were no jewels around her throat or any other ornament, the better to heighten her air of innocence. The French coif she wore with her hair drawn back tightly had been chosen to frame and display her face.

Even the curls that fell down her back beneath the coif's short black veil had a purpose. Slightly tangled and mussed, they were meant to make a man think of how her hair would look tossed wantonly across his pillow. As May's excitement and anticipation had grown, she'd studied herself in the looking glass, and wondered if the girls she'd left behind at the abbey would even recognize her now.

Lastly she'd had to tip her head back so that Poppy could put special drops into her eyes to heighten their allure. Belladonna, Lady Wilyse had called the potion, an Italian word for "beautiful lady," and another bedchamber trick, like the glass *deletti*, used by Italian beauties. May had obeyed, of course, trusting Lady Wilyse to guide her in this new world of the court, and had blinked only once to keep back the tears as the belladonna had stung her eyes. Over and over she'd reminded herself that everything was being done to prove her worth and her loyalty to His

Majesty. What was a bit of discomfort compared to such a noble purpose?

But while the drops might have made May's eyes more alluring, they had also blurred her sight. By the time she had entered the great hall at Lady Wilyse's side, most of the faces around her were so unfocused that to her dismay she doubted she'd recognize anyone to whom she'd been presented when she met them again.

So many gentlemen, so much alike! Desperately she hoped for Jasper to appear and join them, his voice the one she was sure to know from all the others in the haze of the belladonna. She blinked again, struggling to clear her eyes. Alluring or not, she would never let Poppy treat her eyes with belladonna again.

"Come with me, my dearest May," Arabella said, taking her by the hand. "The king grows impatient, and has watched you enough. It is, I think, time you finally were presented."

May walked beside the countess, measuring her steps to match. Even if her sight was not clear, she could still sense the interest their presence caused in the large room. People stepped from their path, clearing an open way for them to approach the king, and the murmur of appreciative voices was like the soft rushing of waves to her ears.

When Arabella stopped and sank deep into her reverence, May did, too, and when the king gave them leave to rise, she remained bent low, as the countess had told her to do.

"Your Majesty," the countess was saying. "May I present your ward, the Lady Margaret Roseberry?"

May's heart squeezed tight in her chest with excitement, and she hoped the king could not see how much she was trembling. Surely even the stiffened arch of her coif must be shaking as she bent before him.

Did anyone else in this enormous chamber realize how much this moment meant to her and her future? Arabella had sworn that the king was handsome, just, and honorable, and that she should not fear him. Over and over, she'd promised May that so long as she trusted the king, he would in turn do what was best for her.

But if His Majesty did not like her, or found some fault or lack within her, then he could give her in marriage to some ancient fellow who could never satisfy her, or to a hotheaded general who would beat her, or, worst of all, he could even send her back to the abbey. If she erred now, then her life would be over before it had fairly begun. Everything depended on this moment, and with an uncertain, tremulous smile, she slowly turned her face up towards the king.

She blinked again, and almost magically her eyes cleared.

The king wasn't young, and he wasn't handsome, not like Arabella had promised. He was old with a big belly. He had small eyes, and the way his jowls drooped around his mouth reminded May of melting candle wax. He was watching her closely, frowning a bit, studying her with such careful interest that she felt her cheeks warm and her knees wobble beneath her.

Oh, she must not faint. Oh, pray God and all the saints, she must not faint before the king!

"I went to St. Beatrice's to retrieve a lady, Your Majesty," Arabella was saying. "How amazed I was to discover that the lady who was waiting for me there was of impeccable lineage and fortune, but also of rare beauty as well."

The king said nothing, gnawing on the inside of his mouth as he studied May.

"Such an English beauty, Your Majesty," the countess continued, her voice purring with praise. "Such fair skin and golden hair, such red lips and melting eyes, such a rapturous face and form! Consider how ripe are her breasts, and how narrow her waist. Surely there could be no more exquisite example of virginal beauty in all your realm."

May's blush deepened. Especially after this afternoon, it was very nice of the countess to compliment her like this, to praise her in such detail to the king. She knew that Jasper had liked these same things about her, so why should not His Majesty as well?

"She is a virgin?" the king asked, his interest keen. "You are certain?"

"Without doubt, Your Majesty," Lady Wilyse assured him. "She is as fresh and as untrammeled as the first dew of morning."

As anxious as she was, May could not help but think of

how heartily she wished to be rid of that distinction, and thought, too, of how close she had come to doing so with Jasper. Her smile broadened; she could not help it, not with Jasper—and Jasper's cock—so alive in her thoughts.

She smiled, and the king smiled, too. He looked younger when he smiled, and less dour. She liked him better this way.

"We welcome you to our court, Lady Margaret," he said. "Or rather, Lady May. That is what you prefer, eh?"

"Aye, Your Majesty," May said, surprised that he had learned this of her. "Thank you, Your Majesty."

"Aye, I knew it," the king said, nodding sagely. "You are no more a Margaret than I."

Around him stood a small circle of his closest gentlemen, and when they laughed in ready appreciation of the king's wit, May looked, and saw with a jolt of recognition that Jasper was among them. He was watching her with the intensity she knew so well, his familiar, pale-eyed gaze alone more arousing to her than any other man's caress might be.

But standing there among the king's gentlemen, Jasper wasn't smiling, not now.

"Rise, Lady May," the king said. "You please us mightily."

"Thank you, Your Majesty," May said breathlessly, forcing herself to focus entirely on the king and to forget Jasper beside him. "I am most honored."

Yet even as she addressed the king, her thoughts were racing back to Jasper. Why should he be so grim, anyway? He knew she'd come here to Hampton Court to join His Majesty's court, and he knew, too, that she was a ward of the king. That had nothing to do with how she felt for Jasper, or he for her. Everyone must put the king's wishes first, and they were no different.

But she did wish Jasper would smile. Didn't he like her gown, or the way Poppy had dressed her hair around her coif? Didn't he still find her desirable?

Because she was quite sure His Majesty did. She'd come to recognize that particular look on a man's face. As old and thick as the king might be, he must still feel the lustful urges of desire, and beneath all his heavy robes and chains of gold and jewels, May was sure his royal cock must be stirring inside his codpiece, inspired by the sight of her.

Daring greatly, she tipped her head slightly to one side. She hoped enough of the belladonna remained in her eyes to make them look as winsome as Lady Wilyse had promised. Just in case, she took another deep breath, or as deep a breath as she could manage, so that her breasts would swell and rise from the neck of her gown. That was an effect she knew every gentleman did appreciate.

Clearly the king was no exception. Restlessly he shifted on his throne, his gaze never leaving May's breasts. Ahh, she thought, he'd not send her back to the abbey now.

"Tell us, Lady May," he said. "Did the holy ladies of St. Beatrice teach you to dance?"

"They did not, Your Majesty," the countess said quickly. "Lady May was woefully ignorant in certain arts when I received her. But since then I have taught her myself, so that she might please you. To be sure, Your Majesty, it has been a hasty education, but Lady May has proved a most willing pupil in every lesson I have offered to her."

The king's gaze shifted to Arabella, a knowing glint to his eyes. "Every lesson, eh?"

The countess nodded modestly, but her pale eyes returned the king's unspoken message. There was nothing modest to her expression, nor should there be, thought May wryly, recalling how she and the countess had passed this very afternoon together in her ladyship's bed. Could even His Majesty know of the many ways in which Lady Wilyse chose to amuse herself?

"*Every* lesson, Your Majesty," the countess said. "Lady May is not complete, but she grows more . . . filled with grace and skill with each day she is in my care."

"Hah, what better teacher could she have?" The king laughed, and rose slowly, holding his hand out to May. He was taller than she'd expected, of a height that matched Jasper's own. "Come, Lady May. Dance with me, and show me what you have learned from your mistress."

With every eye upon her, May took the king's hand and let him lead her to the center of the floor. At once the crowd cleared space enough for dancing, and three other couples joined them to complete the set. She'd a quick glimpse of Arabella, smiling proudly as she stood to the side to watch. She gave May a little nod of encouragement, and May nodded back, pleased to have earned the countess's approval.

The fiddlers began the song, and to May's relief, it was

a tune that she knew and had practiced with Lady Wilyse. She'd succeeded thus far, but she'd no wish now to ruin everything by misstepping with the king before so grand a company.

But as soon as the dance began, she realized she need not have worried. The king himself did not truly dance; though it was clear he knew the steps and the patterns, he moved with difficulty, and May recalled what Jasper had said about the king being troubled by an old wound from jousting. Doubtless this was the reason His Majesty seemed content to turn her around and guide her through the steps, enjoying the chance to admire her more closely from every side. There were several small hops in the dance, and since with each hop May's breasts threatened to bounce free from her gown, he seemed not to notice his own limitations but to relish the dance nonetheless.

"Well done, Lady May, well done," he exclaimed when the fiddles stopped and the dance was finished. He squeezed her hand, his thick fingers swallowing hers in his grasp. His face was gleamed with sweat, and his close-cropped hair clung moistly to his forehead, for all that he'd scarce danced himself. "Truly you do your patroness, Lady Wilyse, justice."

"I am the one who is honored, Your Majesty," May murmured, making her curtsy again. "You are a most admirable partner."

"Aye, but not so agile at dancing as once I was," he admitted grudgingly. "Yet we assure you, my dear, that there are plenty of other areas where we are as strong as ever."

Even May could not miss his meaning, and she flushed. It was painfully easy for her to imagine him huffing and puffing with a woman, and king or not, she'd no wish to experience that for herself. Oh, please, please, might he not give her an old man like himself for a husband!

"Now, that's a true maiden's blush, isn't it?" he said, unaware of her thoughts as he fondly reached out to pat her cheek. "I'll regret that your charming face must be covered at the revels tomorrow night."

"Covered, Your Majesty?" May asked, not understanding.

The king laughed. "Oh, aye, you are new arrived today, and would not know. Tomorrow night we are having a special entertainment in the French manner. We will all take disguises and masks, and only at midnight will our true selves be revealed. It was the notion of Mistress Boleyn, an entertainment to please Her Majesty."

He looked past May, searching among the others. May followed his gaze, and saw him find another lady: handsome rather than beautiful, with dark hair and unusual black eyes. So this was the famous Anne Boleyn, May thought with awe. From here she did not seem the sort of lady to hold a king in her power, but then, as May was learning, there were many ways besides beauty for a lady to enchant a gentleman.

And after a moment the king looked back to May, though whether his smile was for her or Mistress Boleyn she could not say.

"You will enjoy our entertainment, Lady May," he declared. "Lady Wilyse will help you to contrive a costume of your own, so that you might join us."

"Aye, Your Majesty, I am certain she will," May said eagerly, excited by the prospect. "Oh, I cannot wait!"

He laughed at her enthusiasm. "I'll vow there was naught like it at the nunnery, eh?" he said, laughing as the fiddlers began to tune for the next dance. "I shall sit through this next dance, Lady May, and give you over to another partner, so that we might admire you at your steps with more leisure. Blackford?"

"I am here, Your Highness." Instantly Jasper appeared at his side, his expression uncharacteristically serious.

"Aye, and a good thing, too." The king placed May's hand into Jasper's. "You are already acquainted with the lady, Blackford. Dance with her, and put her at her ease."

But before the king left, he took May's chin in his hand. "My pretty Lady May," he whispered. "I'll see more of you soon, eh, pretty poppet?"

She met his gaze as evenly as she could, and when he kissed her, she forced herself not to draw away, but to accept it. He tasted of spices and ale, and he kissed her with a bristle of his beard and a sweetness she hadn't expected. Then he patted her on her cheek, and turned back to his throne and, May suspected, to Mistress Boleyn, leaving Jasper and May facing each other.

"Lady May," he said with a chilly formality she hadn't expected. "Will you honor me with this dance, as His Majesty commands?"

Hoping for a far warmer greeting, May drew back for a moment in confusion. Jasper's handsome dark features were curiously impassive, and he seemed to be looking not at her face or even her bosom but somewhere at the top of her head, perhaps at the crown of her coif. But then it was likely the king was watching them, and Jasper was wise for being reticent before His Majesty and so many other witnesses, including his sister.

Striving to be wise herself, May smiled, but only to the same degree she would to any other gentleman, and made him her reverence to accept the dance.

"I am honored, my lord," she said. Her voice was betraying her, husky with longing, and she couldn't help but press her fingers against his.

But he did not return the gesture, nor did he meet her eye, even as the dance began.

"Are you content, Lady May?" he asked, turning her with the music.

"How could I not be, when I am with you, Jasper?" she confessed in a rush of emotion, trusting that the music would cover her words. "Only a few hours have passed since we did part, but la! It would seem a lifetime away from your company!"

"I meant, are you content with the impression you have made upon His Majesty, my lady, and upon this court?" His words were curt and clipped. "You must be pleased. You, and my sister as well."

"Jasper," she said, her bewilderment growing. "Pray, I do not understand what—"

"Stop, May," he said. "You are no fool to plead ignorance, nor am I to believe it. By now you must be party to my sister's plans for you, and to see the look on His Majesty's face when he watches you, you are already succeeding. I congratulate you, and Arabella, too."

But May only shook her head, struggling to keep her feet moving to the dance as she tried to understand.

"Jasper, I beg you," she said. "Tell me your meaning, for I can find no sense to it."

He stared down at her, barely containing his anger, and that, too, made no sense to her.

"You beg me to tell you, May," he said, "and God's blood, I will. Your presentation to the king was worthy of a Southwark stew, introducing the new slattern from the country. 'Mark her red lips, her ripe breasts, the narrowness of her waist'! As if the king needs my sister to discover your charms!"

"You make it sound so—so wrong, Jasper," May protested. "Your sister was only presenting me to His Majesty."

"Aye, but for what purpose?" he said bitterly. "If that was her purpose, then why did she halt at your breasts and waist? Why didn't she make you lie on your back before the throne and toss up your petticoats before us all, so that the entire court might judge the quality of your cunt before the king possesses it?"

At that moment the music ended and the dance with it. But instead of bowing to May as was proper, Jasper seized her hand and half dragged her away from the other dancers and astonished courtiers, away from the king and the gathering and the great hall itself, and into a corner stairway, where only a single lantern lit the murky shadows.

"Jasper, please, stop, please," May cried, stumbling after him. "Please, tell me where—"

"Nay, you tell me," he demanded. He turned her roughly and pushed her back against the wall, trapping her there with his body. "Tell me everything."

She'd never seen him like this and it almost frightened her, her breath coming in hard, quick gulps.

"You're mad, Jasper, as mad as a hare," she said, and tried to squeeze past him before he blocked her way again.

"Tell me, May," he repeated, his voice a harsh rasp. "Tell me why you would let my sister make a whore of you, there before the entire court."

She gasped, shocked he'd dare say such a thing to her.

"I am not a whore, Jasper," she said, her anger rising to match his own. "Not yours, nor any other man's."

"Nay, not a man, but a king," he said, pushing closer against her so she could feel the hard thrust of his codpiece and the cock behind it. "We all exist to please him, don't we? Why else do you believe my sister came to you at that abbey? Do you truly think she would have taken you if you'd been plain, or if you'd had a father or mother to interfere with her plan? Arabella is clever, May, very clever, and selfish as well. Surely you must know that by now."

She gasped again, stunned by the part that she knew was the truth. Not even May could deny it. Arabella *was* clever, and because she was selfish, too, she used her cleverness to get what she wanted. That was scarce a secret, one that May had deciphered soon after the countess had taken her from the abbey.

But it also meant that the countess would not have brought her here to court if she'd been plain or otherwise unlovable. She would likely have left May—heiress or not—at St. Beatrice's, as much as in a prison, and never spared another thought for her. That kindness, that charity, was not within Arabella, and May had realized that, too.

But this part about making her whore to the king . . . That couldn't possibly be true.

"I am not a whore, Jasper," she said again, more defensively this time. "I am the king's ward until he finds me a husband, and that is all."

Jasper shook his head. "What would my sister have to gain from that, May? Why do you think she and Poppy have made a plaything of you, teaching you Arabella's Italian whore's tricks so that you can please even a man as jaded as the king? Why else would she do that, except for you to replace Anne Boleyn in his attentions, and by it earn more royal favor for herself?"

"Nay," May said, horrified, even as she imagined the

king laboring atop her. Could all the sweet lessons in love-
making and pleasure that Arabella and Poppy had taught
her be meant only for obliging the king? Were all the cunning skills she'd learned only to coax the fading desire of a
man too old to return them? "It cannot be. It must not be!"

"If the king desires you, then it will," he said merci-
lessly. "You've made a fair start of it tonight, flaunting yourself at his feet, shaking your breasts for him to ogle and
letting him kiss you before the whole court. What will you
do when one night the summons comes to the royal bedchamber? You won't be able to refuse him, or you'll be
denounced as a traitor. You'll have to go to his bed, and
perform whatever he asks, even if you must suck his with-
ered cock until your tongue is sore and your cheeks ache
and—"

"Stop!" May cried, raising her hand to strike him, and
stop the hateful words. "Stop *now*!"

But before her blow could reach his face, he caught her
wrist, holding it pinned against the wall over her head.

"Then you stop," he said, his face so close to hers that
she felt his heated words on her cheek. "You stop now, and
cease playing my sister's game before it is too late. You forget the king, and think only of me."

Before she could answer, he was kissing her, furiously
grinding his mouth over hers as if he could possess her that
way alone. Fueled by her anger, she fought him, trying to
wrench herself free, but he held her fast. The more she
fought, the more her anger seemed to shamelessly turn

to passion. Arching against him, she circled first one arm around his shoulders to embrace him, and when he released the other, she used that one, too, to hold him.

He reached down and yanked a handful of her petticoats aside to touch the smooth skin of her bare thigh. He pushed his thigh between her legs to keep them parted, and she arched forward, offering him herself further. She shuddered as his hand covered her cunny, deftly separating her nether lips to glide his fingers between. Her frolic with Arabella earlier had satisfied her for the moment, but had also left her on edge, wanting more, and when he touched her pearl, she gasped, clinging to him for support.

"You're wet," he whispered hoarsely. "You're nigh dripping. Is that for the king, May, or is that for me?"

"For—for you, Jasper," she stammered, her breathing ragged. "Only for you."

This time when she reached between them to unfasten the lacings on his trunk hose, he didn't push her away, but kissed her again while his fingers played in her quim, stroking and teasing her with new purpose. He'd always claimed he wished to take her maidenhead properly, when they'd both have time to savor the experience, but she was so deliriously feverish now that she did not care if it happened here, in a shadowed stairwell in hearing of the music and voices of the court.

She felt his cock spring free, hot and alive beneath her touch. He grunted as she closed her hand around its length, tugging gently the way she knew he liked, and in return he pushed a single finger deep inside her. She whimpered at that intimate invasion, and cried out as he eased a second finger inside her, stretching her. Faith, she did not wish to spend this way again, but she could feel her muscles beginning to tense and her nerves to quiver, and knew she was perilously close.

"Hurry, Jasper," she whispered urgently, panting with excitement. As her silk skirts crumpled and fell around her, she raised one leg and hooked it around his waist, opening herself completely to him. He bent his knees slightly, searching for the perfect angle, and nudged the blunt head of his cock across her slick quim, searching for the opening.

One thrust, thought May as her heart pounded with excitement. One thrust from him, and she'd finally know the joy of being filled and complete, of—

"*Lady May.*"

So close, so close, and yet not again. For over Jasper's broad shoulders she saw the disgusted face of the Duke of Pomfrey, and beside him Arabella's, pale and disapproving.

And no matter how she would wish it, the game had not ended yet.

CHAPTER ELEVEN

*J*asper could not believe this was happening. It was never good to be caught with one's cock open to the air, let alone with a lady who was similarly exposed. But to be discovered with his cock so hard it was near to exploding, and the lady panting and ready to take him with her leg hooked around his waist, and, worse still, for that lady to be Lady May Roseberry— why, it went far beyond disbelief and ill fortune, and all the way to a devil-born curse.

Aye, that was it: devils and demons. Considering his sister was party to the interruption, that must be it.

"Leave us," he ordered sharply, doing his best to shield May as he tried to stuff his cock back into place. "God's blood, sister, leave us!"

"I will not leave you, Jasper," Arabella said indignantly. "Why should I leave you to shame this poor lady further?"

"Aye, Lady Wilyse is right," Pomfrey said, his voice as tense as the expression on his face. "Release the lady, Blackford, before any more harm is done to her. Not even you could escape a charge of rape, and I'll swear that's what I have seen here."

"Nay!" wailed May, pushing around Jasper's shoulder. Her gown was mussed and wrinkled, her hood knocked askew, and tears of frustration trickled over her cheeks, but at least she'd covered her quim from Pomfrey's sight. "There is no rape, Your Grace, and I will swear that by the Scriptures themselves!"

"You are distraught, Lady May, and know not what you say," Pomfrey said. "The word of women in these circumstances is never to be trusted."

"It should be, Your Grace," May exclaimed, dashing at her tears with the heel of her hand, "if it is the truth, and I—"

"Hush, sweet, hush," Jasper warned, resting a cautionary hand on her arm. If only he'd worn his sword, so he might treat Pomfrey as he deserved! "Do not let him bait you like this. I'll address him, and serve him as he merits for his interruption."

"You shall not, Jasper," said Arabella. "All His Grace did wish was to dance with Lady May, and when you carried her off as you did, His Grace came to me in concern, and together we came to find the lady. It's well we did, too."

"Arabella," Jasper said, his temper rising even higher. "You interfere with my affairs."

"I care not a fig for your affairs, brother," she said blithely. "But I do care for this lady's honor. I believe His Majesty will as well. Come with me, my dear. If we return to the others at once, then no one will question where you have been."

May stared at her offered hand with such disdain that Jasper longed to kiss her again then and there as a reward for her loyalty.

"I do not wish to go with you, my lady," she said, pointedly reverting to the more formal address. "My preference is to remain with Lord Blackford."

Arabella sighed. "You still do not understand, do you? You are a ward of the king, and any sin or injustice done to you is by extension a sin or injustice against His Majesty, if he decides to take offense. Thus if you insist on clinging to my fool of a brother—"

"Spoken by my fool of a sister!"

Arabella glared at him for interrupting. "If you insist on this, then you risk seeing him marched off to the Tower in chains, and the only way he shall leave it will be after he has been torn and hacked asunder into four pieces."

Swiftly May glanced up at Jasper. "Is this true?"

But before he could answer, Lord Pomfrey did instead.

"It is indeed, Lady May," he answered brusquely. "Lady Wilyse does not enlarge the truth. My cousin the king protects those closest to him with a lion's devotion. You are his ward. He will tolerate no insults to you."

"Nor will I, Your Grace," Jasper said, his voice rumbling to match his temper. "God's blood, if I'd my sword with me—"

"What a good thing you don't," Arabella said acidly. "Else we'd all be wallowing in blood, and no closer to any true satisfaction. Lady May, pray listen to reason, and come with me."

"Don't heed them, May," Jasper warned. "They serve only themselves."

But he saw at once that May was in fact heeding them. Even by the wavering candlelight, he could see the hesitation and fear cross her face, and indecision with it. He should have been gratified that she worried for his fate, that she didn't wish to put him at risk. Yet all that Jasper felt was anger at his sister and Pomfrey for interrupting them in the first place, and now putting these notions into her head.

"No harm will come to me, May," he said again. "I swear it."

But May shook her head.

"I must go," she said, placing her palm on his chest in a plaintive gesture of farewell. "Even you have told me that the king can act suddenly, and follow his temper over his head. If any harm came to you because of me, I should never forgive myself."

He seized her hand and kissed it. "We are not done," he

said softly, his gaze meeting hers over his hand. "Pray trust me, my dearest. This is not over."

Her eyes widened, just enough that he could see the desire that still burned within them. Then resolutely she shook her head once again to discourage him, and without another word, she fled with his sister.

Pomfrey waited to speak until the women had passed.

"You will not have her, Blackford," he said, his smirk unmistakable. "The lady will not be yours, but mine."

Curtly Jasper bowed, not trusting himself to speak. But duke or not, if Pomfrey had any of this sense his sister seemed to praise so highly, then he'd understand how little purpose there was in making such a claim.

Because Jasper knew the truth. The duke had already lost, and the lady—ah, the sweetest lady May—was already his.

IT WAS NOT an easy night for May in Arabella's bed.

The sisterly friendship that had grown between them during their journey had been shattered, broken by how the countess had so unceremoniously interrupted May and Jasper in the stairwell. Arabella had insisted that they return to the great hall, where May had been addressed once more by His Majesty, and danced several times with Lord Pomfrey, and many others besides.

To May's sorrow, there was no further sign of Jasper.

While Arabella considered the evening a great success, May refused to agree. She felt betrayed and used for false ends, and no matter how many times Arabella tried to explain that everything was being done for May's own protection and betterment, May refused to agree with that, too.

By the time Poppy had undressed them both for the night, the silence between May and the countess had become icy indeed. Once the candles were doused, Arabella had tried one more time to rekindle the delightful passion they'd shared earlier in the afternoon, a gentle gliding caress along May's hip, a kiss on the nape of her neck. But May had steadfastly refused such cajoling, too, and instead had huddled on the very edge of the great bed, her back resolutely towards Arabella like a wall of stone.

It was only much later, when Arabella's regular breathing proved she'd finally fallen asleep, that May had let herself weep, shedding hot, anguished tears of longing and regret that she had smothered in the sleeve of her smock. There in the dark she'd slipped her fingers between her thighs to stroke her cunny, striving to recover some of the joy that Jasper's touch had ignited within her. She tried, and failed, and wept more instead. She had come to court with such bright spirits for her future, yet already it seemed as if all her hopes were turning to bitterest ashes.

The next morning, when Arabella had gone to the garderobe, May quickly asked Poppy in a furtive whisper if there was any fresh message from Lord Blackford for her.

"Nay, my lady, not this morn," Poppy had said, her

expression full of sympathy. Of course Poppy had already heard the entire sad story of last night, because Poppy heard everything.

"But I would not worry overmuch, my lady," she said softly, so the countess would not overhear. "All the gentlemen of the court rode out with His Majesty before dawn to hunt, and most likely will not return until dusk. That's the king's way, you know, and woe to any poor sots with throbbing heads who drank too much last night."

"I suppose not," May said with a listless sigh, her thoughts with Jasper, not the unfortunate sots.

But Poppy had understood that, too, patting May's hand for encouragement.

"His lordship's not forgotten you, my lady," she said. "You'll see. I vow he'll find you among the masks this night."

Burdened with her own woes, May had forgotten the masquerade, and the reminder of it cheered her. Poppy was right. No matter how thick their disguises, she was sure to recognize Jasper among the other gentlemen from his height alone, and that thought also cheered her. Besides, hidden by their masks, perhaps she and Jasper would find a way to slip away from the company to his bedchamber and at last finish what they'd begun in the stairwell.

With such thoughts, May's spirits rose, and she was able to look forward to the day's amusement. Grudgingly she even let the iciness between her and the countess thaw, though she vowed to herself never to return to the intimacy they'd shared before.

With all the gentlemen away with the king, the queen had invited the ladies of the court to join her in her quarters to put the last touches on their costumes for the night, and to display them to one another. Arabella had produced a costume for May, just as she had produced every other article of her dress.

The costume was creamy white sarcenet, simply cut along the same lines as an ordinary gown for court. The sleeves were different, however, having been cut very long and full like wings, with the edges cut to resemble feathers. Silver spangles and glass Venetian pearls had been sewn at random over the entire gown, so that by the candle's light the costume would twinkle with every turn. There was a headdress, too, a version of a French hood with white feathers and more spangles, and a matching mask that covered her eyes.

"What role am I to play?" May asked as she held the costume to her body, imagining herself in it. "Am I a white fairy queen?"

"A queen?" Arabella asked, amused. "Nay, no queen. That would scarcely be proper for a lady so young as yourself. The costume is meant to be an angel or a saint, or perhaps a dove."

"Truly?" May frowned, now disappointed in the costume. How could she hope to seduce Jasper dressed as a saint or a dove? "I would wish to be something more interesting than a saint or a dove."

"It will be interesting enough to gentlemen," Arabella

said drily. "Nothing inflames a gentleman more than a vision of innocence and purity so that he can dream of ravishing it. Surely my brother has taught you at least that much."

But when May saw the costumes of the other ladies, her disappointment only grew. Gathered in Her Majesty's sunny private chamber, the queen's ladies-in-waiting and her other attendants were an impressive group in their own right, ladies of the highest rank and most powerful families. Many were older, as was Her Majesty, and to May they seemed aloof and daunting, and not nearly as welcoming to her as a newcomer as the gentlemen had been the night before.

"It is only because you are young and beautiful that they dislike you," Arabella had said, shrugging away their disdain. "Do not let them intimidate you, for your blood is as good as theirs and your fortune much better. They fear you will tempt their sons and steal away their husbands, and quite rightly, too."

But the queen herself smiled warmly at May, putting her at her ease and asking her questions of her studies at St. Beatrice. May was surprised by Her Majesty's appearance, having always imagined queens to be tall and haughty. But Katherine of Aragon was as short as her royal husband was tall, with a round face, red blond hair, and sad, heavy-lidded eyes, and when May recalled the rumors of how the king was seeking to divorce her on account of her failure to produce a son, May felt only pity for her. What was the good in being a queen if it meant having to be wed to so arrogant a husband?

One by one, the ladies displayed their costumes for the masquerade to the queen, and as May watched, her disappointment in her own costume only grew. These others were the bright colors of precious jewels—rubies, sapphires, emeralds—and dramatically cut with sweeping trains and capes. One that May particularly coveted was made of gleaming black satin with a pattern of scarlet flames appliquéd along the hem, all designed to transform a duchess into a fire-breathing dragon, complete with a fanciful headdress of sparks on trembling wires over her head. How could she be content as a dull little dove compared to that?

The grandest costume belonged to Her Majesty. Cut from purple and gold stripes, the gown was meant to represent a Turkish queen, with tiny golden bells sewn to the sleeves and a headdress wrapped like a turban with dangling silk tassels.

"Her Majesty will resemble nothing but a squat little pincushion in those stripes," Arabella said to May as soon as they left the queen's rooms later that afternoon. "Of course she has no choice but to dress *à la Turque*, to follow the king's choice."

"The king will be dressed as a Turk, too?" May asked, trying to picture the blustering king in such exotic garb.

Arabella nodded. "It's a secret, aye, but a secret that the whole palace knows. His Majesty believes that we will all be fooled, and so we shall pretend to be, and marvel at his disguise and invention."

"What costume will Lord Blackford wear?" May said, unable not to ask.

Arabella sighed irritably. "I do not know my brother's whim, nor do I care, nor should you, either. Especially not you, May. Your only concern must be to look for the Grand Turk, who will be the king. Find him, and attend him, though I dare to believe he shall find you first."

"A *Turk?*" May said, incredulous. "I am to be a dove, while the king will be a Turk?"

"His Majesty may play at whatever guise he chooses," Arabella said, "and it is not your place to question it. Mistress Boleyn, good day."

Mistress Boleyn stepped from a window at the end of the passage, where she had clearly been waiting for them.

"Good day to you, Lady Wilyse, Lady May." Mistress Boleyn curtsied to each of them in turn. May still found it strange to have this sort of respect paid to her, especially by a lady who was whispered to hold such power over the king.

"If it pleases you, my Lady Wilyse," Mistress Boleyn said, "I would have a word alone with Lady May."

Arabella regarded her suspiciously, then nodded. "It is well enough with me, mistress. Lady May, I shall wait for you at the end of this gallery."

Mistress Boleyn waited until Arabella was out of hearing. They were standing beside a window, and the sun through the tiny diamond-shaped panes sent a web of shadows crisscrossing Mistress Boleyn's face. She was older than May had first realized, more of an age with Arabella than herself, and though she was not a beauty, her black eyes snapped with so much wit and cleverness that she seemed prettier than her features.

"You wished a word with me, mistress?" May asked, belatedly realizing that by rank she was the one who must speak first.

"I do, my lady." The sharpness in her voice rivaled a knife's blade. "I will be quick. I saw you last eve in the great hall with His Majesty. I saw how you beguiled him, how you teased him."

"Faith, I wished to please him as my sovereign and no more!" exclaimed May. "I have no designs upon His Majesty, nor wish to."

"Forgive me, my lady, but I do not believe you." Her black eyes narrowed, her mouth hard. "I will not sit by in idleness and watch you try to claim him for yourself, my lady. I warn you that I will not be meek, nor mild in my devices, and if you cross me in this, you will find yourself with more enemies than you can know."

Without waiting for May's permission, she curtsied and withdrew, leaving May shaken and stunned.

"What did the hussy wish to say?" asked Arabella, hurrying back to her side. "La, your face is as white as new linen!"

"She warned me away from the king," May said, staring after Mistress Boleyn's parting figure. "She said that if

I didn't heed her, she would be sure I'd more enemies than I ever could know."

Arabella smiled. "That is most excellent! That means you have done exactly as you should, my dear, and that you are already succeeding with His Majesty, for her to feel so threatened."

"But I do not wish to succeed with His Majesty!" May cried plaintively, remembering what Jasper had told her last night about Arabella's plans. "I would never wish to please him like that!"

"Hush!" Arabella grabbed her by the arm and pulled her to one side. "Do you know what would become of you if you were heard to speak so? If the wrong ears heard you, you would be denounced as a traitor, and my brother and I, too, for harboring you. Is that what you wish, May? To see us all ruined?"

"Nay," whispered May. "But I also do not wish—"

"What you wish matters not," Arabella said fiercely. "You are part of this court now, and your first loyalty in all things is to His Majesty, else you suffer his displeasure and the consequences of it."

Shaking her head, May tried to pull free. "But why can I not be loyal without having to—"

"I'll not let you be a traitor, May, nor will I let you destroy me with your selfishness," Arabella said relentlessly. "You *will* please the king however he desires, and that is an end to it."

She released May's arm with a small shove for emphasis.

"Now come, it's time we dressed for the masquerade. And no more of your treasonous talk, May. Not one word."

"IT's YOUR COSTUME for the entertainment, my lord," Drumble said, standing beside Jasper to gaze down at the costume spread across the bed. "One of the king's men brought it whilst you were hunting."

"I am to wear this?" Jasper asked with disbelief. *"This?"*

"You are, my lord," Drumble said. "Those were His Majesty's wishes. You and three others were chosen special on account of your being the same height as His Majesty. That's the jest of it, you see. You're all to be as twins to the king, so none will guess which Turk is His Majesty, and which is not."

"But this, Drumble?" Jasper said. *"This?"*

"I know, my lord, I know," Drumble said, striving to commiserate. "But if disguising the king is to be the conceit, then it would have to be a robe such as this, on account of His Majesty being so, ah, stout. And perhaps those Turks do know something, my lord. Mind you, they're the fellows that keep the harems full of heathen women for sport, aren't they?"

But Jasper could only stare at the ludicrous costume with growing despair. The day had already been wretched. The king had called for a day of hunting, which had meant rising before daybreak to plunge through the forest in the dark. Ordinarily there were few things Jasper enjoyed more than hunting, and he was good at it, too, which was part of his success at court.

But today when His Majesty had insisted that Jasper ride at his side in his usual place of honor, the reason had not been Jasper's skill at riding or shooting, but that the king wanted to speak of the endless charms of Lady May. The king was besotted, that was clear; Arabella must be overjoyed.

It had been bad enough that Jasper had been forced to listen to the king's mooncalf babblings about a woman he himself desired, but His Majesty had also expected Jasper to contribute as well, fair begging for any tantalizing secrets that he might know of the lady. Of course the greatest secret—that he had very nearly taken the lady's much-vaunted maidenhead last night not a hundred yards from where the king had sat—was one that Jasper had wisely kept to himself, though the effort had given him the righteous headache that plagued him now.

And then this . . . this *costume*. Jasper stared down at it, aghast. He might as well be asked to wear a campaign tent, there was so much fabric put to use in a single garment. The robe would cover him from his neck to his feet in purple stripes, with full sleeves gathered into ruffled cuffs. Matching purple gloves lay beside the robe, with oversized tassels hanging from the gauntlets.

As if that were not gaudy enough, there was a purple turban centered with a winking false jewel and the feather of a peacock, and a silver mask that would cover his entire face from view. He'd never worn such rigmarole in his entire life, and after tonight, he'd pray he never would again.

And how in God's holy name was he supposed to win May tonight if he was hidden away in a costume that, at best, could only inspire her laughter?

Drumble sighed. "Forgive me for speaking plain, my lord, but God's fish, that be a foolish rig for a gentleman."

But Jasper was thinking, not listening. If the point of this masquerade was to disguise and confuse the king's identity for the royal amusement, then why couldn't Jasper take advantage of that same confusion for his own purpose? After last night, Arabella would be guarding May more closely than ever from him, or any other man she felt might dare poach on the royal preserve. But if she believed it was the king himself come to woo her little protégé, then she'd as good as turn back the coverlet for him; she'd be that eager. He could sweep May away from beneath his sister's nose, and with her blessings, too, a sweet irony that would make the ruse all the more delicious.

There would, however, be one trick to it, and a large, disagreeable (if it went awry) trick at that. Jasper must find May and escape with her before the true king did, or the entire ruse would be worthless. But for May's sake, and what he'd planned for them both, he would succeed.

"OF COURSE THE Lady Dove will dance with you, my lord philosopher." Arabella smiled at Lord Pomfrey beneath her mask, acknowledging his dreary costume. "She will be most honored."

As the duke bowed, she gave May a furtive little push of encouragement. The king had still not appeared, but had sent his permission that the music and the dancing might begin before he arrived. While rumors swept through the crowd as to exactly why His Majesty was detained—an urgent meeting with the French ambassador, a quarrel with the queen, an indisposition caused by the roast partridge at supper—the fiddlers had dutifully tuned their strings again in preparation, and chosen the king's favorite song to begin the dancing, whether he was here in the great hall to enjoy it or not.

As soon as the tune was announced, May had looked again around the hall for Jasper. She'd already promised him this first dance yesterday, when they'd parted in the courtyard, only to have it claimed by His Majesty instead. She'd hoped to make that right with Jasper tonight, but she could not dance with him unless he joined the company. Now she was left with no choice but to dance with Lord Pomfrey, and reluctantly she took his offered hand.

She could not forget how he'd been with Arabella last night, when the two of them had hunted Jasper and May to the stairwell, and interrupted them at a most intimate moment. As shadowy as the stairwell had been, May was uneasily certain that the duke must have stolen an excellent view of her open cunny and her other charms besides, and that certainty embarrassed her now.

"Your costume becomes you, my lady," he said. "What role do you take? An angel?"

"A dove, Your Grace," May said, holding her arms out at her sides so the long, fluttering sleeves showed as wings. "Though do not ask me to fly."

Neither doves nor angels could compare to dragons, but May had finally decided that a dove, however meek, was preferable to an angel as a paragon of pristine goodness. At least doves must mate with other doves, or there'd be no dove eggs, a thought she'd much considered as Poppy had laced and pinned her into the costume. To be sure, the notion of mating doves was not nearly as arousing as watching the black stallion mount the mare, but it was better than celestial angels.

And the costume, too, had proved much more beguiling than she'd originally thought. If Arabella insisted that she be dressed in virginal white, then she was glad the costume itself was the least innocent gown imaginable. The white sarcenet flattered her skin, making her seem more roses and cream than pale, and the cut of the bodice was so close that Poppy had had to lace her corset even more tightly than usual. Her waist looked enticingly small and her breasts more ripe, and the gathered pleats to the skirt gave her walk a seductive sway, all effects that she was sure would please and fascinate Jasper. Besides, she seemed to be the only courtier at the masquerade dressed in white, and she sparkled among all the other rich and gaudy colors simply by being so different.

But it was one thing to be admired by His Majesty and the rest of the company, and to imagine Jasper's response to such a provocative gown, and, as she soon discovered, another entirely to see that same effect on a gentleman like Lord Pomfrey. As his lordship led her to join the other dancers, he was staring at her breasts with such ravening desire that she felt as if she were standing naked before him and that at any moment he might fall upon her. He was so intent that he seemed to have forgotten that it was his turn to speak, leaving it to May to continue their conversation, such as it was.

"A dove, aye, Your Grace," she said with a nervous small laugh. She wondered if he'd been drinking already; Arabella had warned her that a man's entire nature could change for the worse from wine or strong waters. "A common bird, of little curiosity, I vow. Everyone has seen a dove."

"But not such a dove as you, Lady May," he said, using the closeness of the crowd around them to press closer to her, too, his hand grazing along her back and lower to touch her bottom through the skirts. It was all done as if by accident, but May believed he touched her instead on purpose, and she slipped away as quickly as she could.

"What is the nature of your own costume, Your Grace?" she asked quickly, desperate for any way to deflect his attention away from her person. It was in truth a drab, dull costume of black stuff with long robes that swept the floor, with no ornament at all. Nor had he bothered with a mask, either, doubtless assuming that, as a duke, he was too grand for such silliness.

"It represents a philosopher," he said with no interest at all. "A learned scholar who reflects upon the great questions of life."

"Then tell me, O learned philosopher," she said, with relief as the dance began. "Pray tell me the greatest question of life."

"I needs not be a philosopher to answer that," he said, smiling as he bowed to mark the dance's beginning. "The greatest question is why you would offer that sweet quim of yours to a knave like Blackford."

She gasped at his audacity, thankful the next step of the dance took her apart from the duke. But when they were rejoined, he continued.

"When I consider what I witnessed, with Blackford's cock so close that your lips kissed it . . . Praise God Lady Wilyse and I came when we did, before with a single thrust the rape would have been complete."

She gasped again, so shocked she'd no words for reply. Jasper had threatened the duke for interrupting them; May couldn't imagine what he'd say now if he could hear what the duke was saying to her.

In all of Arabella's lessons, there'd never been particular advice for a situation like this. May had already made a scandalous scene with Jasper last night when he'd hauled her away, and Arabella had made it painfully clear that she could not risk another such scene this night, not unless she

wished to forget entirely a lasting place here at court. She
had no choice but to remain with the duke until this dance
was done, and no choice, either, but to listen to his scur-
rilous remarks.

The duke turned her neatly around before he spoke
again, stealing his hand along the side of her breast.

"I haven't forgotten that first night in the garden, Lady
May," he said, his face taut and his words coming fast. "I
remember how you tasted, how you felt in my arms, how
your breast filled my hand so well. Most of all I recall the
scent of your cunt, enough to make me imagine how much
I'd like to fuck it myself."

She flushed at the memory and tried to pull away from
him, but he pulled her back so she couldn't help but listen.

"You've made me mad with wanting you, Lady May,"
he said, "mad with wanting to possess you as I wish, to
force you down on your knees and bend you over and take
you that way, like the bitch in heat that you are. Then,
when you are ready, I will thrust my member again and
again into your obedient cunt until you scream my name."

"Nay, Your Grace," she said, unable to restrain herself
any longer. "It will never be so, not between us."

"And I say it will, Lady May." His smile was cold and
ruthless. "You will scream for me, Lady May, and for no
other."

CHAPTER TWELVE

On the other side of the tapestries that hung on the wall of the great hall, Jasper waited as he'd been ordered, dressed in his ridiculous costume. He stood with three others, all clad exactly alike—Lord Wofford, and two yeomen of the guard—all chosen for this peculiar role on account of being the same height as the king. To keep the mystery as long as possible, they'd been instructed not to speak but only to gesture in a royal manner, and for this purpose they'd already been granted permission to do whatever was necessary to maintain their roles, even if it meant not bowing before the true king.

They would enter the great hall together as a group to add to the confusion, and not through the main doorway, but by way of one of the servants' entrances tucked behind the tapestries that hung along the walls. On the other side of the tapestries, most of the court had already assembled in the great hall, and excitement for the unusual entertainment bubbled audibly through the crowd.

At last the king joined them, lifting his silver mask long enough to show that he was in fact the true king.

"I wish to keep the jest in place the entire night, and woe to the man who breaks it," he said, his expression gleeful beneath the tipped mask as he looked from one man to the next. "Courage, my friends, and may luck go with you. Or should I say my fine Turks? Hah, hah, away!"

He flipped the silver mask back over his face and sent one of the yeomen to go first into the great hall. His appearance was met by appropriate cheers, for word had spread throughout the palace that the king would be costumed as a Turkish grandee. But then another tall, imposing Turk appeared from between the tapestries, and another, and two more after that, until five Turks stood before the delighted company. Keeping to their silence for secrecy as had been arranged, the five separated, and began to wander through the crowd.

Jasper moved slowly, trying to mimic the king's slow, lumbering pace rather than his own confident stride, and he made the same royal gesture of acknowledgment with his gloved hand. It amused him to see how courtiers of every rank bowed and scraped before him, guessing that he might be the king, and he was grateful for the mask that hid his grin.

But as diverting as all this was, his main goal was to find

Lady May. He'd limited sight through the eyeholes of the mask, and as he peered about for May, he glimpsed a graceful feminine figure from the corner of his eye, and turned eagerly towards it.

"Your Majesty," said Mistress Boleyn, making him a curtsy that was so surpassing elegant that it was more a dance than a reverence. Even to his practiced eye, her costume was astonishing. In scarlet silk that was at once the king's own color and a hue that flattered her pale skin and dark eyes, her gown was cut so low over her breasts that he marveled her nipples did not pop clear. She'd enhanced the effect even more by wearing a white ruffle around her throat and a red velvet and gold mask over her eyes, so that only the square of skin above her breasts was left shockingly, temptingly bare.

She licked her lips and raised her chin towards him, showing the tip of her tongue suggestively between her teeth. Idly she touched the white ruffle around her throat as if to adjust it, then trailed her fingers downwards until she reached the mounded flesh of her breasts. Languidly she traced the shape of the curves, her fingertips passing back and forth in as brazen an invitation as Jasper had ever seen, or enjoyed. What a shame the true king was not in his place to savor the performance as well!

"Your Majesty," she breathed again, resting her hand lightly on his padded sleeve. "Do not leave me alone too long, I beg you. You know how lonely I can be without you."

She smiled, and licked her lips again. He touched his gloved fingers to the front of his mask as if to blow her a kiss, and she laughed, convinced she'd just discovered the true king.

Slowly he moved onwards, searching for May. She had to be here somewhere. He'd already spied Arabella, dressed in dark gray and silver, engaged in one of her usual flirtatious conversations with a younger gentleman he did not know. He turned towards the dancing, and there she was.

He'd believed he knew her well enough to be accustomed to her beauty. He was wrong. Dressed all in shimmering white, she was almost ethereal, yet also so seductive that it stole his breath to look at her.

The purity of her gown made her skin in contrast glow with tempting, rosy vitality, and the simple cut made her waist seem impossibly small and her breasts above impossibly lush. He alone among the gentlemen in this hall knew the luscious reality that lay beneath that white gown, and he, too, knew the feverish desire so much at odds with May's angelic face.

At once he recalled the night before, how her cunny had wept sweet tears of desire for him, and in answer he felt heat flood his cock and his balls tighten in expectation. He was done with teasing and promises and wrongful interruptions. Tonight he'd take her to his bed, and not let her leave it until dawn.

She turned with the fiddles, her skirts swinging gracefully around her. Only then did Jasper realize that her partner was Lord Pomfrey, and his urgency to take her from the great hall increased. The duke was wearing some sort of don's foolishness, black robes more fitting for a monastery than a masquerade, but what irritated Jasper most was the rascal's possessiveness. Lord Pomfrey kept his arm firmly around May's waist, and took every chance the dance provided to touch her hand, her arm, her hip, even the sides of her breasts. To May's credit, she was doing what she could to avoid Pomfrey, and the expression on her face was fixed and miserable. Being born heir to an English dukedom might entitle Pomfrey to many earthly riches and rewards, but Lady May's person was not one of them.

Purposefully he moved towards her, cutting a regal swath through the crowd. When he reached May, the fiddlers stopped their playing and the other dancers shuffled hurriedly away. All of them remembered the interest that the king had shown in the beautiful newcomer, and all assumed His Majesty was merely acting on that same interest now.

Surely the expression on Lord Pomfrey's face was worth every purple scrap of this ludicrous costume. His customary smugness had vanished, replaced by a fawning smile as he bowed low. Best of all in Jasper's eyes, he released his hold on May.

"Your—Your Majesty," Pomfrey stammered. "This lady did me the honor of, ah, dancing with me whilst we awaited your arrival."

Imperiously Jasper raised his hand, exactly as the king

would do. The duke shrank back, more fearful of his royal cousin than he'd wish anyone to know, while Jasper tried not to laugh inside his mask.

But there was nothing humorous about his effect on poor Lady May. She had curtsied low before Jasper, and rose slowly as he'd motioned towards her. Now she stood with her hands clasped tightly at her waist, the color gone from her cheeks, and the lips of her lovely mouth pinched tight with anxiety.

Jasper held his hand out for her to join him, and with a brave little shrug of her shoulders she took it to follow. She held her head high and tried to smile up at him, but still he saw the glisten of tears in her eyes, and it took all his willpower not to throw aside the mask to reassure her.

Instead he kept to the king's ruse, and nodded for the musicians to resume their play. As they did, scores of excited conversations began once again around them as well, and as they walked from the hall—majestically, Jasper hoped—he felt the gaze of every eye upon them.

Outside the hall in the passage, every red-clad guard snapped to attention, their long staffs and pikes clicking smartly on the brick floor, and the few costumed latecomers to the masquerade bowed and curtsied as they passed. Yet Jasper kept to his disguise, though his fingers tightened around May's little hand as they walked.

"Your—Your Majesty honors me," she said softly, though he was sure he heard the quaver of more tears in her voice. "If it pleases you, might I ask where we are going?"

Still Jasper said nothing, though it grieved him to make her suffer. The risk of being overheard in the palace's halls and galleries was too great.

Beside him she nodded. "Forgive me, Your Majesty," she said, the misery in her voice palpable. "I should not have presumed to ask such a question of you."

When at last they reached his lodgings, he stopped at his door. She looked about, clearly wondering why they were here, and not in the grander portion of the palace that held the king's chambers.

"Is—is this where you would bring me, Your Majesty, to some private place of your own?" she asked, making him wonder what sort of nonsense his sister must have told her of the king's habits for assignations. "Have we come here so—so no one will know us?"

Silent still, he opened the door for her, and she stepped inside. Drumble had prepared the room exactly as Jasper wished, with wine waiting on the table and a fire already in the grate; though it was warm out of doors, there was always a chill inside the palace, and tonight of all nights he wished her to be warm.

She had gone to stand at the doorway to the bedchamber, turned away from him frozen there before his waiting bed. Her back was stiff with a mixture of dread and determination, the long sleeves of her gown hanging like the folded white wings of a dove.

"I will do my best to please you, Your Majesty," she said in a muffled voice that touched him to no end. "As Lady

Wilyse explained, she has taught me much, and they say I—I am of a passionate nature and—and I vow I will please you, Your Majesty. I *will*."

And at last he pulled off the cruel disguise, the mask and the turban and the gloves that had hidden his true self, and began to tear away the rest of his costume as he crossed the room to join her.

But May . . . May knew none of this.

She stood with her back to the bedchamber door, desperately trying to do so many things at once: to be brave and strong so she would not weep and spoil everything, and yet at the same time to be winsome and comely and charming so that the king would desire her, as he was supposed to.

To be chosen like this was a rare honor for any woman, and more rare still considering she'd only just arrived at court. For His Majesty to select her from all the ladies gathered in the great hall, for him to bring her here, to this secret small chamber that he must reserve for those times when he wished to be alone and without a sea of attendants around him—oh, aye, she was honored, honored and blessed among all Englishwomen, highborn or low.

And to think she'd believed Lord Pomfrey was her greatest trouble this night!

Now she must forget everything else, of how frightened she was to be alone in a chamber with a bed and a man who was a stranger to her. She must not worry about what she would do if he could not muster a cockstand sturdy enough to take her maidenhead. She must not think of how he was old enough to be her father, or that his eyes were small and greedy in his face, or that he wheezed when he'd tried to dance, and Merciful Mother in Heaven, what would she have to *do* to please such a man?

Because she *would* please him. No matter what happened, she must please him. He was her king, her master, her monarch—and besides, if he ordered it so, she must obey.

She clasped her hands tightly before her to keep them from shaking before him. No man would wish for a woman who wept in his bed, or trembled like the last wizened leaf that clings to the branch. Arabella had told her, and Arabella would know. She must relax, and be coaxing, and forget her own fears so that she might put him at his ease.

Most of all, hardest of all, she must forget Jasper.

Behind her she could hear the king shoot the bolt to the door, the scrape of iron on the lock. They were alone now, completely alone, and she could hear him begin to undress, the slide of rich fabrics across skin and then to the floor.

Still she did not turn, and she did not look. She wasn't brave enough for that.

"I will please you, Your Majesty," she said again, as much to convince herself as him. "You will see. I will please you, and—"

"Hush, hush," the king said, a gruff whisper so close

behind her that she caught her breath and made a small leap forward.

"*Shhhhhh*," he said again, a gentle soothing sound meant to comfort her. She closed her eyes, warring with herself to be calm, and felt his hand rest on her shoulder. She remembered those hands, heavy and thick with golden rings and jewels on fingers that were like sausages. With a little gulp she opened her eyes and turned her head to look down at the hand resting on her shoulder.

But it wasn't the hand of the king. This hand had fingers that were strong and lean, and wore but one ring of heavy gold with a black stone, incised with a rampant lion.

She gasped and spun around, her hands still clutched together as she staggered backwards from the shock. She did not know whether to trust the proof of her eyes, or if her fears were making her see things that were not there.

"Ah, May," Jasper said. "Is that the best greeting you can offer me?"

But still she stood where she was, too shocked to move. He'd shed the gaudy turban and the mask, and his dark hair clung damply to his forehead from where it had been pressed beneath. Gone, too, were the gauntlet gloves that had concealed him so thoroughly, and the heavy striped robe hung open from his shoulders, over his own doublet and shirt and black trunk hose.

"I saw the king," she said slowly. "He told Lord Pomfrey to step aside, and then he took my hand and led me here."

"It wasn't the king, sweet," Jasper said, shoving free

of the last of the costume. "You believed what you saw. There were five of us dressed alike tonight, on His Majesty's whim."

He smiled crookedly, disarming her as he stepped closer. Even though he'd been hidden away inside the costume, how had she not guessed it was him?

"He will not be angered that you stole me away like this?" she asked anxiously. "To bring me here to these rooms—"

"My rooms," he said. "Exactly as I promised. It is a risk I'm willing to take for you, my lady."

"For me," she repeated in wonder. "For me?"

"I beg you, May, tell me I do not disappoint you," he said, slipping his fingers into her hair to turn her face to his. "Tell me, May, even if it is not true. Say that you would rather have me here with you than His Majesty."

"I would, my lord," she whispered, so overwhelmed that it was the best she could manage. She put her hands on his beard-roughened cheeks and kissed him, feeling the warmth of it flood through her body. She had been so frightened and now she wasn't, and the relief of being with Jasper at last was almost more than she could bear.

Yet she understood what he had risked to bring her here, and what they both might face because of it. Now she was determined to make this one night worth that risk, a night that neither of them would forget.

She took a step back from him, her gaze not leaving his eyes, and began to unfasten her gown, pulling the pins that closed her bodice and then unlacing it from beneath. It was not easy without Poppy to help her, but somehow the time that it took her only spun out the rare pleasure of watching him watch her. Bodice, kirtle, sleeves, petticoat: she shed each piece of her shimmering dress and let it fall to the floor at her feet, until it seemed as if she were poised on a cloud of silvery white silk. Finally she stood in only her smock with her boned corset.

"Here," he said, gently turning her about. "I'll play your lady's maid."

With ease he undid the knot that held the lacings of her corset, and slowly drew the cording through each eyelet in turn, letting her feel her body relax each fraction of freedom. With the last eyelet, he pushed the corset forward and off her shoulders, freeing her from its whalebone confines. She gave a small sigh of relief, and in one swift move pulled her smock over her head, leaving herself naked except for her white thread stockings and heeled slippers.

"Faith, but you are beautiful," he breathed, reaching from behind to fill his hands with her breasts.

"For you, Jasper," she whispered. "Only for you."

CHAPTER THIRTEEN

May sighed as Jasper pulled her back against his chest, relishing how he rubbed his thumbs across her nipples to make them stand. She shook her hair to one side and lifted her hands behind her head to reach his face, arching back against him. To be so freely naked while he was still clothed aroused her more, and he kissed and nipped at the side of her throat.

His hands roamed lower, across her belly and lower still, stroking her thighs as he pulled her closer. She caught her breath in anticipation, and when he covered her fleeced mound with his hand, threading his fingers through her curls, she sighed with a shudder.

He pushed his knee between her legs, separating them, and she widened her stance to give him more. He slipped his hand lower and with a single finger opened her cunny's lips to find her pearl. He pressed it gently, the tiniest of caresses, and held his finger there without moving, letting her feel that much, letting her know what more was to come.

For a long moment she let herself feel, just feel. Then she slipped free and turned to undress him, desire making her clumsy. She'd no experience with a gentleman's clothes, either, the points and laces and rows of tiny, foolish buttons, yet he did not seem to mind, nor did he help. Instead he reached forward to fondle her breasts, distracting her further as she tried to make sense of his clothing, both of them laughing at her ineptitude.

She shoved off his doublet, pulled off his shirt, kissing his now-bare throat in the place that he loved, just below the black line of his beard. From there she could not help kissing the line of his collarbone, his chest below, and lower, lower, across his flat belly to the teasing line of black hair that rose from the top of his trunk hose. Finally he pushed her aside to pull off his hose, finishing what she'd begun, and she laughed again to watch him hop on one foot as he wrestled with it, every bit as clumsy with lust as she had been.

But her laughter faded when at last he stood naked before her.

"You promised this to me, too," she said softly, drinking in the sight of him by the fire's light.

He grinned, justly proud of himself. "I vow I am a man of my word, sweet."

"Aye, you are that," she said, "and far more besides."

He'd called her beautiful, but what was she beside his own manly beauty? She'd never seen anything as divine, his undeniable strength and perfectly formed masculinity. He was hard and muscular where her own body was soft and yielding, his shoulders broad and his arms and legs thick from riding and hunting.

Yet what fascinated her most was his cock, rising tall from the nest of black hair, the head rosy and blunt and already glistening with wanting her. The simple sight of him like this, gilded by the firelight, made her own body ache in response, her breasts heavy and sensitive and her cunny wet and ready for him.

For *him*.

He reached for her and she went to him eagerly, turning her mouth up to meet his. She could feel the hard length of his cock pressed between them, eager to find its true place within her, and she pressed and wriggled against it, remembering other times: when she'd sucked him by the river, and he'd tormented her with his fingers in the stable, and most of all last night, when together they'd come close enough for her to feel that same cock's head pressing close against her quim.

But as delicious as all that had been, she was done with the teasing, done with the play, done with her virginal ignorance. She turned towards the bed, meaning to lead him there, but instead he swept her into his arms and carried her, laughing with delighted surprise, the last few steps before he tossed her onto the bed. She sank into the feather bed, her hair fanning out behind her across the sheets, and then he was with her, too, kneeling between her parted legs.

Gently he parted her quim's lips, and with his cock in his hand rubbed the head of his cock along her opening, stroking her up and down without entering her. He swept the head, wet with her juices as well as the first of his own, over her eager pearl, just enough to make her gasp and tighten her legs around him. She'd never felt anything so glorious, and instinctively she raised her hips forward, seeking more.

With a groan, he found her opening and pressed into her. She was so wet that as he eased his way as much as he could, she still felt the pressure of his thickness, opening her and filling her in a way she could never have imagined. She cried out, more from surprise than pain, and that was enough to make him drive into her, one strong shove. Then he was buried deep in her, thick and hard, with her legs spread wide and his balls against her bottom.

Breathing hard, he propped himself on his elbows above her and kissed her, possessing her at once with his tongue and his cock. He flexed his hips, drawing out only to plunge back in with increasing force, the sweet friction of his cock dragging across every sensitized nerve in her cunny.

She gasped from the raw, dizzying pleasure of it. Nothing had prepared her for this: not Poppy, nor Arabella, nor even the *deletti*. This was fucking, and she could not get enough.

Nothing felt as good as Jasper's cock within her, and she curled her legs around his waist to take him deeper. She cried out each time he drove into her, arching her back to meet him, and when at last she felt her body tense and tighten until she felt she could not bear another thrust, he gave her one, and she felt herself explode with the violent joy of it and more pleasure than she could have dreamed. The ripples hadn't begun to stop when she felt him give one last, powerful shove, and he filled her with his seed, hot and wet and slipping from him.

As soon as he could, he propped himself on his elbows to look down at her, kissing her lightly as they both gasped for breath.

"Did I hurt you, May?" he asked, so contritely that she grinned back at him.

"Nay, not at all," she whispered. "Not one bit."

"You were a maid," he said. "You were so tight, you could not be otherwise."

As if to prove it, she felt his cock make a kind of lurching twitch within her that was so unexpected—and so wonderful—that she gasped aloud, her fingers tightening into his shoulders.

"Yet I've made you weep," he said, brushing aside the tears from her cheeks that she hadn't realized she'd shed.

"With joy, not pain." She smiled up at him. "But I've made you weep, too, it would seem."

She shifted her hips beneath him by way of taunting demonstration.

"I did not cry," he said, chuckling. "I spent, sweet, and there is a world of difference."

He pushed into her again, letting her feel how he remained hard inside her.

"Oh, Jasper." She stared up at him in wonder. "Can you do it again?"

"Aye," he said, "and a good thing that is, too, since I meant to keep you here through the night."

Once again he kept his word, and kept her occupied as well. To May's astonished delight, he seemed to be ready to try most everything with her, with only a brief time for recovery. She told him of the books that his sister had shown her, books with pictures of people fucking in every imaginable position. Jasper had laughed, and explained that these were famous books by a gentleman named Aretino, from Italy, where people felt more free to please themselves in different ways.

Yet he had not laughed when May had described the picture that had intrigued her the most, of a woman with her legs raised so high that they had rested on her lover's shoulders, the better to show his thick cock half buried in her quim. Instead, he'd been intrigued as well, and determined to please her. He'd taken the looking glass from the wall and propped it in a chair beside their bed where May could see herself. Then with her direction, they'd replicated the same posture she'd remembered from the book, with her slender ankles over his shoulders as he'd entered her.

May did not know whether it was the position itself

that was so exciting—for to have her legs raised so high had made her already narrow cunt even tighter around his cock—or whether it was being able to watch themselves in the glass, Jasper's cock hard and glistening with her juices as he pumped it in and out of her golden nest, the plump lips of her cunny clinging to his length as if loath to let him leave.

Yet as delicious and inventive and amorous as all this had been, at some point they had fallen asleep, twined and tangled in each other's arms. Jasper had promised to keep May in his bed until sunrise, but they had been so active during the night that they slept through the cock's crow and later—so late, in fact, that it wasn't the rooster that woke them but Drumble, thumping desperately on the door to be let in.

Swearing and stumbling with drowsiness, Jasper had left May still sleeping to go open the door.

"Why in the devil's name are you here?" Jasper demanded in a hoarse whisper as the servant came rushing into the room. "Why can't you ever leave me in peace?"

Drumble bowed quickly, and stole a quick glance from his naked master through the bedchamber door and at May still sleeping with blissful abandon.

"Forgive me, my lord," he said, "but it's not in the devil's name that I come, but in His Majesty's. You're summoned to the king at once, my lord, or leastwise as soon as you cover yourself."

"I'll cover you, you impudent rascal," Jasper said, as

Drumble swiftly began to pull fresh clothes from the chest. "What do you mean that the king wishes to see me?"

"I mean exactly that, my lord," Drumble said. "I was sitting outside your door when one of his servants brought the message. He wanted to deliver it to you himself, but I said you was occupied, and he gave it to me instead."

Jasper groaned, and swore again. It did not take a wise man to guess why the king wished to see him so soon after rising. His role as a Turk who wandered from the masquerade, how he'd carried off the prize lady of the night before His Majesty could so much as speak to her, and how that same lady now lay sleeping in his bed—oh, there were so many possibilities for their meeting.

"I do not recommend taking the time to shave, my lord," Drumble said, holding out a clean shirt. "His Majesty is seldom patient when he rises."

"His Majesty is never patient, regardless of the hour." Jasper plunged headfirst into the shirt, holding out each arm in turn so Drumble might fasten the cuffs. "I'd better go to him before he sends the guards for me next."

He washed and finished dressing as quickly as he could, deciding what would be safest for May. He could leave her here to sleep in peace as long as she wished—which, after last night, would be the kindest course—and join her again when he'd returned from speaking with the king. But there was always the chance that he might not return at all, and in that case, he'd not want her to waken here, alone and unprotected. Nay, better to send her to the one person he trusted to be able to guard her nearly as well as he would himself.

He went to her now, hating to wake her. She lay on her back with her hair tangled around her and one lovely breast uncovered, her cheeks flushed with sleep and the most contented smile imaginable on her face. He couldn't help but smile fondly in return, his heart tight in his chest.

It was curious, the feeling she inspired in him. With every other woman in his past, his usual response after a night of passion would be to hurry away as soon as he could, before the woman developed any sort of embarrassing attachments or misplaced conclusions.

But with May, he felt differently. Just looking at her now as she slept, he realized that. Somehow, without him realizing how, she had become impossibly dear to him. He didn't want to leave her, even with the best excuse he'd ever had in the king. He wanted to stay, and spend this day with her and the next besides, and many more after that. But no matter his feelings, he'd no choice in this, and with a sigh of regret, he sat beside her on the bed and kissed her lightly, brushing his lips over hers just enough to wake her.

She stretched drowsily, letting the sheet slip from her other breast as well, and made a small purr of contentment that almost drew him back to her side, king or no. Then she opened her eyes, saw him bending over her, and smiled.

"My own Jasper," she said, her voice charmingly thick. She raised her hands to loop them around his neck and draw him back to bed.

"You must rise, sweet," he said with regret, gently removing her arms from around his neck. "His Majesty has summoned me, and I must go to him at once, and it would be better for you not to be found here."

"The king has summoned you?" Instantly she was awake, pushing herself upright and shoving her hair back from her face. "Surely he must wish to speak of me. I will go with you, Jasper. Together we will explain, and make him see reason."

Her confidence charmed him, impractical as it was. What kind of argument could be made on behalf of reason for a night of fucking?

"Nay, my dearest, as much as I wish your company," he said, kissing her again. "But at this hour the king will still be among his gentlemen of the bedchamber, and not fit for receiving ladies. I want you to go to my sister, and stay there until I come to you again."

Though he tried to keep his voice light, she must have heard the seriousness in it. "Why? Do you fear? Will the king—"

"Do not worry, May," he said, rising from the bed. "It's likely nothing. But I've tarried long enough, and must go now. Drumble will help you to dress. He's familiar with ladies' things, and could likely teach your Poppy a few niceties. Perhaps he already has."

He smiled, putting on good cheer he did not necessarily believe.

Neither did she.

"But what if things go wrong, Jasper?" she cried plaintively. "What if the king blames you for me, and punishes you, and sends you to the Tower, and—and—"

"None of those things will happen, May," he said firmly, though he, too, had his doubts and fears. One never knew for certain with the king. "Drumble will see you back to my sister. Farewell, my darling, and God be with you."

He touched his fingers to his lips, and had already begun to turn through the doorway when she spoke again.

"I love you, Jasper," she whispered forlornly, her voice breaking with emotion. "Whatever else happens, know that—that I love you."

He looked back to her, there in the middle of the bed with a pillow clutched tightly in her arms and every feeling and emotion writ plain on her lovely face. And before he'd quite realized it, he'd said the same to her.

"I love you, too, May," he said, words he'd never spoken to any other woman. "I love you."

Then with the heaviest heart imaginable, he left.

MAY HURRIED THROUGH the hall of the base-court with Drumble beside her. The distance between Jasper's rooms and the ones she shared with his sister was not far—it had turned out they were very nearly across the courtyard from each other—but she hurried still, too anxious and distraught to walk slowly.

Jasper had been right about one thing: Drumble did

make an excellent lady's maid, and had pinned and laced
her back into her costume as expertly as Poppy herself had
done. But in the unforgiving morning light, the ethereal
white gown that had seemed so beautiful by the lights of
the great hall looked crumpled and forlorn after having
spent the night tossed aside on the floor of Jasper's bedchamber. The few other courtiers she had passed in the
hall had leered pointedly or raised their brows in disapproval, realizing at once from her dress that she'd spent the
night in a bed other than her own.

She paid them no heed, scarce even noticing their
reactions. Her thoughts were entirely with Jasper and his
audience with the king, and her prayers were with him as
well. She could not believe her good fortune to have fallen
in love with Jasper and he with her, especially after the
rapturous night they'd spent together. But if that was to
be their only night because of the misplaced rage of their
intemperate king, then surely that would be the worst possible fortune as well.

"His lordship will be well enough, my lady," Drumble
said as if reading her thoughts. "You will see. His lordship
always wriggles free of trouble, he does."

May smiled forlornly. "You sound exactly like Poppy.
She would say that, too."

"Well, then, my lady, we'd both be speaking the truth,
wouldn't we?" The small man smiled at her and winked.
"His lordship will be right again with the king before we
know it."

"Thank you, Drumble," she said softly, and opened the door to Arabella's lodgings. Clearly Poppy was likewise awake, for the fire was made in the hearth, the water in the ewer beside the wash bowl had been replenished, and the countess's breakfast tray was on the table. But Poppy herself was not to be found, and with a frown, May called her name. The door to the bedchamber was ajar, and carefully she pushed it open, unsure whether Arabella might still be asleep.

Aye, the countess was still abed, her spangled mask from last night still tied crookedly over her face, but she was hardly alone. Sprawled beside her in the bed with one arm thrown over her hip lay a ginger-haired young man that May recognized as one of the yeomen of the guard. Another purple-striped Turk's costume lay discarded on the floor at the foot of the bed. It was just as well May hadn't returned here last night, else she likely would have ended up in the bed with them.

Once this idea would have been wildly exciting. The guardsman appeared a well-made man, and Arabella knew no end of ways to discover pleasure. But since May had been with Jasper, she'd realized that she was not as much an adventuress as she'd once thought. She wasn't cut from the same bold cloth as Arabella, and the prospect of reserving her favors for the single man that she loved seemed much more to her liking.

The guardsman yawned, and flopped onto his back. May's eyes widened. The man was indeed armed with a splendid pikestaff, and even at ease it matched the rest of him for length. At least Arabella had found the right Turk for her, too, thought May, gently closing the door after them. Jasper would scarce believe this when she told him.

If she could tell him. The magnitude of what she faced struck her hard, and she pressed her hand over her mouth to keep from sobbing.

"Good morn, my lady," Poppy said, setting the well bucket beside the door so she might hurry to May. "Praise God you are safe! Oh, now, what has happened?"

May buried her face against Poppy's shoulder, letting her tears spill out.

"There, there, my poor dove," Poppy said, folding her arms around May. "I know it was not what you wished, but it is an honor to be chosen as you were by His Majesty, even if—"

"But I was not chosen by His Majesty," May said. "That was what everyone was to think, and I did, too, when I left with him. But inside the costume was Lord Blackford."

"His lordship!" Poppy stared at her, aghast. "Oh, fie, fie! To play at being the king, only to use that favor to press his suit with you! What her ladyship will say to that—what His Majesty will say!"

Fresh tears welled in May's eyes. "Oh, Poppy, that is what I fear the most. If he suffers because of me—"

"Then it will be his own undoing, the wicked, thieving knave," Poppy said furiously. "Did he force you, then? Did he hurt you?"

"Nay, not at all!" May cried. "I went to his bed willingly, eagerly, exactly as you and her ladyship would wish me to go to my lover."

"Your 'lover,'" Poppy said. "Lord Blackford has helped you to your own ruin, my lady, and now you're no more than another of the black lion's broken doves, soon to be cast aside like all the rest."

"But he won't do that, Poppy, not with me," May protested. "His lordship is perfect, perfect for me, and . . . and I love him, and he loves me!"

"What a wonder," Poppy said with disgust. "I'm sure His Majesty will be most pleased to hear of it."

May nodded miserably. "His lordship is with His Majesty now, and I—I know His Majesty will be furious, and—and if I am the cause of him punishing his lordship, then, oh, Poppy, how shall I live?"

"You'll live, so long as his lordship does, too." She sighed, and drew May to a nearby bench, sitting her down with her arms around her quaking shoulders. "There, now, it's done, and can't be undone. Best to look forward, and plan for what will come next. His Majesty does possess a hot temper, no doubt of that. But Lord Blackford has always been a clever fellow, and has his ways of slipping free of trouble quick as any eel."

May sniffed back her tears. "That's—that's just what Drumble said to me, too."

Poppy used the corner of her apron to blot May's tears. "Drumble's a wise fellow, and if he says a thing, it must be true. But if you've a prayer to spare for Lord Blackford, than I would say it."

ON THE FAR side of the palace, in the king's dressing chamber, Jasper would have welcomed that prayer as well. Before him sat the king, still in his dressing gown woven with tulips and a red velvet cap on his head. They were together, facing each other in the small chamber, the king having dismissed all his other servants and attendants so that he might address Jasper alone. But His Majesty had asked that his guards remain outside the door, at hand and at the ready, and that particular afterthought had made Jasper's hopes plummet.

Oh, aye, he thought gloomily, before this day was done, he could be leaving the palace with his hands chained behind, tossed in the bottom of a boat to be taken to the Traitors' Gate of the Tower, and for what? Because he'd dared to fall in love?

"Blackford," the king said, rolling Jasper's name on his tongue with disconcerting relish. "Tell me yourself what became of my favorite fellow Turk last eve."

Jasper took a deep breath. He'd already decided that the truth would be his best companion before the king.

"As you know, Your Majesty, I entered the great hall with you and the others, all of us dressed alike," he began. "I followed the ruse as you had exactly ordered, never betraying my identity. Then I came upon Lady May Roseberry."

The heavy folds that framed the king's mouth seemed to deepen with disapproval. "At which point you chose to forget my orders, and follow your own desires with the lady."

"Aye, Your Majesty, I did," he admitted, letting a note of sadness creep into his voice. "Such were the powers of the lady's charms, that I weakened, and succumbed."

"Hah." The king worried the inside of his cheek. "Do not speak to me of the powers of ladies."

"Forgive me, Your Majesty," he said as contritely as he could. "I did not intend Lady May as my excuse."

The king made a barking laugh, his eyes glinting. "That was not my intention, either, Blackford. Far from it. I speak from what befell me last eve. I'll grant that I was displeased when you removed Lady May from the great hall. Sorely displeased! Yet with that lady gone, it was as if I'd my true sight restored."

"Indeed, Your Majesty," Jasper said cautiously, the conversation taking an unexpected turn.

"Aye, indeed," the king declared. "Before me I once again saw Mistress Boleyn in her most ravishing glory, the lady who has held and returned my love and devotion for many months' time. I saw her, and she dazzled me anew, like the most rare jewel that she is. Thus I thank you, Blackford, thank you with all my heart."

Jasper stared. "You would thank me, Your Majesty?"

"I would, and I do." He leaned forward, the corners of

his mouth twitching. "It is not often a rascal like you can escape our wrath for disobedience, eh?"

"Nay, Your Majesty, not often at all." Jasper grinned, a wave of relief sweeping over him. "Thank you, Your Majesty."

The king swept his hand through the air. "No thanks, man, no thanks. But tell me. Did you enjoy the lady? Was she all that she seems?"

"She was, and she is." Jasper inhaled, steeling himself for the favor he would ask. "There can be no other woman that I can regard more highly. In truth, Your Majesty, since Lady May is your ward, I would ask of you the honor of her hand in marriage."

"Hah, you would, would you?" He smiled broadly. "Now, that is a fine notion, an excellent notion, and one I would be happy to oblige save for one obstacle. You are too late, Blackford, and another man has come to claim your bride."

Jasper stared in disbelief. "Name him, Your Majesty," he demanded. "Name him, so I might know the rogue who presumes to steal my claim to the lady."

"The Duke of Pomfrey," the king said, watching shrewdly for Jasper's response. "An excellent, thoughtful gentleman. He is our cousin, you know, of our blood. He is a rich man, with many lands. He needs a wife to secure his title with an heir."

"Then he will find a score of other ladies at court to

help him achieve that," Jasper said, more warmly than was wise. "He need not claim Lady May. He has no reason to beyond his own greed for the lady's inheritance, and spite for claiming the lady I love."

"Ah, love," the king said, musing. "A fine thing, love, though not one that has a part in the arrangement of marriages. Lands, titles, power, influence: those are what make fortunate marriages. You've already sired three sons by your first wife. A new wife would surely wish for a place closer to the title for any son she might bear herself. You may find the lady is more practical in considering her prospects."

"Then I have land as well to offer the lady, Your Majesty," Jasper said, "and a fine estate, more than sufficient to support a score of children."

"But I must look after the lady's future," the king said. "Pomfrey can make her a duchess."

"I can make her a countess," Jasper said, "and give her children born of love."

"Pomfrey is likewise a man in his prime. I expect he will do the same."

"But I may already have filled her belly last night," Jasper countered. He hadn't considered that until this moment, but a child, his child, growing within May was an enchanting idea, so long as it didn't become a magpie in Pomfrey's nest. "I can assure you of that. And unless Lord Pomfrey is content to look at his eldest son and heir and see a lad taller than he, with my dark hair and pale eyes, then I—"

"You did fuck her, then?" the king asked, his expression

darkening. "Confess it, Blackford, for I know well what manner of cockerel you are among the she-hens. You took my ward's maidenhead, and spent your seed in her womb?"

"I did, Your Majesty," Jasper admitted, adding a little bow to his confession for good measure. "She is well and truly mine, in a way that Lord Pomfrey can never now achieve or—"

"I did not give Pomfrey my blessing," the king interrupted again. He settled back in his chair. "I knew of your attachment to the lady, and the fondness of your regard. The entire court saw you were in love with her the moment you arrived among us. Now it seems you've laid your claim upon her person by filling her belly as well as her heart."

Wildly Jasper's hopes swung upwards again. "Then you will bless my union with the lady?"

The king grunted. "Nay, I did not give that, either," he said. "But I will tell you this, Blackford, exactly the same as I told Pomfrey. It will be between the two of you to decide Lady May's fate. You must prove to me, and to the lady, which of you two gentlemen is the most bold in his wooing and the most worthy of her hand and her fortune with it. If Pomfrey still wants her after he learns you've already had her, then I'll send the lady back to her convent for three months' time to see if she quickens with your child or not. Pomfrey may not care, but I'll not have bastards among my peers."

"I vow it will not come to that, Your Majesty," Jasper declared confidently. "Lady May will choose me. No other man could show the love, the desire, the patience and friendship, that I have showed the lady."

But the king only grunted, no answer at all. "I'll give you a day's time to prove yourself, Blackford, to the lady and to me. Twenty-four hours from this moment, by the clock in the courtyard, the same as I have granted to Lord Pomfrey. At the end, I will decide which of you will claim the bride, with her at my side."

"I thank you, Your Majesty," Jasper said, bowing again. He was sure he'd win—he loved May, and she loved him, and last night he'd proved it in the best way possible. How could Pomfrey compete with that?

CHAPTER FOURTEEN

"You *fool*!" raged Arabella, and hurled the goblet crashing against the wall. "You thoughtless, selfish little fool! You know what you have done with my brother, don't you? You have ruined us, May, all of us, and for what? For what?"

"Because I love him," May said, standing as straight as she could before the countess. For her, Jasper's love meant everything. She had never known a parent's love, or the love of any other relation, and now when love, real love, was finally being offered to her, she would never give it up. She knew this conversation would not be easy, but she hadn't expected this madwoman's fury. "I love him, and he loves me."

"*Love!*" Arabella practically spit the word. "Then truly you are a fool, if you believe in my brother's love. I've known Jasper since he was born, May, and he has not once loved anyone beyond himself. Now that he has fucked you, you will be as nothing to him, another sad little creature whose name he won't be able to recall. And to think you could have had the king himself!"

"But your brother does love me," May insisted. "He told me so himself."

The countess stared at her, her gaze hard as flint. Sitting in her smock, she looked much older this morning, the bright morning light harsh on her face. Her hair was tangled and full of snarls, last night's paint was still smeared across her cheeks, and the shadows and lines beneath her eyes were proof enough of whatever excesses she had shared with her guardsman before he'd been unceremoniously hurried from her bed not a quarter hour before.

"And what will that earn for you?" she demanded. "Wealth, power, place, influence? Those are the things that last, May, not the poet's fancy of love. He will not marry you, you know. He never speaks of marriage, not to you or any of the others."

"I spoke not of it, either," May said, and she hadn't. She was so content with his love that she'd not thought onwards to the complicated material permanence of marriage, of banns and betrothals and contracts and jointures.

"Then you are double the fool," Arabella said with such reproach that if there had been another goblet within her reach, it, too, would have been hurled across the chamber. "Now your pretty *love* could land us all in the Tower for displeasing the king, and all because you could not keep your legs together when my brother came sniffing between them."

"But I don't want power or place or influence, and I already have wealth," May said defensively. "All I wish for is love."

"You will have nothing if you rely on my brother," the countess said, "and even less—Hark, who is that at our door, at this hour?"

May gasped, and so did Poppy behind her, mopping up the spilled wine.

"Should I answer it, my lady?" Poppy asked, rising.

"Of course you should, Poppy," Arabella said, swiftly plucking a shawl from a chair to fling over her smock. "Likely it's the king's guards, come to haul us away. May, here, by me. No matter that you have wronged His Majesty with your sins, I vow we won't make this easy for them."

The knock at their door was commanding, exactly as May imagined a soldier's to be, and with a terrified little cry she hurried to stand beside Arabella. To her surprise, the countess took her hand, linking their fingers together.

Poppy waited by the door until the countess was ready, then slowly opened the door a crack.

"Is Lady Wilyse within?" the man asked, his face still hidden. "I wish to speak with her."

May closed her eyes, struggling to control her fear. So this was how it would end, here, now.

Poppy opened the door the rest of the way, and curtsied.

"His Grace the Duke of Pomfrey, my lady," she

announced loudly, as if they were in a grand house instead of a single room. "His Grace wishes to speak with you, my lady."

May's eyes flew open. Lord Pomfrey stood solemnly before them, as impeccably dressed as ever, with a pair of attendants accompanying him.

"Good morn, Your Grace," Arabella said, her voice now silky and engaging as she sank into a graceful curtsy, as if she weren't dressed in only her smock and a shawl. May might have ruined her opportunity with the king, but clearly Arabella was already considering the duke in his place. "Pray will you join us?"

She motioned to the armchair before the fire, and belatedly May curtsied, too, wondering what the duke could possibly want at this hour.

But Lord Pomfrey continued to stand as if the countess hadn't spoken at all, his gaze intent not on Arabella but on May.

What could he want of her? May wondered, her heart racing. She remembered the wicked things he'd said to her last night as they'd danced, and how determined he'd seemed to make his desires come true. Had he some fresh news from the king that she had not? Had he already learned of Jasper's downfall?

"Forgive me for this early hour, Lady Wilyse," the duke said, "but there are times when I believe haste is the only course. Lady Wilyse, might I ask your permission to walk with Lady May about the courtyard? You can watch us from this window, and I vow to keep her always within your sight, as is proper."

"Of course, Your Grace, of course," Arabella said with an encouraging nod. "I would trust you further, if you would wish to walk with her in the gardens."

"Thank you, Lady Wilyse, but the courtyard will suffice for what I must say." He nodded solemnly to the countess, and held his arm out to May.

With little choice, May rose, but before she joined the duke, Arabella turned her aside, her face full of concern.

"Heed what he offers, May," she whispered softly. "All I wish now is for you to be happy."

May stared with surprise. "But what of the king, and your plans and plots?"

"You are not me, sweet." The countess sighed, and leaned forward to kiss May's cheek. "Choose what will make you happy, and keep you safe."

The duke cleared his throat. "Lady May, will you join me?"

May nodded. Her heart still racing with uncertainty, she took his offered arm, and together they left. He said nothing as they walked down the hall and the steps and into the courtyard. Others bowed as they passed, watching them with respect as well as curiosity, and little wonder, thought May, considering how curious a pair they must make with her in the hopelessly wrinkled costume from last night's masquerade. Likely any who saw it could guess what they'd been doing, including the duke himself, and her cheeks flushed with shame.

As soon as they were outside, his servants fell back from hearing, and May glanced up at the countess's window. Arabella was there watching, as the duke had bid her to do, and at the next window was Poppy's red hair as well. How ironic that now she'd have such careful supervision while she walked with a gentleman in this open, public place, while last night no one seemed to have known at all where she was, even as she was enthusiastically enacting Aretino's postures before a looking glass.

And how fortunate, too, that the duke could not read her thoughts. He smiled gravely at her, seemingly ready at last to speak.

"Lady May," he said as they walked. "It should not surprise you to learn that I admire you greatly, and have done so since first we met."

"Thank you, Your Grace," May said, still thinking more of Jasper and Aretino than the man beside her. "You honor me."

"I would wish to do far more than that, Lady May," he said. "You possess beauty, rank, and wit, and you appear to be of excellent health for childbearing. In short, you possess every quality that I seek in a wife, as I have already explained to His Majesty. Lady May, will you do me the greatest of honors, and agree to become my wife and duchess?"

Stunned, May stopped walking, and drew back her hand from his arm. "Forgive me, Your Grace, but I fear I do not understand. Are you asking me to wed you?"

"I am, Lady May," he said, his foxlike face so serious he

almost looked pained. "I wish to marry you and take you as my wife."

"That is—that is generous of you, Your Grace," May said quickly, "and a great honor. But I do not know you, Your Grace, nor do you know me."

"I know enough, Lady May," he answered, undeterred. "You will be mistress of my lands, and mother of my children. You will have my name, and my protection in all things. You will be linked by marriage to His Majesty himself. You will want for nothing."

"Except for love, Your Grace," May said. "You do not love me, nor do I love you."

"That will surely come in time," the duke said, "as it does for all spouses. His Majesty said that as well."

"His Majesty? You have already spoken to His Majesty of this?"

"I have, Lady May." At last he smiled, his lips tight as they always were. How had she ever kissed him? she wondered. "This very morn. You are his ward. It is his decision to make, and he agrees that it is a most advantageous match for us both."

"But not to me!" she cried, her voice so anguished that others across the yard turned to stare. "Not to *me*!"

The duke looked uncomfortable, and unhappy, too. "Now, now, none of that," he said, reaching to take her hand again. "I've surprised you, I know. But when you have time to consider—"

"The man in the purple Turk's costume last night was

not the king, Your Grace," she said, desperation guiding her words now. "It was Lord Blackford. And after I left you, he took me to his rooms and fucked me, over and over, and— and I'm not a maiden any longer."

He stared at her, his eyes narrowing slightly.

"I do not believe you, Lady May," he said at last. "I will concede that you left with Lord Blackford in disguise, but the rest—nay, I do not believe it."

"Even if it is the truth?" she demanded. "Even if I still wear the masquerade costume from last night, crumpled and soiled by his hands?"

His gaze flicked down over her person. "That is nothing. I surprised you before you'd time to dress yourself properly."

"Very well, then." She glanced about to make certain she'd not be overheard. "Lord Blackford sat on the edge of the bed and I knelt between his legs and took his cock into my mouth and sucked and licked it and dandled his cods beneath it in my hand until he groaned and grew hard in my mouth, but did not spend. Then he bid me climb over him, my bottom to his front, and as I held the lips of my cunny open, I lowered myself upon his cock, taking it slowly so I might feel each inch as it stretched and filled me while he held my breasts in his hands."

Though Lord Pomfrey's expression had not changed, his face had flushed and his lips had parted, his breath growing faster. "I still do not believe you. A month ago you were still in the convent."

"But not last night, Your Grace," she said, determined to finish telling him. She didn't know why it suddenly seemed so important that Lord Pomfrey know exactly why he'd never be a true rival to Jasper, or why, too, it was exciting her to tell him, and how it would excite her more in turn to confess her telling to Jasper himself. "After I'd taken the whole length of him into my cunny, he spread his legs beneath me, forcing my own legs wider to tighten my passage around his cock."

She was so lost in the memory now that she'd almost forgotten she was describing it to the duke, there in the middle of the palace courtyard. She glanced up at Arabella's arched window, and the two women's faces watching her. What they saw must have seemed ordinary, even mundane: her standing before the duke, her white skirts sparkling incongruously in the sunlight, her hands clasped before her, her long trailing sleeves weaving gently in the breeze. They wouldn't hear her words, not from there, but they'd see her speaking and the duke listening intently, respectfully, with his servants standing ten paces behind. It would appear the most innocent of conversations, but there was nothing innocent in what May described.

"Imagine it all, Your Grace," she said, her words tumbling out at a feverish pace. "Imagine my golden nest mingled together with his lordship's black thatch, his ballocks hanging full against my nether-hole, his cock buried deep in my cunny with my lips swollen and ripe around it. With my widespread legs braced beneath his, I could raise myself up, sliding along his pole, and then sink back down again to swallow him up."

She smiled to herself, remembering so vividly that she could feel the moisture gathering again in her cunny, almost as if Jasper were there with her again. "Because I was so wet, Your Grace, I took his lordship with ease, for all that he was so large and I'd been so late a maid. You must imagine it all, Your Grace, imagine it well. I knew how we did look, for his lordship had propped a glass upon a chair, so we might watch ourselves at play, and I . . . I saw it all, Your Grace, and felt it, too, when I spent, and he filled me so full with his seed that it spilled over, from my cunny to my open thighs and then to the floor below, and—"

"I would do that to you, Lady May," the duke said, his voice harsh and his fingers twisting restlessly at his sides. "I'd fill your cunt, and make you forget Blackford ever touched you."

She blinked as if waking from a dream, and in a way she had, a dream of her own making. The duke had stepped closer to her, and May had never seen such raw hunger on a man's face before. She'd described one of her couplings with Jasper to discourage the duke, to show him he could never compete with Jasper, but instead of discouraging him, her words seemed only to have inflamed him more. It frightened her, seeing him like this, and she was sure that if they'd not been standing in so vast and public a place, he would have fallen on her like some wild and savage beast.

"I will have you," he said roughly. "I will not be refused, Lady May. You will be my wife, not Blackford's. *Mine*."

"Nay, Your Grace," she said, jerking free of him. "I will never wed you. I will *not*!"

Before he could stop her, she turned and fled, her heels biting into the cobbles as she ran from the courtyard and back into the palace. She did not know where she was going except away from the duke, and away from a marriage without love, too. Tears again blurred her eyes, and as she ran, she nearly tumbled over a page who stood in her way.

"My Lady May Roseberry," the boy said, holding his ground before her. "I have a message for you from Lord Blackford."

"Lord Blackford!" May seized the boy's shoulder. "Is he unharmed? Is he well? What do you know of him? Oh, tell me, I beg you, tell me all!"

The boy's eyes were round with surprise. "I know nothing of that, my lady. All I know is what he bid me tell you, that he wishes you to meet him at once at the garden maze near the river."

May nodded eagerly, her heart filling with joy. "Do you know where that is? Can you take me there?"

"Aye, my lady," the boy said, turning to lead her. "This way, my lady."

She followed him down another passage and from the palace and along a walk beneath nodding trees. The gardens ran out as far as May could see, great empty plains of flowers, greenery, and neat-kept paths that at this time of day were devoid of any company, save her and her trotting page. Before them lay the river, shimmering in the late-morning sun, and to their left rose a wide, tall hedge of hornbeam.

"Where is this maze?" May asked the boy, wondering if perhaps he had pretended knowledge, or simply misunderstood. She was hot and tired and disappointed, and had begun to fear that the page's message might be only a trick of Lord Pomfrey. "Where is Lord Blackford?"

"There, my lady," the boy said. "There's his lordship now."

And there indeed was Jasper, suddenly appearing through a break in the tall hedge. She ran to him and he caught her in his arms, gathering her so tightly against his chest that she wondered if he'd ever release her, nor did she wish him to.

"What has happened, Jasper?" she begged when, at last, he set her back down on her feet. "Is the king angry? Are you pardoned? Are you free?"

"It was a miracle, May," he said, laughing. "His Majesty gave me thanks instead of a pardon, and a challenge."

She drew back, skeptical. "You make no sense."

"Nor did the king," Jasper said. "Come with me, and I'll explain it all in good time."

"Faith, you would torment me!" she exclaimed. "Tell me now, and then I will tell you my own marvels."

"In time, in time," he said, kissing her into silence. "Not a word of the king or any other marvels, not yet. All I wish for now is that you come with me."

"But where, Jasper?" She looked around, wondering where in this great empty garden he expected her to go with him.

"Here, my love," he said grandly, and taking her by the hand, he led her into the opening in the hedge. To her surprise the hedge had been grown into a kind of walkway, so tall and thick as to mask the rest of the world beyond it. But as soon as they reached the end of the leafy passage, two more lay beyond it, and another turning beyond that.

"Where are we?" she asked, mystified.

"We're in the maze," he said, grinning at her confusion. "A kind of garden-puzzle wrought of greenery. If you don't take care to keep your bearings, you can become lost for hours. You did not know what a maze might be, did you?"

"Nay," she confessed. "But I do not see—"

"You will," he said, "if you'll but trust me."

She looked up at him for a long moment, then smiled. Aye, she would trust him. She'd trust him to lead her anywhere, even if she hadn't already lost track of the twistings and turnings of the hedges, this way and that, with his hand firmly clasped in hers. Surely trust must be a part of love, for her to trust him as she did now.

At last they reached a small clearing, shaded by a pair of spreading trees, with a wooden garden bench beneath.

"A lovesome place, isn't this?" Jasper said as he seated May on the bench. "We might as well have a moat about us—we're that far from everyone else in here."

But May did not care about the moat or everyone else.

Nothing really mattered except Jasper himself, and he'd scarcely sat on the bench beside her before she'd twisted around to face him. She laid her hands flat on his shoulders, studying him as seriously as if seeing him for the first time. His pale blue eyes with their dark lashes, the bow of his lips and the line of his jaw and the tiny black hairs of his beard and the little moon-shaped scar on his cheekbone, all the parts that made his face so endlessly dear to her.

She felt his hand on her back, steadying her, and with that for encouragement she began to slide across into his lap. Effortlessly he lifted her, settling her so she was sitting astride him with her knees on either side of his thighs. He chuckled, then groaned, and she leaned closer, whispering his name like a private incantation against his neck. He turned her face to find her lips, and soon was kissing her, kissing her so hard that she felt herself melting against him.

Kissing him made all her senses more acutely aware. She heard not only his groan as he deepened his kiss but the leaves rustling over their heads and the whispering *shush* of her sarcenet gown as he pulled it higher to bare her legs. She could taste his desire in his kiss, and she could not breathe enough of his scent, the musky, masculine scent of his hair and his skin and his cock besides. She shifted on his lap, and was rewarded with his hand moving along her back to her waist and then over her hips, stroking her and pulling her closer until she sat snug against him.

Somehow while they'd kissed, he'd pushed the front of her gown down far enough that he could ease her breasts

free of the stiffened bodice, but still mounded provoca-
tively high by the whalebone stays of her corset. His lips
moved from her mouth to her throat, to the place he knew
could make her breath catch, then slipped lower to suck
on her offered nipples, his tongue teasing their tips while
he lightly played the edges of his teeth across the crests.
She cradled his head, afraid he would stop, until she was
moaning and writhing with excitement. When at last he
broke away, her nipples were red and wet and tight, and the
breeze on them made them cool just enough to tighten still.

He pulled her skirts higher and slid his hands beneath,
above her stockings and garters to the smooth warm skin
of her thighs. Higher still he reached, until he found her
cunny between her widespread legs and made her gasp.

"You're wet," he said. "You're fair dripping."

"For you, Jasper," she breathed. "Only for you."

She sat back long enough to reach between their bodies, opening the front of his doublet and pushing aside his
codpiece to tug down the front of his trunk hose. Grate-
fully his cock sprang free, already thick and stiff between
them, and she played along its heated length to tease him
as he'd teased her.

He caught her wrist, stopping her.

"Enough," he ordered hoarsely, and he pulled her forward, lifting her. "Ride me."

She opened herself to him, guiding the blunt head of
his cock to slip between the greedy lips of her cunny. But
he was done with teasing and play, and instead he grasped

her hips, his fingers spread over the soft flesh, and pulled her down hard onto his cock, filling her completely in a single stroke. He groaned at her tightness around him, his eyes closed and his head bowed, and she gasped, clutching his shoulders.

"Ride me," he said again, and she did, rising up on her knees to draw along the length of him as far as she dared before he pulled her back down and drove into her again. As their rhythm built, he closed his hands over her breasts, squeezing her nipples with every thrust so that the pleasure raced from her breasts to her quim and back again.

She could feel the tension building within him as he pumped her harder, his breath coming in ragged bursts, and her own excitement grew in response until she was crying out with each of his thrusts, her hands braced on his shoulders and her head thrown back in abandon. He caught her hips again, holding her down as his hips bucked up with his release, and as she felt the jet of his seed within her, her own crisis came, making her cry out with the joy and the power of it.

With her body still trembling, she fell forward against him, her cheek to his chest and the sound of his racing heart beneath her ear. As she calmed, he stroked her hair and held her close, and she listened as his heart slowed and his breathing with it. His seed slipped wetly from her cunny, and she could feel his cock shifting and sliding from her, too. Her skin was cooling now and her legs ached from being held so widely apart, yet still she did not want to move, but stay here with him forever, drowsy and sated and safe.

"I love you," she whispered against his chest. "Oh, how I love you."

"Then marry me," he said.

She pushed back from his chest to stare up at him. "What are you saying?"

He smiled, brushing her hair from her forehead. "I'm saying that you should marry me."

She stared at him, still not believing. To have two lords propose marriage to her in a single morning would make most ladies incredulous.

"Your sister said you'd never marry again."

"I'm not marrying Arabella," he said. "It's you I wish for my wife. Will you?"

She smiled slowly, unable to answer. It wasn't that she was uncertain of him—she'd no doubts at all—but that she could not believe the fate that had brought her here, to this place with this man. That, and the tears that welled in her eyes.

"Will you, love?" he asked again. "Will you marry me?"

Her smile widened. "You must ask the king first."

"I have," he said. "Before he would agree, he said I must win you."

That made her laugh through her tears. "Faith, what more must you do?"

"I must do nothing," he said, fondly brushing aside her tears with his thumbs. "Not now. But you must say yes."

"Yes," she said. "Yes, your lordship, I will marry you."

She reached up and kissed him, a kiss that was as full of love as it was of passion, and promise, too, for the future they now would share. She could feel his cock stirring, too, rousing within her, and in response she began to move as well with languid purpose.

But Jasper groaned, and reluctantly broke the kiss. "We can't, May, not now. We must go to His Majesty and tell him."

She lowered her chin and looked up at him through her lashes. "Fie on His Majesty. This once he can wait."

Yet Jasper did not laugh as she'd expected. "Perhaps the king can wait, but I cannot. There is, you see, another suitor for your hand."

"Lord Pomfrey." She sighed. "He has already asked me."

"He has?" Jasper asked with disbelief. "The dog! When? How?"

"This morning," she said. "He came to our lodgings and asked to walk with me, and I went with him into the court, and he asked, and I refused. And then I came here to you."

"Where you said yes, may the heavens bless you a thousand times for it," he said. "But now we've double reason to go to the king, before Pomfrey turns sly and tells him some lie or another."

They put their clothes to rights as quickly as they could, or as quickly as they could while pausing frequently to kiss.

"Are you certain you know the way out?" May asked as at last they left the bench. "Faith, I know I don't."

"It's not so very hard," he admitted. "So long as you keep your right hand to the hedge and follow only those turnings, you'll find your way."

"Truly?" she said, placing her fingers to the shiny leaves of the hedge. She grinned over her shoulder at him. "If that is all the secret to it, my lord, then try to catch me!"

Laughing, she bunched her skirts in one hand and ran, her fingertips whipping over the hornbeam leaves as he'd told her to do. She could hear him close behind her, laughing as well, and while she suspected he could have caught her with ease if he'd wished to do so, he stayed just far enough behind her to make it seem as if he were chasing her for real. By the time she reached the entrance, she was breathless from running and from laughing, and half stumbling as she raced out to the path.

"I won, Jasper," she crowed, looking back into the maze for him. "I won!"

"Aye, Lady May, you have," said Lord Pomfrey, and with a gasp she turned round. The duke stood waiting before his horse with three of his men—not his usual liveried servants, but armed guardsmen on horseback—and with them was the young page who had led May to the maze. The duke was dressed now for a journey, and he wore a sword as well as he bowed briskly to her. "The prize is to be my duchess, and you have won it just as I have won you."

She gasped, and turned to run back into the maze to find Jasper, but the duke grabbed her arm and pulled her back.

"Nay, Your Grace, release me!" she cried, fighting to

free herself. "I refused you then, and I refuse you again now. I will not marry you!"

His grasp on her arm only tightened. "I know you were at first overwhelmed by the generosity of my offer," he said, his anger making him stronger. "But in time I am sure you will accept that you were meant to be my wife, and no other's. Now come, madam, and no more of this. I have a priest waiting who will lawfully marry us."

"Nay, I will not!" cried May. "Jasper, Jasper, here!"

At once Jasper appeared, lunging from the maze towards her. The duke drew his sword, the scrape of the blade from the scabbard enough to make May stop fighting. Jasper stopped, too, his fists knotted with frustration yet unable to attack the duke as he wished without putting May at risk.

"Let the lady go," he said. "And for God's sake, put that blade away."

But the duke only smiled and jerked May closer to him. May gasped. She did not know which frightened her more: this bullying by Lord Pomfrey or the fury she saw on Jasper's face at his own helplessness, and silently she prayed that he'd not risk himself by perpetrating some heroic foolishness.

"The lady is mine, Blackford," the duke declared, "and she answers to me, not to you. His Majesty told you that she would go to the man who showed more boldness, which clearly makes her mine. Now keep back, else I'll use this on you."

"I am not yours, Your Grace," May cried, still struggling

to break free. "Can you not understand that? I have refused you once, and I shall refuse you every other time."

"There," Jasper said. "She doesn't want you. What more do you need to hear?"

"What do I care for a woman's words?" the duke said, dragging her stumbling towards his horse. "She will be my wife, not my adviser. Come, Lady May. This willfulness does not please me."

"The king comes, Your Grace!" exclaimed one of the duke's men, pointing across the gardens. "The king!"

There was no mistaking any party that included the king. He was easy to spot himself—a large man riding with daring skill—but he was accompanied by attendants with the royal standard and several other courtiers. Even on the rare days that His Majesty did not hunt, he would spend his mornings riding out across his parks and gardens, and clearly he was returning now. But just as they had spied His Majesty, his people in turn had spied the duke's men and horses near the maze, and drawn by curiosity, they changed their course to join them, the king at the forefront.

"You'd best release me now, Your Grace," May said acidly. "His Majesty will not like to see you treat his ward so basely."

The duke released her as swiftly as if she'd been made of hot coals.

"His Majesty will see what is fair and just," he said defensively. "That is what he will see, Lady May, and act upon as well. You will be yet declared my wife."

But May wasn't listening. Instead she'd run at once to Jasper and his embrace, flinging her arms around his waist to hold him close.

"You will be my husband," she said fiercely. "So I'll vow to His Majesty, too. I'll have you, Jasper, and no other."

"You will, sweet," he said, his face filled with fresh determination as well as love. "I'll vow as well to make it so."

Then suddenly the king was there before them, on an enormous bay gelding that made His Majesty all the more imposing. The gentlemen bowed, and May curtsied, feeling woefully self-conscious in her bedraggled costume.

"What manner of gathering is this?" the king asked, gesturing for them all to rise. "Pomfrey? Blackford? I gave you each leave to court my ward, not haul her along the riverbank."

"I was rescuing the lady when you arrived, Your Majesty," Lord Pomfrey said quickly. "As you see, she is in a most lamentable condition. But as you advised boldness, I had come to take her before a priest who is waiting to marry us."

The king scowled down from his horse. "You presume, Pomfrey. You were to woo my ward, not carry her off on your saddle like some pagan captive. If that is your notion of wooing, then God's foot, I should be loath to see how you would consummate the match."

Still scowling, he shifted his gaze over to Jasper and May, pointedly looking at May's stained and crumpled gown. "And you, Blackford. You look as if you've put your wedding night before the wedding. Is that your idea of wooing? To swive the lady on the grass before you've made her your wife?"

"Forgive me, Your Majesty," Jasper said, bowing again. "But the lady and I are already so joined by love that the vows of marriage before a priest will serve only to confirm the union of our hearts."

The king snorted. "What say you to this, Lady May? It would seem that you have been barbarously misused by them both."

"Nay, Your Majesty, not at all!" May exclaimed, stepping forward to speak. "Both of these lords have protested their devotion to me, and both have asked for my hand."

"Aye, they have asked me as well," the king said, smiling down at her. "Both are worthy gentlemen, lords with much to recommend them as husbands."

"Aye, Your Majesty," May said. "But one alone does love me as a husband should, and the other does not. One I have already accepted with all my heart, and one I have refused."

"Your Majesty, I protest," the duke said, coming to stand beside May. "Such a solemn choice should not be made by the foolish whims of a girl, but on the sober merits of her suitor."

"Well spoke, Your Grace." Now Jasper joined May, slipping his arm familiarly around her shoulder, while she nestled close to his side. "For if we are to be judged on our merits, why, then I am confident both the lady and His Majesty will come to the same rightful conclusion."

"Hah, you are a confident rogue, Blackford, aren't you?" the king exclaimed, laughing. "Very well. Since the lady must abide with one of you for the rest of her mortal days, I leave the decision to her. Lady May, which will be your husband?"

"The man who holds both my heart and regard," May said. "I joyfully give my hand to Lord Blackford."

"And I shall welcome her hand with equal joy and love," Jasper said, kissing her fingers. "My own, dear Lady May."

"This cannot be, Your Majesty!" sputtered Lord Pomfrey. "To let the lady fall into the hands of this rascal, this knave, this—"

"Do not question my will, Pomfrey," the king said, then turned to beam at Jasper and May. "You have our blessings for this union, and our wishes for your joy and contentment. And make haste with your wedding, too. The black lion should be wed to his lioness before the first litter of cubs appear, eh?"

"Aye, Your Majesty," Jasper said. "You will agree to change from my dove to my Lady Lioness?"

May smiled, her heart overflowing. "I will, my lord. So long as we oblige the king regarding the cubs."

"Oh, aye, I plan to sire an entire litter or more," he said, laughing as he swept her into his arms to kiss her. "Whenever you wish to begin, my lady wife. Whenever you wish to begin."

Want more from Charlotte Lovejoy?
Read on for a tantalizing peek at

MADAME BLISS

Available from Signet Eclipse

The summer sun still hung low and lazy in the Devonshire sky, the shadows cast by the oak trees long across the meadows and the dew nodding heavy on the tall grasses. Yet it was not like any other morning, for in those same tall grasses lay a squalling, woeful female infant.

This sorry newborn babe knew nothing of men, for even the father who sired her had refused to give her his name. Of a mother's love, she knew little more, for her mother, poor woman, could contrive no better course for her child than to cast her away at three days' age, and abandon her against a hummock at a lonely country crossroads. The tender infant had no sustenance, no comfort beyond a tattered blanket to shelter her from the elements, and if she'd not been intended for greater things, she surely would have perished from thirst or hunger or mongrel dogs, with none to mourn her tiny corpse.

But on that particular summer day, Fate sent the traveling coach of Lady Catherine Worthy rumbling over the crossroads, and near to where the babe lay. Frightened by the thunderous sound of the coach's great ironbound wheels, the babe cried aloud so shrill that it drew the attention of Lady Catherine Worthy. The lady thrust her head from the coach's window, crossly mistaking the babe's pitiful wail for the squeak of an axle purposefully misaligned by wheelwrights determined to cheat her.

"Stop, there, stop!" she shouted to her driver. "Stop at once, I say!"

The great coach lumbered to a halt, yet still the sound persisted, shrill and vexing. Her Ladyship leaned farther from the window, the lace-trimmed lappets on her cap flapping on either side of her face, and waved her hand imperiously at the footman who rode on the box behind.

"You there!" she called. "Someone has tossed away a pup by the road. I see it myself, there in those weeds. Go back and fetch it now, haste, haste! There is nothing I loathe more than some low villain discarding a pup like rubbish."

The footman trotted back and plucked not a dog, but the babe, from the grass. Bewildered, he looked back to the coach, holding the wriggling (and quite damp) infant at arm's length away from his splendid silver-laced livery coat.

"It's not a pup, m'lady," he shouted. "It's a baby."

"A baby, you say?" Disappointment filled the lady's voice. "Not a pup?"

"No, m'lady," the footman said, squinting warily down at the wretched child in his arms. "Do you still wish me to bring it, m'lady?"

"A baby." Her ladyship sighed mightily. "I do not suppose we can leave it here, else wild pigs shall eat it, and there's another soul lost from Heaven. Is it a boy baby or a girl?"

With a single indelicate finger, the footman lifted the baby's swaddling blanket to peer inside: the first ever to ogle this poor infant so, but far from the last. "A girl, m'lady."

"A girl." Her ladyship sighed again. "Very well. Our Christian duty demands that we offer assistance to those who cannot provide for themselves. We shall keep her, and order her baptized this Sabbath."

Thus through the charity of her ladyship, the foundling girl came to live among the serving staff at Worthy Hall. She was duly baptized, and named Mary, for Our Lord's Mother, and because that was the name her ladyship called all serving girls. As a surname, she was given Wren, because her ladyship deemed that a proper bird for an orphan to emulate: small, humble, industrious, and plain.

Alas for Lady Catherine's careful plans! As Mary Wren grew, it became clear that there was very little of the humble wren in her. Her temper was not given to humility, but to spirit, and though she was too often corrected with the rod by her betters, she still spoke freely whenever she perceived injustice or unfairness.

Yet the unfairness often fell towards Mary herself. While she toiled hard at every task presented to her as the lowest scullery maid, working from before dawn until long past sunset, her labors were never judged sufficient by Cook or Mrs. Able, the housekeeper. No matter how hard Mary worked, she never could seem to please, and she despaired over how sorry a character they would give for her if ever she dared to leave for another place, at another house.

Least wrenlike of all was Mary's appearance. By the sixteenth anniversary of her coming to the Hall, she had grown into the rarest beauty, and much more a swan than a wren. Her complexion was clear and bloomed like a damask rose, her hair dark and curling, her teeth even and her eyes the brightest sapphire. Further, she'd grown into a lushly ripe young woman, her breasts full and high and her waist small, and despite her modest servant's dress and cap, she was remarked by men of every station wherever she went.

Pray recall that at the tender age of sixteen, Mary was still innocent, a virgin in every possible way. She did not seek the constant attention she received, nor did it please her. Instead it made her feel uncertain and confused, even shamed, so much so that her cheeks were constantly ablaze with her misery.

To no surprise, the footmen, grooms, and other men on the staff soon discovered this, teasing Mary whenever they could. They'd torment her even in the servants' pew at church each Sunday, contriving ways to pinch the round-est part of her bottom each time she knelt at prayers, or snatch aside her kerchief from her bosom to reveal more of her softly rounded breasts to their prying eyes.

Thus one summer morning, when Mary heard the other women in the kitchen giggling and whispering about a rare handsome young gentleman who was among the party of visitors new arrived at the Hall, she didn't join their gossip, but concentrated instead upon shelling the beans for the servants' nooning.

"They say Lady Nestor won't stay a night away from home without Mr. Lyon at her side," said Betty, a chambermaid, as she sipped her dish of watered tea with a true lady's daintiness. "Her ladyship claims she would perish without his counsel and his succor; he's that pious a young gentleman."

"Oh, aye, succor," scoffed Susannah, the cook's maid, as she sliced onions into neat white rings. "I've seen that Johnny Lyon, the handsome rascal, just as I've seen how her ladyship fawns and dotes upon him, though she's old enough to be his mother. The only succoring between those two comes with her mouth tugging upon his pious prick."

"Not before the lass, Susannah," Betty cautioned, even as she laughed raucously. "Don't sully Mary's maidenly ears."

Maidenly or not, Mary's ears had already heard their fill of Mr. John Lyon. Another orphan like herself, he'd been taken up by Lady Nestor, Lady Catherine's oldest friend. But while Lady Catherine had made Mary a servant, Lady Nestor had decided her orphan showed uncommon promise, and had paid for Mr. Lyon's education as if he'd been a gentleman born. She'd determined him for the clergy, but her servants as well as the ones at Worthy Hall judged him far too handsome to be wasted in a pulpit.

This was all Mary knew of Mr. Lyon, nor did she care to learn more. She'd heard enough. She bowed her head and pretended not to listen, a ruse the other two women at once saw through.

"*Those* maidenly ears?" Susannah jabbed her knife in the air to signify the maid. "Why, Mary's no better than the rest o' us. You'll see. Some pretty lad will catch her fancy and tickle her between her legs, and she'll be on her back with her petticoats in the air faster'n you can speak the words."

"I will not!" Mary said warmly, her head still lowered over the bowl of beans. "I've vowed to Lady Catherine with my hand upon the Holy Scripture that I'll stay a maid until I wed, and not be tempted to sin."

"Vows so foolish as that are made to be broken, Mary," Betty said, not unkindly. "You shouldn't swear to oaths that can't be kept, even if her ladyship asks it of you."

"I've a notion to test her," Susannah said. "Mr. Lyon's coffee is almost ready, Mary. You take it up to him in the drawing room."

Betty gasped. "Mary can't go above stairs," she said indignantly. "She's kitchen staff."

"This once she can," Susannah said, determined to have her so-called test. "Mr. Lyon wants his coffee, and has been ringing and ringing for it, and Mary here's the only one in the kitchen who could take it up. Unless you be too timid to do it, Mary?"

"I'm not frighted by this Mr. Lyon." Mary set her bowl on the table with a thud, and untied her apron. "He's only a mortal man of flesh and blood, and no more."

"Oh, aye, he's *flesh* enough," Betty said, chuckling. "Charming, luscious, manly flesh, in all his glory. But I warrant even a maid like you will soon see that for yourself. Go now. Take the tray, and mind you keep clear of her ladyship."

"And mind you come back directly to tell us everything. *Everything.*" Susannah thrust her tongue from her mouth and touched it to her lips, suggestive enough to make Betty burst with fresh merriment.

Like the cawing of two crows, their laughter followed Mary as she climbed up the back stairs with Mr. Lyon's tray in her hands. She was much vexed by their amusement, coming as it did at her expense, and she thought of a score of clever retorts she should have made to end their teasing. She'd not been tempted by any man or boy heretofore. Why should she weaken now?

But by the time she reached the front hall, her temper had cooled. Test or no, she didn't belong here, and she hurried across the black-and-white marble floor towards the drawing room as swiftly as she could. Her plain linsey-woolsey gown seemed woefully out of place amongst the upstairs splendor, and even the painted faces of long-ago Worthys hanging on the walls seemed to sneer their disapproval down from their gilded frames.

She'd face consequences enough if Lady Catherine came upon her, but the ones she feared more were from

Mr. Punch, the butler, and the housekeeper, Mrs. Able, both more exalted in her world than the mistress. If either one discovered Mary so far from the kitchens, she'd be thrashed for certain, and likely be burdened with extra tasks for punishment as well. With such a threat to spur her on, she was close to running by the time she scratched on the drawing room door, and woefully out of breath, too.

"Enter," came the deep masculine voice inside. With the tray balanced clumsily against her side, Mary turned the knob, and pushed the door open with her hip. But because the day was warm, or perhaps only because she was so anxious, the door stuck tight in its jamb. Fearful at being faulted by Mr. Lyon for this delay, she swung the full force of her hip against the recalcitrant door, and turned the knob again.

Of course the door chose that instant to give way, and Mary flew headfirst into the room, staggering and bumbling like a wayward sot as she struggled not to drop the tray with the coffeepot, dish, and sweet biscuits. She lurched forward across the oaken floorboards, her gaze intent upon the tray, her horrified face reflecting back to her in the distorted curve of the polished silver pot. Like a windblown sailor dancing along the foretop spars, she finally found her footing, steadying herself and the tray with a happy small sigh of relief and accomplishment.

But oh, what peril still awaited her next, more wrenching and hazardous than a thousand falls and stumbles combined!

"Are you unharmed, miss?" he asked, his voice rich with his concern. "Not injured, I trust?"

Mary looked up from the coffeepot, and tumbled again, this time into the endless green pools that were the gentleman's eyes. Struck dumb, she could only nod in wordless agreement to his query, and marvel all the more at his face and person.

He was neither so beautifully perfect as to be an Adonis, nor of such a warrior's sturdy physique as to qualify as another Hercules. Yet the young gentleman who stood before her possessed more charm and masculine grace than any other of his sex that she ever had known. Perhaps twenty years in age, he was tall and well made, his shoulders broad and his belly flat, and Mary could not help but marvel at how well muscled his legs and chest appeared to be, such as is the case in gentlemen much given to riding. He was dressed with sober elegance, in a dark gray superfine suit of clothes that only served to accentuate the sea green of his eyes, and he wore his own hair instead of a London gentleman's fashionable wig, his gilded curls tied with a black silk ribbon and becoming nonchalance at his nape.

"You are certain you're unharmed?" he asked with the sincerest concern. "Quite well?"

Once again Mary nodded. Mr. Lyon—for so, of course, it was he—smiled, a single dimple lighting his cheek, and the poor smitten girl felt herself sway beneath its charming beacon. He sensed her weakness and seized the tray from her to place it on the table behind him. Then with great gentleness, he took her arm and guided her to a nearby settee, conveniently placed beside a tall arched window.

"There," he said, joining her. "Now breathe deeply, and collect yourself."

Mary closed her eyes and leaned towards the open window, breathing deeply as he'd instructed her. When at last she felt more restored, she opened her eyes, only to realize those same breezes had mischievously disordered the kerchief around her neck, and her breasts, scarce contained by the sturdy barriers of her stays and her bodice, now lay impudently bare before him. Beside her, Mr. Lyon's eyes were wide at such an unconscionably brazen sight, his lips pressed together so tightly Mary feared he'd forgotten to breathe as well.

"Oh—oh, sir, please, forgive me," she stammered as she fumbled to restore her scattered modesty. "I'd no wish to be so bold, especially before a gentleman of the church!"

"Not yet, my dear, not yet," he said, raising his gaze with effort back to her face. "To serve Our Lord is my greatest hope, true, but I've still much more study before I make my final choice."

"Indeed, sir," she said. "I've heard her ladyship has complete confidence in your gifts."

"Her ladyship is most kind," he said, touching his forehead with humble respect. "I can only hope to approach the regard she has for me."

She smiled shyly. "I'm sure she's every reason to admire your abilities, sir."

"Her ladyship is most generous in her praise." He

shrugged with that self-deprecatory charm that is so rare in handsome men. "But here, perhaps you can help me."

Mary nodded eagerly, too ready, alas, to oblige him in all things.

"I need an audience, you see," he began. "Someone who'll listen, and criticize my work where it's lacking so I might improve it."

"Oh, sir," she said sadly, "I'm but the lowest scullery maid, sir, and unschooled in literary matters as that."

"Nonsense," he declared. "Even a hermit in a cave has taste of one sort or another. You'll do better than any Cambridge don. I'm sure of it. What name does your cook call you by?"

"I'm Mary, sir," she said, flushing again beneath his attention. "Mary Wren, sir."

"And I am John Lyon, your servant, Miss Mary Wren." He grinned and winked, as if to show he understood how foolish and teasing a statement that was to make to one who was in fact a servant.

"Yes, Mr. Lyon." She laughed with delight, for she'd never been called "Miss Wren" in all her life. How pleasing it sounded to her ears, and how especially sweet for being in his voice!

He laughed with her. "How vastly agreeable you are, Miss Mary Wren. How could I ask for a finer audience?"

To Mary's sorrow, he rose from the settee, but ventured away only long enough to gather up a sheaf of papers from the desk, and soon returned to sit beside her. The settee was small, and as he shifted to better arrange himself on the cushions, the narrowness compelled his knee to press against hers. She said nothing, not wishing to appear rude, nor was there space for her to move away even if she chose to.

"I've written about the temptation of Eve by the serpent," Mr. Lyon said, fanning the pages in his hand. He paused, and looked over the papers at Mary. "You do know of Eve, and her mate, Adam?"

"Oh, yes, sir," she said promptly. She liked how his knee pressed against hers, and the strange feel of eager excitement that came with so simple a touch. "Adam and Eve lived in the Garden of Eden, until the serpent beguiled Eve into biting the apple of sin, and God cast them out into the darkness."

"Very good, Miss Wren!" He seemed surprised yet pleased by her recitation, as every man does when discovering a woman who understands the nicety of sin. "A fine, concise telling."

She smiled and basked in the glow of his approval. "Lady Catherine made certain I learned my letters, sir, so I could read Scripture."

"Then you're scholar enough to counsel me, Miss Wren." He looked back at the papers, turning them towards the light through the window behind them. The sun was slipping below the trees, and to catch its fading rays, he needed to twist and turn his arm until it rested along the curving back of the settee, behind her shoulders.

"Now then," he began, his face contorted in an academic scowl. "My thesis is that Eve could not help being weak and succumbing to temptation, because that is woman's natural flaw."

"That she be weak, sir?" Mary exclaimed. "You would blame mankind's fall from eternal grace upon women's weakness?"

"Why, yes," he said evenly. "That is common knowledge, Miss Wren. Adam, being of stronger resolve, would have resisted the serpent's temptation. Now, if I may continue, then—"

"You may not, sir!" she cried, forgetting herself in her indignation. "Not until you admit that men can be every bit as weak as women!"

"Is that so?" He leaned closer to Mary so that his chest pressed into her arm and their faces were almost touching. "Would you care enough for your argument to risk a proof?"

"A proof, sir?" she asked, not understanding his question. Her ignorance was not quite complete, for she did understand that his nearness was making her heart quicken, how her skin warmed where his body brushed against hers, how she felt at once eager and languid, and ready for she knew not what. "And—and what is that, sir?"

"Oh, it's a simple enough test, sweet." His voice was low and coaxing to her, his words a feathery brush over her cheek. "You do your best as a woman to lead me into temptation, and I shall see if I can be the stronger as a man, and resist."

She frowned a bit, for his very male argument was still new to her, one she'd not yet heard from any man. Besides, by then she realized she was slipping back into the soft curve of the settee's arm, or perhaps it was Mr. Lyon himself who was easing her backwards with his insinuating presence.

"Don't frown, Mary," he said softly, almost troubled. "Where's the temptation to a man in that?"

"I didn't mean to frown, sir." She smiled up at him to show she meant well, and rested her palm on his cheek as further consolation. "Not to you, sir."

His smile in return was dazzling, like a rainbow after a storm. "Ah, Mary, you are so sweet, you make me believe not only in temptation, but in love."

"Love, sir?" she asked, startled to hear such a word uttered by him so soon in their acquaintance. "You are in love, sir?"

"With you, dear Mary," he whispered, his arm slipping around her waist to support her. "I was lost the moment you came through that door."

Before Mary could offer up her reply, he was kissing her, the first time ever she'd permitted any man to make her such a freedom. His lips moved over hers with a heated urgency she'd never known before, and as she gasped with surprise at the unfamiliar sensations, her lips parted as she sought more air. Of course he chose to misread her amazement, taking it for a welcome she didn't know enough to extend. Soon his tongue was sliding between her lips and against her own, as sure and fiery as Cupid's dart of love.

Of *love*: surely that must be what she felt! Mary's head seemed to spin so that she feared she'd swoon, and she clung to Mr. Lyon for support, her fingers clinging to his shoulders as if for her life.

With her hands to hold them steady, she felt his slip between them, and ease itself most cunningly beneath her kerchief and inside her bodice. Yet though her conscience cried out against such impunity, her heart had heard that magic word LOVE, the key that would unlock most any maiden's lock.

And Mary was no different. She let him push aside the straining cloth, and felt her new-ripened breasts spill out to meet his eager touch. She'd always wondered why men should be so fascinated by these baubles, which she believed were fashioned for the nourishment of babes and little else.

It didn't take long before she understood it all. She sighed as his clever fingers began their winning caresses, pulling and teasing her tender flesh until her nipples had tightened and grown stiff and proud. She arched against him, aching for more, even though she'd still no notion of what that *more* could be as she began to gasp and writhe beneath him with unmitigated delight.

"See how you tempt me, Mary," he said, his breathing harsh against her throat. "I wish to be strong, yet love makes me weak. Your love, Mary, you and— Ah, sweet, what's this?"

Again his eyes widened with surprise as he drew back from his attentions. She knew at once what had caught his eye, and with her ardor instantly dowsed, she struggled to cover her secret shame.

"No false modesty, Mary, please, not between lovers," he said, holding her wrist to keep her shielding hand away. "What a delicious secret you've kept hidden, sweet!"

"Can you fault me for so doing, sir?" Mary cried, finally pushing herself away from him to sit and put her clothing to rights. "Oh, please, sir, I am so shamed!"

He had discovered her birthmark, the spot that had showed upon one side of her left breast as long as she could recall it: a tiny, perfectly formed heart placed not far from the true one that beat within. In Mary's complete innocence, she'd always suspected that Nature's coquettish placement of this little heart must be a sign, a brand to show a wanton temperament, and a tendency for affections too freely given and received. This birthmark had always tormented her, and to this moment she'd taken great care never to reveal it to others. But now—now to her considerable sorrow—she'd carelessly let Mr. Lyon uncover her secret, and her humiliation with it.

"Why should you be so shy, when it's the most delicious birthmark I've ever seen?" he asked in perfect honesty. "To be so marked by Venus herself, in a place where only a true lover's eyes might discover it."

Mary looked at him sideways, uneasy, with her arms still crossed protectively across her breasts. "You do not find it ugly, sir, or distasteful?"

"Oh, my poor dear, not at all!" he exclaimed. "Was

there ever another woman so rapturously blessed with such tribute from Venus? Was there ever another man so honored by this fascinating revelation?"

"You're certain, sir?" she asked, still unconvinced. "You are not speaking so from kindness or pity?"

"Of course not," he declared heartily. "Come, I'll give you proof of my lover's devotion. Show your dear secret heart to me again, and I shall kiss it as a solemn pledge of my admiration."

Surely, she told herself, she could ask for no more than that, and with trembling fingers, she once again revealed the coy little heart and her tremulous breast with it. With worshipful murmurs meant to calm her anxiety, he lowered his lips to the site, and offered the most dedicated and respectful tribute imaginable. From the birthmark, he swiftly shifted back to the nearest rosy nipple, suckling first with his lips and then flicking lightly with his tongue while with his hand he offered equal delight to her other breast.

Overwhelmed by sensation, she closed her eyes in modesty, and to better comprehend his sweet devotion. Clearly Mr. Lyon wasn't like the footmen and grooms who tormented her so. Clearly he didn't deserve the smirks and lewd jests that the older women in the kitchen cast his way. Clearly he was a gentleman, who cared for her sensibilities, to treat her with such tender regard.

She sighed sweetly, giving herself over to his attentions, and circled her arms around him. She'd never before held a gentleman (or any other man, for that matter) with this familiarity or freedom. She was amazed by the difference in his body from her own, the hard, lean muscles of his arms and shoulders, the manly strength she discovered beneath her hands, as if he were eager to follow her every bidding.

Daring further, she slipped her hands inside the skirts of his coat to his breeches, and discovered the round, firm cheeks of his buttocks, snugly covered by the soft wool of his breeches. She spread her fingers open, delighting in the neat way the splendid, taut curves filled her hand, and in response he groaned aloud, grimacing as he released her nipple from his lips.

"Oh, sir, have I injured you?" she whispered breathlessly, loath to let him go. "Have I hurt you in some way?"

"Not—not at all," he said, though his ragged breathing betrayed a distress similar to her own. "But here, let me guide you."

Swiftly he shifted apart from her, only long enough to draw her hand around to the front of his breeches.

"There," he said. "See the proof of what you have done to me."

She saw, and she touched, and she marveled. She had, of course, come across unbuttoned footmen who were either too lazy or too drunk to find the privy making their water behind the stables. Likewise she had glimpsed their male members in their hands or limply stuffed back into their breeches: shriveled, limp affairs, unlovely to any eyes but their possessors'.

But here indeed was proof that Mr. Lyon's staff must be

wrought of much finer flesh and blood. Behind the buttoned fall of his breeches, its blunt head pushed proudly forward, its height and breadth barely contained, and fair ready to burst free of the buttons that struggled to contain it.

At such a sight, Mary blushed, more from wonder than from lingering modesty. At once Mr. Lyon caught her hand in his, and led it to his straining cock. She touched him gingerly, curiously, but enough to make him groan again. This time she did not draw back, but swept her hand along his hard length, marveling at the heat she could feel even through the cloth. He pushed hard against her palm, his hips rising to meet her caress.

Yet even more astonishing was that by stroking him in this fashion, she felt her own pleasure growing in perfect sympathy. Her heart was quickening, her bared breasts growing somehow heavier and more sensitive. Though the window beside them was open to the breezes, the most extraordinary sensation of heat was building low in her belly, as if her private parts were possessed by a fever that made her ripen with longing. She felt strangely swollen, even damp, with an almost unbearable desire to touch herself for surcease.

"You suffer, sir," she whispered, her eyes wide, her breathing ragged, her legs shifting restlessly together as she sought to ease her own distress. "Yet I do as well. I feel as if I burned with a fire's heat, sir, as if flames did lick me from within, as if—"

"Mary." He stopped her words with kisses that were

now demanding rather than tender, pressing her back farther into the arm of the settee. The wool of his coat grazed
her nipples, another kind of sweet torment, and she arched
upwards against his chest, seeking more of him than she'd
words to explain. She felt the window's breezes on the bare
skin above her heavy stockings as he threw aside her apron
and petticoats and bared her thighs as he had bared her
breasts. When he slipped his knees between her legs, opening her more widely to his advances, she welcomed him,
shifting so as to give him better access to her charms.

The fever of urgency made them both clumsy, throwing
both caution and clothing aside in their haste. Her kerchief
and cap fell from the cushions to the floor, two buttons
tore from his coat in his hurry to pull that garment from
his body, and yet neither paid any heed. An hour before,
and Mary would not have known him from Adam, yet now
she could think of nothing more than the pleasure this
handsome gentleman was bringing to her.

With teasing deliberation, she felt his fingers glide along
her inner thigh and dally briefly in the curls of her mound
before, at last, coming to settle on her cunny. She caught
her breath as those artful fingers parted her, opened her, in
a way that she'd never realized was possible.

The moisture she'd sensed welling within now eased
the way for his touch, taking him deep within on its slick
and honey-sweet path. Lightly he stroked the tiny nubbin of flesh that held her pleasure, making Mary gasp and
clutch at his hand: not to stop, not at all, but to continue

on, *on*, like any good huntress with her quarry in reach. She arched against his hand as he pressed deeper into her cleft, and clung to his shoulders, her knees tangled around his brawny forearms; and if a moan of delight escaped her lips, why, then it was the glad hosanna of a happy acolyte to the one freeing her from the thrall of innocence.

But then there came another sound, another voice from the hall, a voice so fearful that Mary's eyes flew open with horror. She pushed Mr. Lyon aside and jumped to her feet, frantically arranging her bodice and cap.

"What the devil?" her dear gentleman demanded, his voice hoarse and rasping with his unfulfilled need.

"It's not the devil, sir, but the butler," she cried in a desperate whisper. "He's tipping the blinds against the sun in each room on this side of the house, same as every afternoon, and if he should find me here, so far from the kitchen, why, he will scold me, and thrash me, and—"

"Hush, sweet, hush," said Mr. Lyon, his green eyes flashing with outrage on her behalf as he rose, too. Even as he buttoned the fall on his breeches, he was more than equal to the challenge of Mr. Punch. "You'll not suffer at that rascal's hands, not on my account."

But Mary had no wish to send him against such a fearful foe, not when it seemed she had only begun her delicious acquaintance with Mr. Lyon.

"Please don't, sir, I beg you," she said breathlessly, tugging her bodice back in place over her breasts as she fished behind the settee for her kerchief. "Consider the scandal, sir, pray do. I won't have you risk your glorious future for my sake."

He scowled at being restrained, but at once saw the logic to her appeal.

"Then flee, if you must," he said with open regret. "But swear to me, my love, that you'll not forget me."

"Forget you, sir!" Mary cried with astonishment. "Never, sir, never."

"Then come to me this night, when the others are asleep," he urged, seizing her once again in his arms. "We can meet in the garden, or the orchard, or the loft over the stable."

She shook her head, her ear still primed and listening for Mr. Punch's footfall. "I cannot, sir, not to those places. I'm watched too closely by the others. What of your bedchamber above stairs?"

His expression turned dark. "My chamber is too near to Lady Nestor's rooms for that. She's a good woman, aye, with every care for my welfare, but watchful as a cat."

At the mention of his benefactress, Mary guiltily recalled her own savior, and her solemn oath to Lady Catherine now pressed like a stony weight upon her conscience. It had been as nothing for Mary to swear to preserve her maidenhead when there'd been no temptation to do otherwise. But Mr. Lyon was temptation indeed—as handsome and virile a temptation as any wavering virgin could want—and tears glazed Mary's eyes at the awfulness of her sacred (if rash) oath.

On this very settee, she had tempted a pious Christian gentleman to sin with her. She'd wantonly spread her thighs for him to please her, and in turn she had touched and stroked his prick as if it were the most luscious plaything imaginable. Worst of all, she'd no regret save that they'd been interrupted at their sport by the coming appearance of Mr. Punch. Surely by now her mortal soul must be in peril of damnation!

"Oh, sir, I cannot," she whispered sorrowfully. "I cannot."

He struck his fist to his chest, over his heart. "Do you doubt me, Mary? Do you question my love for you?"

"No, no, sir, never that," she declared, raising his hand from his chest to her lips. "It's that I have sworn—oh, Heavens, there *is* Mr. Punch! I must go, sir, else be caught, and sent away!"

She leaned forward and kissed him quickly, a kiss stolen from him as others had so often been stolen from her.

"I will contrive to see you again, dear sir, and soon," she promised in a desperate whisper. "You have my pledge upon it."

Then before this splendid gentleman could say more nectar-sweet words to tempt her to linger, Mary turned and fled the room. Yet even as she ran, she was already plotting and planning towards the next moment she could slip away to meet her darling Mr. Lyon, her LOVE, and with every worn step upon the kitchen stair, she likewise took another step on her giddy journey towards her own irreparable ruin.

ABOUT THE AUTHOR

CHARLOTTE LOVEJOY is the pseudonym of an award-winning novelist. She lives with her family in an old house outside Boston, where she is currently writing her next erotic novel.